For my mum, Anna Way, with love

1

They stand there, the three of them, looking at the dead man, his blood creeping slowly across the floor. Despite the savagery of his death the room is very still, almost peaceful after the violence that has led to this.

Soon the police will come. They will charge into this nice expensive kitchen in this rather lovely London town-house with their boots, their batons, their loud authority, and will want to know what happened, whom to hold responsible.

It's Vivienne who speaks first. 'What will we do?' she asks, her teeth chattering with shock. 'What will we tell them?'

The seconds drip by slowly until her mother at last replies. 'We will tell them that this is the man who murdered Ruby,' she says.

TWO MONTHS EARLIER

2

It's almost closing time. Outside on the dark Peckham street rain falls on flickering puddles. A man, weaving in and out of traffic and clutching a can of cider, thumps his fist on idling cars. Beyond him the Rye lies abandoned, its rain-soaked lawns and gardens, ponds and playgrounds cloaked in darkness now.

Vivienne checks her watch: ten to six, only three tables occupied still. Walton, the elderly Trinidadian who calls in most days, finishing his slice of vanilla sponge; a teenage couple on table number four, eyes locked, hands clasped over tea long gone cold. And the doctor. Her gaze flickers over him then away again as it has for the past hour, as it does every time he arrives and takes the same corner table, asking for strong black coffee, pulling a notepad from his jacket pocket and beginning to write. His fingers barely pause as the words flow in a language she doesn't recognize. She has noticed herself waiting for him each day.

Soon Vivienne begins to shut up shop, pulling the blinds down, collecting menus and sugar bowls. 'Closing now,' she calls.

The teenagers leave first, with Walton close behind. 'Goodbye, Elizabeth Taylor. Goodbye!' he says. 'See you tomorrow!'

She smiles and waves him off, turning back to find the doctor standing only a few feet away and she jumps to find him suddenly so close. 'Sorry,' she says. 'Two coffees, was it? Three eighty, please.'

'Elizabeth Taylor?' he asks as he hands her the money. It's the first non-coffee-related thing he's said to her. 'Reckons I look like her, daft sod.' She laughs to show the absurdity of it, and he smiles politely.

'This is a nice place.' He nods towards the pink neon sign in the window that says *Ruby's*. 'And this is your name? Ruby?' His accent curls around the words. Is he Russian, she wonders. Polish?

'Oh, no, I'm Viv. Ruby was my sister but she died when we were young.'

He glances at her. 'I see. I'm sorry for your loss.'

She waves her hand breezily to show how over it she is, though in truth the very thought of Ruby makes her throat thicken, even now. 'You live near here?' she asks, to change the subject.

'I work at the hospital.' He nods in the direction of

King's College and she affects a look of surprise, as if she hadn't already clocked weeks ago the NHS tag hanging around his neck, the name Dr Aleksander Petri in black type.

'Well,' he pats his pockets as if looking for something and she lets her gaze flicker over him again. He has a kind face, she thinks; his almond-shaped eyes thick-lashed and so dark as to be almost black, his mouth— 'I must go,' he says, jolting her from her reverie. 'Thank you for the coffee,' and then he is gone, the door thudding gently closed behind him.

Her friend Samar arrives moments later, his hair wet with rain. 'Was that him?' he asks, clapping his hands together for warmth. 'Dr Feelgood?'

'Yep.' She fetches the broom to sweep the floor.

'And?' He looks at her expectantly. 'Any progress?'

'Nope.' She pronounces the word so that it ends with a satisfying 'puh' and Samar rolls his eyes.

'Ask him out, for God's sake.' He follows after her, helping her lift chairs onto tables. 'Did I tell you Ted's taking me to Paris?' he says after a while, with unconvincing nonchalance.

She stares at him. 'You've only just got back from Amsterdam! Jesus, how many romantic mini-breaks does one couple need?' But she sees the glow in his eyes, sees how the person he was has been transformed by love, and sighs. 'Ask if he's got any single straight friends, will you?'

*   *   *

7

Half an hour later Viv turns the corner into Chiltern Avenue. It's a wide, tree-lined street, the Victorian semis large and impressive, set amongst spacious, well-kept gardens. She sees her mother's house ahead and quickens her pace as the rain picks up. Her mum's corner of Peckham has changed almost beyond recognition in the quarter of a century that she's lived here, the slow and steady creep of gentrification transforming what was once a shabby, unfashionably edgy part of south-east London into something shiny and desirable, the original demographic squeezed out family by family as loft and kitchen extensions, four-by-fours and a general sheen of exclusivity and wealth has taken its place.

Only her mother's house stands out from the homo-genized, sanitized crowd. Number 72 is a faded kaleido-scope of colours; the paintwork a peeling turquoise, the guttering a weather-beaten red, the door a washed-out yellow. In the front garden rainbow-striped windmill spinners tatty with rain and mud poke up through banks of weeds, and the bent browned husks of long-dead sunflowers bow before a brass sculpture of a naked woman, her breasts and belly green with the passage of time. A trio of wind chimes hang from the branches of a leafless sycamore, their music mingling with the rain.

As usual the front door rests on its latch and Viv pushes it open with a sigh of disapproval but steps into the light, high-ceilinged hall to feel the house's familiar pull, its peaty, musty smell of boiling pulses; the spicy sweetness of sandalwood and patchouli, and she relaxes into its warmth and familiarity. Her mother runs a sort of boarding house for the waifs and strays of South London: the abused, the addicted, the lost and the lonely. Sent to her by local refuges, psych wards and rehab centres, her guests take up residence in one of the many light and airy bedrooms, some for a few weeks, others for a few months, until they are deemed fit to return home or are found a more permanent place elsewhere. The most cursory of glances reveals this is not a lucrative enterprise, yet somehow the house's colour, character and atmosphere transcends the worn furniture, the splintering floorboards and grubby paintwork.

To the right of the hall is the kitchen and Vivienne enters it now to find her daughter Cleo seated at the large pine table, her head bowed over her school books, half of which are obscured by an enormous ginger tom lying supine across them, his vast furry belly vibrating with loud contentment. A lightshade made from many pieces of coloured glass throws rainbow squares across the wide, well-worn floorboards. The walls are covered in a jumble of art prints and black-and-white photographs, an Amnesty International poster, a framed Maya Angelou quote. Books crowd together on the shelves; texts on feminism and politics and spiritualism and psychology, and Vivienne doesn't know if her mother has ever read these books, has never in fact witnessed her read any of them, but supposes that she must have, once.

She goes to her daughter and kisses the top of her head. 'Where's Gran? Sorry I'm late, Sammy popped in.'

Cleo looks up at her distractedly, her school tie tugged half out of its knot. 'That's all right. Can we go home now? I need to—'

She's interrupted by the appearance of her grandmother. Stella seems to sail rather than walk into any room she enters. She's an impressive sight; tall and statuesque, her long grey hair dyed a faded magenta. She wears a voluminous kaftan in shades of green and red with a necklace of brightly painted African beads. She's in her mid sixties but, rather like her home, the heady mix of colour and flair surpasses the general wear and tear of age and one is aware only of her attractiveness.

Stella's voice is deep and rich, and seeing her daughter she says, 'Oh, hello, darling. Now, I came in here for something, but I have absolutely no idea what it is.' She wanders over to the stove to poke at something simmering there with a spoon. 'Would you like some nettle and elderflower tea? It's homemade.'

They are alike, physically, although at five foot six Viv doesn't quite have her mother's impressive stature, something she's both relieved and a little regretful about. 'Christ, no,' she says, then takes a seat and asks, 'who've you got staying here at the moment, anyway?'

'Just four: a new woman came last night, the others I think you've met – we still have Shaun, of course.'

She says the name fondly, just as Vivienne inwardly shudders at the mention of Stella's long-standing guest.

Hastily she turns back to her daughter. 'Did you manage to finish your project, love?' she asks.

But before Cleo can reply, Stella interjects with a crisp, 'I doubt it. She's spent most of her time fiddling with that phone of hers.'

As if on cue, Cleo's mobile pings and she snatches it up eagerly, while Stella sighs.

Vivienne has noticed a hint of discord recently, like a cold draught blowing between her daughter and mother. It's nothing she can put her finger on, just an occasional, troubling tension that she's not entirely sure she's imagined. She looks at Cleo, tapping furiously on her phone, her school books abandoned. She doesn't share her and Stella's pale skin, dark hair and violet-blue eyes, but instead has the same strawberry blond curls, the creamy, freckled complexion and wide, pale green eyes of Ruby. In fact, in recent months a passing expression or angle of Cleo's face will bring Viv's dead sister back so vividly that it sometimes makes her heart stumble. Perhaps that's what's behind the occasional frost she detects in her mother's tone when she talks to her granddaughter: perhaps pain is at its root; the three of them have always been so close, after all.

Stella's landline rings and she picks it up to embark on a long and involved conversation about a mindfulness workshop she's hosting, and a few minutes later a young woman comes in, dark-haired and painfully thin, her small awkward frame a collection of sharp angles clothed in black. She startles at the sight of Vivienne, her eyes

11

darting from her to Cleo with a look of panic as she backs away. 'No, please don't go,' Viv says gently. 'Are you OK? Would you like something?'

The woman plucks anxiously at her skirt. 'No. I . . .' She turns to leave, but just then Stella hangs up the phone and goes to her. 'Jenna, how are you feeling?' She puts an arm around her. 'Headache gone now, is it?'

Visibly relaxing, she looks at Stella gratefully. 'Yes, thank you,' she whispers. 'I thought I'd make a cup of tea.'

She has that effect on people, her mother, on the waifs and strays that she collects, has always collected, in one way or another. They all adore her. Even before she turned this house into a refuge, they would find her, seeking her out, sensing within her a place of comfort and safety. Viv watches as the young woman is steered towards the kettle, Stella's hand upon her shoulder.

Cleo looks up to check that her mother's attention is elsewhere, then turns back to her phone. It vibrates to indicate there's a new message, and her heart leaps.

Cleo?

Hey.

Hey. Where were u yesterday? Missed u.

She stares at the words in surprise. He's never said anything like that before. Had to do something with Mum, she writes.

K. Wot u up 2?

Nothing much. Homework. 😊

😊

She beams back at the little smiling face. They met on a Fortnite board on a gaming site a few months back. It's only recently they've begun private messaging. His name is Daniel and he's a year older than she. He's told her he lives near Leeds and she's told him she's in London. Yesterday he sent her a picture of himself – a blond-haired boy smiling shyly beneath a beanie hat – and she's been thinking about him ever since.

U there?

Yeah.

Thought I'd scared U off wiv my pic. Lol.

Course not. It's nice.

Thanx. U got one?

She hesitates, but nevertheless her thirteen-year-old heart feels a thrill of excitement. Maybe, she writes. She glances at her mum, sees that she's watching her, and hastily drops the phone.

'Who's that you're texting, love?'

'Just Layla.' She's a bit scared how easily the fib trips off her tongue. She doesn't usually lie to her mum, or that is, only about how many sweets she's had, or if she's got any homework to do. But her mother only nods and turns back to the weird thin lady who looks terrified of everything.

Cleo knows she's not got much time. She wants to give him something more and quickly writes, Gtg, spk 2mrw and then, before she can stop herself, she adds a 🖤 then stares at it in horror. Why did she do that? Seriously, why? That's not cool. That's so babyish, so . . . and then he's replied. And he's put a 🖤 too and she grins in relief.

'Come on,' her mum says to her, handing her her coat. 'It's time to go.'

Viv watches her daughter gather her books with painful slowness and tries to hide her agitation. She can hear Shaun's voice from somewhere above, a door opening and then closing again, the sound of footsteps on the stairs. She resists the urge to drag Cleo away, her coat half hanging off her.

It happened a few weeks ago. Stella had gone away on a weekend yoga retreat and, as Cleo was on a rare

14

visit to her father's, had asked Vivienne to look after the house and guests in her absence. She'd been doing the books for the café at the kitchen table with a glass of wine when Shaun appeared.

He'd been staying there for a month by then, but they'd never made much more than small talk before. She tried to remember what Stella had told her about him: a recent spell in rehab for drugs, she thought. He had walked into the kitchen and stopped when he saw her, then leaned against the fridge, appraising her, a rather cocksure smile upon his face. 'You in charge of the asylum tonight then?' he'd asked.

She'd laughed. 'Something like that.'

He sat down opposite her then, and she was slightly taken aback by his sudden proximity. He was tall and well built, with a broad Mancunian accent and was, she would guess, in his late thirties, tattoos covering his muscular arms, a somewhat belligerent air.

She'd looked back at him levelly. 'So, how're you finding it here? Settled in OK?'

He shrugged. 'Yeah, it's sound. Your mum's all right, ain't she?' He stretched and yawned, the hem of his T-shirt rising up to reveal a flash of taut stomach. 'She's a character, any rate. Looks like a right old hippy and talks like the queen. What is she, some kind of aristo, slumming it with the proles?'

Viv had smiled and murmured a non-committal, 'Hardly.' The fact was, Stella's parents had most certainly been wealthy, but Viv had never met them. Stella had been estranged from them since before she was born, and her and Ruby's childhood had been anything but privileged.

'Well, any road,' Shaun said then, 'knows what she's about, don't she?' He nodded at her ledger book. 'What you doing there, then?'

So Vivienne had told him about her café.

'Done all right for yourself, haven't you?' Though he'd been smiling, there was a hint of resentment in his tone. He'd pulled out a tin of tobacco, begun rolling a cigarette, and started telling her about his misspent youth in Manchester. He was entertaining; funny and quick-witted, though she sensed this was a well-worn charm offensive, that there was an unpredictability hiding behind his smile and his mood might change in an instant. She'd met men like him before. She had, too many times in her youth, slept with men like him before, the sort whose swagger and bravado was a front for damage and gaping insecurity, who triggered her instinct to appease, pacify and bolster.

He was exactly the sort of man, in fact, that she had trained herself to avoid. 'Your problem is, you go for lame ducks,' Samar told her once. 'It's your saviour complex. You must get it from your mother.' It was unfortunate that Shaun was so very good looking.

He had just finished telling her about how he and his school friends had stolen a milk float when suddenly he'd disarmed her by saying, 'You're one of those women who don't know how fit they are, aren't you?'

And it was so clichéd, such an obvious *line*, yet even as she'd rolled her eyes she'd felt a reluctant thrill. Probably because she'd recently turned forty and no one (apart from Walton) had said anything even vaguely complimentary to her for quite some time. And she hated herself for it, saw by the flash in his eyes that he'd seen his words had hit their mark, and if she'd drunk a little less wine, or been a little less giddy at finding herself childfree for the first time in months, she might have put him firmly in his place.

Instead she'd laughed, 'Oh do me a favour,' and he'd grinned back at her, the air altering between them, both of them knowing now what the score was. She'd poured herself another drink, enjoying the back and forth of flirtation, telling herself it would only go so far: she would finish her wine then go upstairs to bed, alone. But, of course, it didn't happen quite like that.

And when she'd woken up the next morning in his bed she'd been full of self-loathing and regret. Sleeping with Stella's guests was about as stupid as it got, and her mother would be furious if she found out. She'd slipped from the bed, silently scooping up her clothes and escaping to Stella's room – where she was supposed to have slept that night. Knowing that her mum was due back later that afternoon, she'd fled for home as soon as she could, before Shaun even had time to surface.

She'd managed to avoid him for a while after that and life had gone on, though she'd shuddered whenever she thought of him. She'd only just begun to forgive herself, to hope she'd got away with it when, unexpectedly, he'd called her.

She'd answered her mobile as she was rushing to fetch Cleo from a party.

'All right, Viv. How's tricks?'

'How did you get my number?' she asked, before remembering with a sinking heart that it was pinned to the corkboard in her mother's kitchen, the 'in case of emergencies' contact for when Stella was out.

'Well, that's not very friendly, is it?'

'Sorry. I . . .'

'Wanted to know if you fancied a drink.'

'Um, I'm not sure that's a good idea,' she'd replied slowly.

'Oh, right, like that is it?' His voice was instantly hard, the fragile ego she'd sensed lurking there revealed in a heartbeat.

'No, of course not,' she'd said hastily. 'I'm just not . . . I'm sorry, but I don't want to get into anything, we probably shouldn't have . . .'

He'd given a belligerent laugh. 'Think you're too good for me, is that it? Should have been grateful, saggy old bitch.' His sudden aggression had stunned her. He'd cut her off, leaving her to stare down at her phone, her heart pumping with shock and anger.

That had been two weeks ago. She'd not seen him since, had managed to avoid coming to her mother's house until today. But as she and Cleo finally get to the door, Shaun appears at the top of the stairs. He stops, looking her up and down insultingly, and she feels a flash of cold dislike.

'Going so soon?' he says, sauntering down towards her.

She puts her hand on Cleo's shoulder and steers her towards the door. 'Yep, gotta run. Bye.' She and Cleo go out into the night, and she closes the door firmly behind her, a shiver of disgust prickling her skin.

Their house is a twenty-minute walk from Stella's, on the other side of the Rye, and Vivienne pushes Shaun from her thoughts as she links her arm through her daughter's. 'How was school today, love?' she asks.

For a while they chat about a history project Cleo's been working on and how she thinks her team will do in an upcoming football match, and Viv smiles down at her, her happy, popular child, always tumbling from one enthusiasm to the next. She'd been twenty-six when she'd become pregnant, a result of a brief and unhappy fling with one of the suppliers for her café, a handsome but feckless Irishman named Mike who was a few years younger than herself. He'd run a mile at the news of her pregnancy and had kept only sporadic contact with his daughter since. It had always been the two of them after that, and as a result they'd always been close – as close as Viv was to her own mother, in fact.

As they draw nearer to their street Vivienne shivers in the cold November night and murmurs, 'Thank God it's Friday. I can't wait to get home. We'll have spaghetti for tea, shall we?'

They pass beneath a street lamp just as Cleo looks up at her and smiles, and there is, again, something in the angle of her face, in the expression in her eyes, that takes Viv's breath away. Her daughter looks in that split-second so exactly like Ruby that her sister is brought back to life with sudden, shocking force.

It's a new thing, Cleo's random expressions triggering this heart-jolting reaction in her. Out of the blue a memory will turn up, glinting and sharp, to stop Viv in her tracks. Tonight she's transported back to the little house in Essex where she and Ruby spent their childhood, a white, ramshackle cottage on the edge of a stretch of fields. In this memory Ruby is sixteen and heavily pregnant, dressed in a blue cotton dress and standing by the window that's crisscrossed with iron latticing, the light falling on her red-gold hair, her hand resting on her swollen belly.

Viv, aged eight, had gone to her sister and pressed her cheek upon her tummy, gazing up at her as she listened intently. And then it happened: as Ruby smiled down at her with the exact same expression that she'll see mirrored in her own daughter's face thirty-two years later, Vivienne felt something move beneath her cheek and squealed in excitement. 'Did you feel that?' she asked. 'I felt him! I felt the baby kick!'

And Ruby grinned and said, 'Yes, I felt it too. Not long to go, Vivi. Two weeks and you'll be an auntie.'

An auntie at eight years old! How important and grown-up and wonderful that felt. She would love this baby with all her heart; she did already.

But she never got to meet her sister's child, never had a chance to call him by the name Ruby had so carefully chosen. Noah. Her nephew would have been called Noah. Because almost two weeks later, a few days before her due date, Ruby would be dead, and Noah with her.

Now, walking along the dark street with her own child, a passing motorbike rouses her from her thoughts. Seeing that they've nearly reached their gate she swallows back the shards of pain that have risen to her throat. 'Come on,' she says to Cleo, opening the door. 'Go and get changed and I'll make dinner, then we'll watch something on Netflix, shall we?'

Alone in the kitchen, she puts the radio on and pours herself a glass of wine. She hates it when this mood descends upon her. It's the anniversary of Ruby's death on Monday and it always upsets her, no matter how prepared for it she is. Noah would have turned thirty-two this year, and as she has done every single year since it happened, she imagines the person he might have become – from toddler, to schoolboy, to teenager and young man – a sadness gathering inside her that's hard to shake off. 'Come on, Viv, get a grip,' she tells herself and, tuning the radio to a music station, she turns the volume up, then starts to put together the ingredients for spaghetti bolognese.

3

There's so much of that day that she doesn't remember. She knows that she was the only other person in the house when Ruby was killed. That it was she who found her sister's body, hugely pregnant, splayed out across her bedroom floor. She knows that it was her evidence that helped put Ruby's murderer away. But though Viv knows what she said she saw, she cannot link those words to any clear, concrete images, as though the details are locked inside a box she has no access to. She's been told that this is common; the mind's way of protecting her from the trauma of that day, but still those buried memories won't let her be, tapping and scratching at the box's lid, as though willing her to relent and let them back out.

Even the time before the murder is hazy, her life in that little white cottage only returning to her in flashes.

They were very poor, she remembers that. Viv and Ruby, eight years between them, each had different fathers; men who were bad and made their mother sad and who they learned never to ask about because they were gone and that was all. The house was down a narrow lane with four other cottages. She sees the patio tiles outside it, dandelions poking through the cracks, an old, abandoned swing set on the patchy lawn, the fields stretching out beyond. Inside, the rooms were sparsely furnished, the panes loose in the casement windows, the wind whistling through the gaps. In her bedroom under the eaves a pattern of pink and red roses crept across the walls. Her sister's identical one was across a narrow corridor, a quilt on the bed of orange and turquoise and green.

And what does she remember of Ruby, before it happened? She knows that she loved her sister more than anyone or anything, that Ruby would take Viv into her bed to comfort her at night when she was sad or frightened. She remembers Ruby's collection of china pigs lined up on her dressing table, the posters of handsome pop stars on her walls, the sweet floral perfume she used to wear, how she'd throw her head back and laugh wholeheartedly, her green eyes dancing. All those things he took from her; all her spirit and love and smell and warmth and kindness, Jack Delaney took them all.

Everything changed when Jack came into their lives. Overnight, Ruby seemed to become someone else;

someone else's. From the moment she met him her sister glowed, her eyes dreamy and lit with something Viv couldn't guess at, her thoughts seemingly always filled with him. Ruby would wait for Jack at the window, ignoring Viv, staring eagerly down the lane for his car to appear, or else sit next to the phone, willing it to ring. Ruby told her that they'd met at the pub where she worked on Saturdays collecting and washing glasses. Jack had been sitting at the bar with the three other Delaney brothers, and Viv would picture him with his cigarette and his black hair and his thin-lipped smile and his stupid car parked outside, and feel a hard knot of dislike grow ever tighter in her belly.

Until then Vivienne's experience of men had been confined to the ghostly, forbidden spectres of her and Ruby's unmentionable fathers, her teacher Mr Kendal, or the kindly dads of her friends, or even Morris Dryden, the butcher's grown-up son whom everyone said was soft in the head but whom Viv liked best of all. But Jack was different. Even at eighteen he oozed a complicated, threatening thing that was linked somehow to that new light in Ruby's eyes, and the time Viv caught them kissing, Jack's hands up her jumper as though rummaging for change. Slowly, however, Ruby began to alter, her usual glow and happiness seeming to ebb away until bit by bit it had disappeared completely.

Their mother hated Jack, she remembers that too; how she'd hear her and Ruby argue, Stella saying he was a thief and a troublemaker and that everyone in the village knew what he was like, what he and his brothers got up to, fighting and stealing and causing trouble. And Viv would think that her mother didn't know the half of it, that when she went out to work Jack's oily smile and fake politeness vanished and the real him would appear, like worms slithering from under rocks. She would see how he would change, a black mood creeping over him like the sun had gone in, how Ruby's voice would turn pleading and tearful at his meanness and his temper. He was always cross with her about something: about how she'd looked at one of his friends or spoken in a way he didn't like. And yet Ruby loved him, wanted to make him happy, her voice appeasing, cajoling, desperate to the end.

When Ruby got pregnant their mum said Jack Delaney was never to set foot in her house again, but as soon as Stella went off to the care home she worked at, there he'd be, Vivienne sworn to secrecy. He seemed to get worse, the bigger Ruby's belly got. Viv would sit in the living room in front of the black-and-white TV and listen to their arguing; his rough, bullying voice, her sister's tearful apologies, and her little hands would ball into fists, willing it to stop.

And what does she remember of that day, the day of Ruby's murder? She remembers her sister waiting for Jack upstairs at her bedroom window as usual, running down to answer his knock and calling, 'Don't tell Mum, Vivi, OK? Don't tell Mum that Jack was here.' How she'd heard the disappointment in Ruby's voice when she discovered it was only sweet, daft Morris Dryden, come to drop off some chops for their mum. A few minutes later, after Morris had left, she heard the second knock at the door, Jack's voice this time, Ruby's high, anxious one after she'd returned downstairs to let him in.

Viv had stayed in the living room, keeping out of his way, but still she heard when they'd begun to argue, heard Ruby's desperate tears, Jack's relentless, mocking cruelty. That day there'd been something different about their fight though, something terrible and out of control that made Viv's heart hammer, made her chew her lip until it nearly bled. And then a scream, a heavy thud, followed by the worst, deepest silence she'd ever known. She'd waited, scarcely breathing, until she heard his tread on the stairs then the front door swinging shut behind him and as soon as she'd dared, she'd crept from the room and tiptoed up to Ruby's. She'd known she was dead, felt it deep inside of herself, a scream of horror trapped in her throat as she stood at the door, gazing down at her sister's lifeless body, her poor, bleeding head where she'd hit it as she fell, her green, sightless eyes.

It was the police who found Vivienne eventually; navy blue arms plucking her from the safe darkness of Stella's wardrobe where she'd gone to hide, clothes brushing against her cheek as she was pulled into the cold brightness where the rooms were full of police and the air full of her mother's sobs at what she'd found when she'd returned home from work.

Later, Vivienne would be told that she'd said nothing

when they found her, that she'd continued to say nothing except for the one word she repeated over and over: '*Jack*.'

Over the following days and weeks, a kind and patient lady with thick round glasses, a turquoise jumper and a gentle voice had, while Stella held her hand, coaxed from her the evidence they'd needed to put Jack Delaney away for good. She'd told how she'd heard him in the house that morning, had heard him shouting at her sister, then Ruby's terrible cry, the thump as her body hit the floor. Of course Jack had killed Ruby; who else could it have been? There was Morris Dryden's account too; the butcher's son telling how he'd passed Jack in the lane after he'd dropped off his delivery. And Declan Fairbanks, their neighbour, who'd seen Jack running from the house ten minutes later, and all the other locals who'd witnessed his bullying behaviour towards his pregnant girlfriend in the months leading up to her death.

Jack Delaney was responsible. There could be no mistake.

After the trial, Stella would sit immobile at the kitchen table for hour after hour, week after week, steeped in grief. It seemed to Vivienne as though all the darkness in Jack had poured into her mother: when Viv looked into her eyes she saw the same dull fury that had once burned in his.

The letters began to arrive soon after. Folded pieces of paper deposited like petrol bombs through the letter box during the night. At first she would bring them to Stella, who would turn away without looking at them, so Vivienne would go to Ruby's room, where the row of china pigs still stood on the dressing table, where the handsome pop stars still grinned their 100-watt smiles, and she would sit on the bed and wrap the orange and turquoise quilt around herself and begin to read.

They were all from the Delaney family, from Jack's mother or uncle or brothers. Those from his mother were pleading, desperate. *You've made a mistake. Please please tell the truth. He's only 18. He never did it. You know he never did it. He'd never kill no one, please, please make them see.* But the ones from his brothers and his uncles were angry, threatening; written in thick black capitals that all but tore through the page: *Your daughter's a lying little bitch. Make her tell the truth.* And, *You and your brat are fucking liars. Watch your back.* She would read them with terror rising inside her. At night she'd lie in her bed and tremble, listening for the letter box to rattle. But Viv hadn't lied. She had heard him that day. She had told the police she did, so it must have been true.

In a matter of months, the life Viv had always known would be gone forever, though she didn't know then the changes that were to come. Meanwhile, neighbours and kindly villagers helped take care of her. They looked at her with misty-eyed pity, picking her up from the village primary and taking her home with their own kids; to warm, busy, noisy houses with Danger Mouse on the telly and fish fingers in the oven. *Your mum just needs a bit of time*, they'd say. *She'll be all right, you'll see.* Later, Viv would be taken back home, to where the temperature seemed to drop twenty degrees and the silence pressed against the walls, to where Stella hadn't seemed to move from her position at the kitchen table in weeks.

Stella never went back to her job at the care home. The letters from the letting agency piled up on the doormat amongst brown ones with 'Final Demand' stamped upon them. When bailiffs pounded on their door Stella behaved as though she couldn't hear them and Viv was too afraid to let them in herself. Similarly, she learned not to pick up the phone when, relentlessly, it rang, and neither of them noticed when the line was finally cut off.

Only one day stands out from the grinding darkness of those weeks. On an April morning five months after Ruby's death, Vivienne came downstairs in her uniform ready for school to find a surprising sight. Her mother, up and dressed and ready to go out. 'Put your coat on, Vivienne,' she said without looking at her.

Viv hadn't moved. 'Where are we going?'

The reply had been astonishing. 'To see your grand-parents,' Stella had said.

The journey had been a long one, taken first by train then coach to a faraway rain-drenched city and followed by another journey by bus to a small village. She could tell by the look in her mother's eye that it wasn't the time for questions, so she'd sat quietly next to her, holding her hand, trying not to worry. She'd never met her grandparents before and she wondered what they might be like. Her mother had only ever told her that they lived far away, and that she hadn't seen them for a long time, and something had made Viv know not to push for more.

When they'd arrived, the house had been very large and beautiful, surrounded by rolling countryside. Vivienne, told to wait at the gate, had watched as her mother traipsed up the long drive, approached the door and knocked. A grey-haired man had answered, and Viv never knew what was spoken between them, only that minutes later the door had slammed shut, Stella had returned to where she waited and said in a voice as heavy as stones, 'Get up, Vivienne. There's nothing for us here.'

They'd made the return journey mostly in silence, her mother lost in thought and unreachable. It was late when they got back to their cottage and for some time they had stood staring at the front door, the moonlight revealing what was painted there in vicious foot-high letters: *LIARS*.

4

It was a few weeks after that when Vivienne's life in Essex came to an abrupt end. Viv had returned home from school one day to find Stella packing their one and only suitcase. 'We're moving to London,' she'd said as Viv watched her, wide-eyed. 'Take that uniform off and throw it in the bin.' Then she'd tossed her Ruby's little green rucksack. 'Put whatever you can fit in there, the rest we'll leave. Let that pig of a landlord deal with it.'

They left there and then, taking a bus to the nearest station to catch a train to a new life. She had sat across from her mother, her bag of belongings on her lap, and tried to make sense of it all. Were they leaving because of Jack's family? Or because they had no money left to pay the rent? She had sneaked a glance at her mum, and thought she understood: Ruby's death was too sad, too terrible, to do anything else but run from.

For the first few months of their new London life they'd moved from place to place, to the spare beds or sofas belonging to 'friends of friends', or the sister of someone Stella used to work with. Sometimes Viv thought about the toys and bedroom she'd left behind, she thought of her friends and the people she knew in their village, but then she remembered the cold dragging misery of Ruby's funeral, the cross bearing her and Noah's names, the mound of earth covered in irises, her sister's favourite flower, and she knew she never wanted to go back there again.

Stella never said how she found the commune in Nunhead and Vivienne didn't ask, it was just another surprising turn in this constantly twisting new life of theirs. It was 1985, Nunhead a grubby pocket of southeast London tucked between New Cross and Peckham. The occasional small and dusty pub filled with small and dusty old men; clusters of council estates, Afro-Caribbean barber shops that stayed open half the night, lights and music and laughter spilling out across the pavement, narrow streets of dirty-bricked terraces, punctuated here and there by a greasy spoon, a bookies, a launderette. It was as far away from their rural Essex lives as Mexico or the moon.

Unity House had been on the border of New Cross, along a wide street lined with tall Victorian houses with steep steps to the door, from where you could look down at the barred windows of the cool dark basement area far below. Viv and her mother had arrived there one rainy Tuesday afternoon. They'd stood staring up at its yellow front door, they and their bags growing steadily damper in the drizzle.

Suddenly the door had opened and a young, pretty woman with a mass of black curls tied back with a red bandana and huge silver hoops in her ears had said, 'Hello! You must be the new recruits. I'm Jo. Looks like you could do with a cuppa.' And Viv had looked into Jo's smiling face and something tightly bound inside her had unloosened a fraction for the first time since they'd left Essex and she'd thought, *Thank you, oh thank you, thank you.*

Unity House had been the start of it all, the start of their new life, of Stella's transformation, though they hadn't known that then. Jo had led them to an enormous kitchen with lime green walls and a long table covered in books and mugs and gardening gloves, a tomato plant someone was in the middle of repotting. Off the kitchen was a brick outhouse, and spying a wooden hutch, Vivienne had let go of her mother's hand and dropped to her knees to find the biggest rabbit she'd ever seen.

When she returned she'd stared up wide-eyed at the posters pinned to the kitchen walls. One, bizarrely, was of a fish riding a bicycle, another was about something called Greenham Peace Camp. After a while she'd tuned into her mum and Jo's conversation and was shocked to hear Stella haltingly tell her about Ruby. Viv had held her breath; her mother never talked about these things, not ever, not even to her. But Jo had leaned forward and put her hand on Stella's arm, her eyes shining with compassion. 'You've come to the right place,' she said. 'We're all survivors here, one way or another.'

When they'd finished their tea, Jo had shown them around their new home, which they soon saw was much bigger than it had appeared from the street: four floors of large, light and airy rooms, linked by narrow passage-ways and three steep flights of stairs. In the living room one wall was entirely covered by a mural of a naked woman, a white dove in each hand. Everywhere she looked were piles of books, an abundance of pot plants, large, dramatic abstract oil paintings in vivid primary colours, a broken guitar here, somebody's bike there. Indian throws were pinned across the large bay windows, turning the room's light a pale mauve, orange, green. Viv can still recall the house's singular woody, musty smell, feel the fresh air blowing through the always-open garden door.

One by one they were introduced to the others. There was Sandra and Christine, who, strangely, had a son together, a round-faced two-year-old named Rafferty Wolf who called one of them Mummy and the other Mama; they lived on the first floor. Soren, a slender, bright-eyed woman in her sixties, wore her grey hair in a long plait to her waist and was clearly responsible for the artwork displayed throughout the house; her attic space was lined with dozens of canvases, a smell of turps in the air.

On the second floor lived Hayley. A student in her twenties, she had purple spiky hair, a nose ring and a wide smile that showed large and gappy teeth. Her room was thick with cigarette smoke and through its fug Viv saw that her walls were covered in posters and flyers with slogans like 'Maggie Out!' and 'Ban the Bomb!' and 'Fuck Capitalism!' Across the hall was Jo's room. In the basement lived Kay, who had a man's haircut, shy brown eyes, wore a man's suit, and barely spoke. 'You'll meet Margo later,' Jo had promised as she showed them to the room that would be theirs.

That evening a dinner was thrown in their honour. The long table now cleared of gardening things, the nine of them crowded around it, everyone – apart from Viv, her mother and Kay – talking at once while Jo ladled something called goulash onto their plates. Vivienne sat close to her mother, overwhelmed by the hubbub of voices, the good-natured jostling for space, and she'd watched wide-eyed as Sandra, mid conversation, lifted her top to reveal her bare breast for Rafferty Wolf to feed hungrily from.

And then Margo had entered the room. Though in her fifties, her black skin was still luminous, her long dreadlocks only lightly peppered with grey. She was, Viv thought, absolutely beautiful. Her movements slow and languorous, she wore a long billowy blue dress with mustard embroidery at the bodice. She took her seat at the head of the table and while Jo poured her a drink, she had turned her large dark eyes to Viv and her mother.

'Welcome, Vivienne and Stella, I'm so pleased to have you here,' she'd said.

Candles flickered and spilled red wax down the necks of wine bottles, their flames casting shadows of the women against the lime green walls. Margo told them how she'd started the commune 'as a place of shelter, somewhere we can live without violence or fear or censure. Everyone is equal here. We all contribute, we pool our resources, our time and our skills . . .' She had a slow, sonorous way of talking that was almost hypnotic. Somebody put some music on, a female voice rising and falling along with a flute and a guitar. Vivienne, sleepy now, leaned her head against her mother's shoulder as she listened to Margo talk.

One by one, the women had told their stories that night, describing how they'd come to find each other, how Margo and Unity House had changed their lives. Viv must have fallen asleep, because the next thing she knew she was being carried up to bed, a blanket pulled over her, her ears full of the music and the rise and fall of the women's voices.

They would stay at Unity House for almost a decade, and during that time the strong, clever, loving women who lived there would each, in their own way, help to shape the person Vivienne would become. But, just as that first night it was Margo who'd made the greatest impression upon eight-year-old Viv, it would also prove to be Margo who taught her the most valuable lesson of all – that people aren't necessarily always who they seem.

5

When Viv wakes the next morning to the sound of Cleo showering down the hall, she lies in bed staring at the ceiling for a while, thinking about Ruby and the black hole of memories she'd fallen into the night before. The little white Essex cottage, their sudden escape to London, the decade spent at Unity House. She looks at her alarm clock and, remembering it's Saturday and that Cleo has a football match she needs driving to, groans and pulls herself from the bed. She drank too much again last night. After Cleo had gone to bed she had thought about Monday's anniversary and one glass of wine had turned into another and then another, as they so often do. Wrapping a dressing gown around herself, she stumbles downstairs to the kitchen where she finds the empty wine bottle and shoves it guiltily in the recycling box with the others.

As she makes herself coffee she gives herself a mental shake. Ruby's death was so long ago; they had survived it, both she and Stella. Jack Delaney had been found guilty and sent to prison, and that was that. It was all in the past.

She'd been in her thirties when he'd finally been released, thanks to an extra eight years added to his sentence for an attack on a fellow prisoner so vicious it had left his victim in a coma, permanently blinded in one eye. On Jack's release, Viv had avoided all news stories about him, even taking Cleo, ten by then, on holiday to France in case the papers decided to print his picture. She had only vague memories of what he looked like: dark hair, a thin, cruel mouth and heavy brow, but nothing substantial; his image had been banished to the part of her brain where her darkest terrors lived and the shadowy figure who stalked her nightmares was frightening enough without furnishing it with the details a photograph would provide. Her mother later heard he'd emigrated to Canada, and though that should have given Viv comfort, it hadn't, not really: as long as he was alive she would fear him.

She carries her coffee across to the table and sits down. A pale morning sun casts its glow across the parquet flooring and the kitchen has a gratifyingly warm and cosy feel. This morning, she thinks with satisfaction, her house looks exactly like the tasteful, comfortable, middle-class home she'd spent the past fifteen years and an awful lot of money trying to create. In fact, every room of her pretty Georgian townhouse is a testament to the hours spent lovingly restoring each period detail, or trawling auctions and eBay for the perfect antique lampshade or table or chair. A million miles from the little white cottage, the large and chaotic commune – the sort of home where nothing bad ever happened and never would. A perfectly nice, perfectly safe place in which to raise her daughter.

She hears Cleo come clattering down the stairs seconds before she bursts into the room, stuffing her football kit into her bag. Her curls still wet from the shower, she takes one look at her mother and wails, 'Oh Mum! You're not even dressed! You're supposed to be taking me to footie!'

Guiltily Viv jumps to her feet. 'OK, OK! I'll be ready in two minutes. Jeez, relax!' She gulps her coffee and hurries from the room.

Five minutes later as they are leaving the house, Cleo impatiently rushing ahead, Viv spies their new neighbour, Neil, cutting his hedge. Not having the heart to ignore his eager smile, she gives him a wave, 'Hello there!' He's a slightly chubby man who looks to be in his late forties with badly dyed brown hair and a rather grating laugh, but he's harmless enough; a welcome antidote at least to the self-satisfied hipsters who'd descended on the area in droves in recent years.

Ignoring Cleo, who's scowling and rolling her eyes, she says, 'You're up and at 'em early, Neil. How's it all going with the renovations?'

'Oh, slowly, slowly, you know how it is.'

'You've done wonders with the place.' She glances up at the sash windows he's recently installed. It is, in fact, quite astonishing what he's managed to do in such short a time. Before he'd moved in, the property had belonged to a sweet elderly Cypriot woman who, due to ill health, had allowed the house to fall to rack and ruin over the fifty years she'd lived there. By the time she'd died it had been almost derelict. Shortly after the funeral her daughter had put it on the market for a price Viv had thought extortionate, considering the work that needed doing to it, and it had languished on the market for over eighteen months before suddenly it had sold, to the entire street's surprise, for the full asking price. A few months later, Neil had moved in.

He's looking at her hopefully. 'You and Cleo will have to come round for a cup of tea sometime. I can show you what I've done inside.'

'We'd love to,' she says, beginning to edge away. 'That'd be great.' She smiles apologetically, 'I'm afraid we've got to run now, footie practice, but let's definitely do that soon, thank you.'

She feels him watching her as they get into the car. Oh, God, does he fancy her? She doesn't really get that vibe, though she's not quite sure what vibe she does get, exactly. Perhaps he's just a bit lonely: she never sees any friends dropping by, no one who looks like family for that matter either. She finds herself hoping very much that he doesn't fancy her; there's something about his high-pitched giggle, his eager-puppy eyes that creeps her out a little. Immediately she feels a twinge of self-reproof: *You're not exactly beating them off with a stick yourself, Viv.* And then she thinks of Shaun and cringes.

There's a short warm-up before the match starts so Viv decides to wait in the car. The icy rain that had begun to fall on the journey over there begins to pick up pace and she turns up the heater, savouring these last moments of warmth and dryness before she's forced out into the freezing cold to watch her rosy-cheeked daughter run around the sodden sports field, happy as a pig in mud. Cleo certainly hadn't inherited her love of sport from her.

She changes the CD she'd been listening to and idly thinks about what to cook for Samar and Ted later when they come over for lunch – something she'd organized to distract herself from the looming anniversary of Ruby's death. Before long her thoughts turn to the café and the refurb she's planning, and she feels a pleasurable tug of excitement.

She sometimes has to pinch herself when she considers how well her life has turned out. A beautiful daughter, her own house and business. For a terrifying time, it had seemed likely that she might not make it through her twenties alive – in fact, if it hadn't been for Stella and Samar, she doubts she would have done.

In 1991, when she was fourteen, she had received completely out of the blue, a letter telling her that both her maternal grandparents had died and left all their money to her. An astonishing sum of £500,000, to be held in trust until her eighteenth birthday. Half a million pounds! She had called for her mother, remembering the journey they'd made to her grandparents' beautiful home, senseless with grief and shock, in the aftermath of Ruby's murder. How her mother had told her, 'There's nothing for us here.'

Stella had read the letter in silence. 'Well,' she said neutrally, when she'd finished. 'Looks like you're going to be rich.'

'But why didn't they leave it to you?' Viv had asked incredulously. 'They didn't even know me!'

Stella dropped the letter to the table and said, 'I don't want their bloody money.'

In the silence that followed they heard Margo walking to and fro in her bedroom above and Vivienne saw her mother's whole bearing tense at the sound. 'What happened between you and your parents?' she asked her tentatively. 'Why did they treat you so badly?' It was a question she'd tried to ask her mother many times over the years, but had never received a satisfactory answer.

But to her surprise Stella said, 'I didn't do what they wanted – university, a career, a good marriage. I was so young when I fell pregnant with Ruby. I let them down. They couldn't forgive me.'

'And they punished you forever after?' Viv said hotly. 'Well, they were bloody bastards, then! I don't want their money either!'

'Take it.'

'No way. Or if I do, we'll share it.'

And though it had taken her a long time, eventually Stella had been persuaded, and at eighteen, Viv had found herself in the astonishing and very dangerous position of having more money than she knew what to do with. Now, as she waits for Cleo's football match to start, she pushes the memory away. What had followed had been one of the darkest times of her life and wasn't something she liked to dwell on.

After the muddy, wet and interminable football match, Viv and Cleo return home, Viv to make a start on lunch, Cleo to get straight on the phone to invite her friend Layla over. 'To help me with my English essay,' she explains, somewhat unconvincingly.

Viv's peeling potatoes when Layla arrives. She pops her head around the door on her way up to Cleo's room and Vivienne waves hello. 'How's it going, sweetheart? Nice to see you.' Layla and Cleo have been friends since nursery school. She's a slight girl, with neat tight corn-rows, lavender-framed glasses and a terrifyingly high IQ. Layla holds strong views on everything from fracking to the Gaza Strip and isn't afraid to air them. Though her parents – a jolly, extrovert couple from Mozambique – run a dry-cleaner's and her older sister Blessing is training to be a beautician, Layla intends to be a human rights lawyer when she grows up, and Viv has absolutely no doubt whatsoever that this will happen one day.

'Samar and Ted are coming over soon,' she tells her. 'Do you want to join us for lunch?'

Layla narrows her eyes. 'Will it be vegan-friendly, Vivienne?'

'Erm, no. No, I'm afraid it probably won't.'

Layla looks at her severely through her glasses. 'In that case, no thank you. I've been reading about the effects of meat consumption on the environment and frankly want no part of it.'

Viv smiles, and notices that Layla is carrying a small duffle bag. 'What've you got in there?'

But before she can reply, Cleo appears and pulls her friend by the arm. 'Come on, let's go to my room.'

A moment later Viv hears Cleo's door close and the stereo being switched on, and she relaxes, relieved that Cleo seems to have bounced back after the disappointing visit to her father's a few weeks before. Mike had recently had a new baby with his girlfriend Sonia, and Cleo's last visit had been her first introduction to her half-brother. She'd been quiet when she returned, and evasive to Viv's gentle questioning. She absolutely doted on her dad, despite the myriad ways he'd let her down. Viv sighs and gets the chicken out of the fridge ready for roasting, shuddering when she remembers that had also been the weekend she'd slept with Shaun. *Should have been grateful, saggy old bitch.* Jesus. She shakes her head: she certainly knew how to pick them.

*   *   *

Upstairs, Layla is watching Cleo rummage through her duffle bag. 'What do you want all this stuff for anyway?' she asks her. 'My sister will go crazy if she finds out I've taken it.'

Cleo pulls out a handful of cosmetics and looks at them in wonder. 'I want you to take a picture of me, I'm sick of looking the way I always look. I've been watching YouTube videos on how to put this stuff on.'

Layla frowns. 'But what's the picture for?'

'Just . . . OK, promise not to freak? I've been talking to this boy online, on the Fortnite forum, you know? His name's Daniel and he sent me a picture of himself and he's amazing. Now he wants one of me. And I don't want to look like some stupid kid. I want to look cool.'

Layla's unimpressed. 'I think this is a very bad idea, Cleo. It's highly likely that this Daniel person is what's known as a catfish. They made us watch that documentary about it at school, remember?'

But Cleo only shrugs. Yes, he could be a fake, but she doesn't think so, and in a way, it doesn't really matter. It's like a game she's caught up in. She's never going to meet him, so what's the harm in it? It's almost like getting lost in a film or a book, a fun, easy way to talk to a cute boy without the embarrassment of having to do it face-to-face. And she's found she wants to be different, suddenly, from the same old Cleo who plays football and gets good grades and looks much younger than everyone else in her year. She'd heard a few boys at school talking about her as she walked past them a

45

week or so ago, sniggering, saying she looked like a boy and had no breasts, that they wouldn't touch her with a bargepole. And even though she knew deep down they were idiots, it had triggered something inside her, a restless anxiety that she was being left behind. She wished she could be more like Layla and not care, but the truth was she did. 'I just want to try it,' she says to her friend. 'Will you help?'

Sighing, Layla picks up a tube of mascara and a lipstick, and shrugs her agreement, surprising both of them over the next twenty minutes by being a dab hand with it. 'No idea why Blessing needs to go to college to learn how to do this stuff,' she mutters, running some straightening irons through Cleo's hair. 'It's not exactly rocket science.'

Cleo smiles and listens to the sounds of her mother preparing lunch downstairs. She thinks about how over the past few days her mum's face has taken on a familiar, distracted look. Every year at this time it's the same: the sadness of an awful, unimaginable thing that had happened a lifetime ago to someone she had never known sweeps through their house, pressing itself against the window panes, drifting up between floorboards, dimming the lights and chilling the air. And this year, like all the ones before it, she'd had no idea what to say to make her mum feel better.

'Do this,' Layla instructs her, pushing her lips into a pout as she brandishes a shade of lipstick called Hubba Hubba!

As Cleo obeys, her thoughts turn to her recent visit to her dad's house, how much she'd been looking forward to meeting her new brother, how when she'd arrived it had been nothing like she'd thought it would be.

Her dad and Sonia seemed to exist in an exhausting cycle of nappies and feeding and sleepless nights, beset with anxieties about sniffles and temperatures and something called colic, something called croup. The baby had been clamped to Sonia's breast for what seemed like hours on end and Cleo had felt in the way, an inconvenience. When she talked, her voice was too loud, her movements too clumsy. When she'd finally been allowed to hold Max, he had screamed so hard that Sonia had taken him back with a sigh of exasperation and she'd started to cry herself, only for her dad to say, 'For goodness' sake, Cleo, don't you start; you're a big girl now, grow up!'

And despite his exhaustion, she'd seen how her dad gazed down at his new son, felt the love that bound the three of them so tightly, and something inside her had hurt, as though the more warmth there was in their little house, the colder she felt inside, and she'd wanted to go home to London, feeling guiltily relieved when her dad drove her to the station and tiredly waved her off.

'Right,' says Layla briskly. 'All finished.' Eagerly Cleo goes to look at herself in the mirror and grins in amazement. Her hair is sleek and sophisticated rather than its usual mess of curls; the eyeliner, mascara and lipstick

Layla's used has definitely made her look prettier as well as older – at least fifteen, she thinks. She runs to her mother's room and returns wearing a red, scoop-necked T-shirt, then again gazes at her reflection in the mirror, delighted with herself. 'OK, now take a picture of me,' she says excitedly.

Later, when Layla has left, Cleo sends the picture straight to Daniel. His response is almost instant – Wow, you're so beautiful! – and happiness fizzes inside her. Then she hears her mum calling from downstairs. 'Cleo? Sammy and Ted are here. Come down!'

G2g xx, she writes, then runs to the bathroom and scrubs the make-up from her face, before returning the T-shirt to her mother's closet and heading for the stairs.

In the kitchen, Samar is telling Vivienne and Ted a story about a well-known theatre actress he'd once worked with. A long career in stage management has provided him with a seemingly endless supply of salacious gossip, but even by his standards, today's tale is pretty hair-raising. 'But I mean, how is that even possible?' Viv muses when he's finished. 'And with a Great Dane, for Christ's sake?' She sighs wonderingly and pours Samar a glass of wine, then offers the bottle to Ted. 'How about you, Ted? You joining us today?'

'Oh, better not, I'm on a diet.' He pats his round stomach regretfully.

When Viv turns back to Samar she's surprised to see the wistfulness in her friend's eyes as he gazes over at

Ted. It occurs to her suddenly that they'd both been quieter than usual today and she wonders if they've had a row. Samar has always been uncharacteristically unforthcoming about their relationship. When he'd first introduced him to her she'd been dubious; Ted hadn't seemed the most obvious match for her friend. While Samar was skinny as a whippet, habitually dressed in black and had a sense of humour verging on depraved, Ted had a lilting Welsh accent, was balding and over-weight, and favoured comfortable clothes in various shades of beige. He'd always struck her as a bit staid for someone as extrovert as Samar.

She also couldn't help feeling that Ted didn't entirely approve of her and Samar's close friendship. He often avoided joining them whenever they got together, sending Samar with an apologetic excuse that never quite felt authentic. When he did appear she sometimes had the nagging sense that he was there under sufferance and couldn't help wonder if he might not like her very much. She takes a sip of her wine and tries to push the thought away. Samar is clearly head over heels, things have moved fast between them and on the whole they both seem happy together. The slight atmosphere today is probably down to a lover's tiff, she decides, as she catches Samar's eye and smiles. She gets to her feet and, sliding the chicken from the oven, bastes it with sizzling fat before slamming it back in. 'So, tell me about this trip to Paris,' she says to Ted. 'Can't believe you're whisking him off again.'

'What can I say? I like to spoil him.'

'God, you lucky sod,' she says to Samar enviously.

Ted shakes his head. 'I'm the lucky one.' At this she sees Samar beam with pleasure, whatever tension there'd been between them apparently forgotten.

Samar and Viv had met aged fourteen when he joined Deptford Green Comprehensive in Year 9. Both of them had been easy targets for the school's bullies – Vivienne for wearing handmade clothes courtesy of Soren, having her hair cut by Hayley with the kitchen scissors, and for living in a house with 'a bunch of weirdo lezzers' that 'didn't even have a telly', and Samar for being Pakistani, gay and seemingly unapologetic about both. Together they'd bunk off to hang out in Nunhead cemetery where they'd sit within its vast, overgrown sprawl amidst the broken angels and mausoleums, smoking spliffs pilfered from Hayley's stash and pouring over copies of *The Face* and *i-D*, dreaming about what better, cooler, well-dressed people they'd be when they grew up.

Samar never said much about his home life but it hadn't taken Viv long to get the gist – three sisters and an unhappy mother in a two bedroom flat in New Cross, a father who was perpetually drunk and full of a nameless rage that he liked to take out on his skinny, rebellious son. Samar had loved the commune, loved Stella with a fervour close to hero worship. He'd become one of her original devotees, first in the long line of waifs and strays she'd counsel over the years, and even now remained one of her most ardent fans.

Aged seventeen, in the mid-nineties, they'd discovered London's gay scene, embracing every bar and club the city had to offer, returning faithfully every Saturday night to be transported to a world where neither Ruby's death nor Samar's dad could follow them.

When, after barely scraping through her A-levels, Vivienne inherited her grandparents' money, life had been wonderful at first. Viv found them a flat to rent in Deptford and she and Samar partied by night and slept by day, their lives an exciting whirl of recreational drugs, booze and men. But then, suddenly, things had changed. Samar landed his dream job as a stagehand in the West End, and didn't want to go out quite so much any more. He began to nag Viv about the drugs and drink she was consuming, the strange men waking up in their flat every weekend. In turn, she thought he was a boring, nagging hypocrite who needed to lighten up. Eventually, they'd had a major falling out. Samar had moved out of the flat and Viv had carried on partying without him.

And then, entirely out of the blue, or so it had seemed at the time, Vivienne, now twenty-two, had fallen into a darkness so thick and bottomless that she could find no way of dragging herself out. For weeks she'd stayed at home, sinking lower and lower, a sadness pressing on her chest that made her unable to eat or wash or countenance the world outside her flat. When she slept her dreams were plagued by horrors from which she'd wake breathless with fear, tears in her eyes, her sister's name on her lips.

Finally, wanting to build bridges and concerned when she didn't answer her phone, Samar had called around, using his old key to gain entry when there was no response to his knock. Within minutes he'd bundled Viv into a cab and taken her straight to Stella's, and over the next year the two of them slowly helped put Vivienne back together. When Viv thinks back to that time she shudders to think what would have happened if Samar hadn't rescued her, if her mum hadn't been there to take charge.

It was a time in her life she never wanted to return to, especially since having Cleo. Sometimes though she feels the darkness like a black beast circling her, waiting for its chance to pounce. Only her need for alcohol remains from those dark days and nights of sex and booze and drugs; wine was the one thing she'd not managed to relinquish, not while her nightmares continued to haunt her.

The chicken out of the oven, Viv is about to call Cleo down to eat when Samar says quietly, 'It's the anniversary on Monday, isn't it?'

She nods, touched that he remembers every year.

'How're you feeling?'

'Oh, you know. I've no idea why I still get so upset every time. Why I can't just move on. She died thirty-two years ago, for God's sake.'

'Have you never had therapy for it?' Ted asks.

She glances at him. 'No, but I've always had my mum to talk to, and you know how brilliant she is.' Even as Viv makes this remark it occurs to her that Ted, in fact, hasn't met Stella yet. Before he came on the scene she, Stella and Cleo would enjoy frequent Sunday lunches around at Samar's flat, but that hadn't happened in months. Again the worrying thought occurs to her that Ted, though perfectly polite to her face, might not quite approve of her and Samar's closeness and she feels a lingering disquiet that the friendship that had survived since their schooldays might not endure if he tried to come between them.

But Ted merely nods. 'Even so, maybe someone totally neutral wouldn't be a bad idea.'

'Oh, don't bother,' Samar tells him. 'She won't go. I've tried to talk her into it a billion times.'

Viv smiles and shrugs. The thought of talking to a stranger about her sister's death has always made her feel intensely uncomfortable, though she's not sure why. She'd been grateful that her mother had never insisted on it when she was young.

'You sure you're OK, though?' Samar asks again, coming over and putting his arm around her.

She leans her head on his shoulder. 'I hate this time of year.'

'What you need is a bit of excitement in your life. How about that doctor guy from the café? Are you going to ask him out?'

She laughs. 'No, Samar, I'm bloody not. For one thing, I don't even know if he's single.'

'Well, get yourself on a few dating websites, then. It worked for me and Ted.'

'Yeah,' she says, 'maybe you're right.' But her thoughts linger on the doctor, and she's not sure what it is about him that intrigues her so, only that there's something about his grave smile, the calm brown of his eyes that she can't quite let go of.

Much later, after her guests have left and Cleo is sound asleep, Viv goes about turning off the lights and locking the front door. Outside, the November wind bounds and batters along the street, she hears a bottle rolling to and fro along the pavement, a dog's distant bark. Before she goes to bed she glances in at Cleo sleeping before softly creeping away.

No matter how hard she tries not to think about it, her mind returns again and again to the day her sister died, a familiar niggling doubt worrying at the peripheries of her consciousness. This strange uncertainty is something that has dogged her all her life. Perhaps it was Jack's continued assertion of his innocence – he had appealed three times against his conviction – or his family's unwavering belief that she had lied, but she's never quite been able to shake it off.

As she gets undressed she reminds herself of how badly Jack had treated Ruby, how both Morris Dryden and their neighbour Declan had said they'd seen him in their lane at the time of the murder. She reaches for her sleeping pills, wanting only oblivion. The right man had gone to prison; there could be no mistake.

She wakes to darkness, her head slow and foggy from the pill, to feel fingers gripping her shoulder and she jerks away in alarm.

'Mum, wake up! Wake up, Mum, it's OK, it's only me.'

Sitting up, Viv gazes around her in confusion. 'Cleo? What's the matter?'

'You were shouting in your sleep again.'

'Oh, God, love, I'm sorry.' She leans over and switches on the bedside light to find her daughter crouching by her bed, blinking in the sudden brightness.

'It's OK. You were really screaming. Are you all right?'

'I'm fine. I'm sorry, darling. I'm OK.'

Cleo straightens and yawns, her face swollen with sleep. 'Sounded like a bad one this time.'

'It was. Thanks for waking me, I'm so sorry I disturbed you. Go back to bed. I'm fine.'

When Cleo leaves, Viv waits for her heart to cease its frantic hammering. The nightmare had begun the way it always did. She's a child again, sitting in the living room while Ruby and Jack argue in the room above. A slow dread creeps through her. She knows that her sister is about to die but she's unable to move a muscle, to do anything at all to stop it. What happens next always varies; occasionally she'll go to Ruby's bedroom to see a dark faceless figure standing over her sister's body, sometimes she'll run from the house knowing that her sister's killer is on her heels, his hand reaching out to grab her.

In tonight's dream though, just as she'd heard her sister's scream she'd looked up to find their old neighbour, Declan Fairbanks staring in at her through the living room window. For a moment she'd held his pale blue gaze before being hit by the overwhelming rush of fear that had caused her to scream out so loudly that she'd woken Cleo – and probably half the street too.

It was not the first time she'd dreamt of Declan; he often appeared in her nightmares, always with an accompanying feeling of disquiet. Sometimes she'll dream that Morris Dryden is there too, his happy grin and rosy cheeks incongruous with her terror.

This, of course, is not surprising, tied as Morris and Declan are to that day, their witness statements playing a key role in Jack's conviction. But she's noticed lately that her unease when she dreams of Declan is laced with something else – a queasy kind of revulsion. She remembers little about him: a rather severe-looking man in his fifties, dark hair peppered with grey, very striking pale blue eyes. She has a dim recollection of him shouting at her once for kicking a ball at his window. Perhaps that's where her aversion springs from, the childish memory of being chastised mixed with the general horror of Ruby's death. Perhaps that was all it was.

For a long time she lies staring at the ceiling, only

the street lamp below her window casting its weak glow upon the blackness. The wind has stopped; the world outside is silent now. But when at last she starts to drift off back to sleep, a sudden noise from the street jerks her back to full consciousness. What was that? Her window is open a crack and she lies very still, listening, until another sound from outside has her sitting up, suddenly alert. There it is again: feet shuffling on the pavement below, then the sound of someone clearing their throat. Her nostrils prickle as she detects the faint trace of cigarette smoke. Slipping from her bed she creeps to the window and looks out.

There is someone standing by her gate and she feels a jolt of shock when she realizes that it's her mother's boarder, Shaun. He's looking away down the street, the red glow from his cigarette rising and falling as he takes a drag, and she quickly steps back from the street lamp's glare. *What on earth?* She waits, heart pounding, until she hears him move off, his footsteps on the pavement gradually retreating, and when she dares to peer out once more she sees him rounding the furthest corner, before finally disappearing from view.

6

Vivienne's disquiet continues throughout the weekend, no matter how hard she tries to distract herself. What the hell had Shaun been playing at? Was he *stalking* her now? The thought is as baffling as it is frightening. She knows that all of her mother's guests are carefully vetted before they're sent to her; that Stella's never given anyone with a history of violence – or any other serious crime, for that matter – yet what did either of them really know about him? When her alarm wakes her on Monday morning these questions are still weighing heavily upon her as she heads for the shower.

Thirty minutes later she and Cleo hurry out of the house only for Viv to come to an abrupt halt before the door has closed behind them. 'I've forgotten my phone. Get in the car,' she says, handing Cleo the keys and turning back inside. 'I'll give you a lift to the bus stop.'

But when she reappears twenty seconds later, it's to find Neil and Cleo in deep discussion at the gate.

They stop when she approaches and she smiles. 'Hey, Neil, how are you?' She puts a hand on her daughter's shoulder and propels her towards the car. 'Sorry to rush off,' she tells him, 'we're running late as usual.'

'No problem,' Neil calls after them. 'Have a good day!'

Viv smiles and waves, but once they're in the car she turns to her daughter. 'What were you two talking about so avidly?'

Cleo shrugs. 'Just Fortnite, gaming, that sort of thing. He knows quite a bit about it because his son's into it.'

Viv puts the key in the ignition and glances at her in amazement. 'He has a son? He never said.'

'Yeah, he lives with his ex-wife, apparently. Why, what's wrong with that?'

'Nothing's wrong with it, it just seems odd he's never said so before.' Neil was someone who *really* liked to chat about himself, and it did seem strange he hadn't mentioned such a huge part of his life. She can't stop mulling it over as she pulls away from the kerb and checks her rear-view mirror, where she sees Neil grinning enthusiastically after them. He'd once told her that he was an IT consultant, but it occurs to her that in all the time he's lived next door he's never seemed to have a job to go off to, or at least, not that she's noticed.

After she drops Cleo at the bus stop she edges slowly through the morning traffic towards the café, and her mind returns to Ruby. Her sister would have turned forty-eight this year, Noah would be a grown man. Perhaps he'd have had kids of his own. For years afterwards, Viv had tortured herself with 'what ifs'. What if she'd called an ambulance straight away? What if she'd tried to get help rather than running off to hide? Might Noah have been saved? As a child she would be plagued with thoughts of Noah's tiny heart beating on even after Ruby's had stopped, until it too had ceased. It was a thought that made her breathless with pain. Later, much, much later, she'd read that no baby can survive longer than fifteen minutes in utero after the death of its mother, that no ambulance would have reached their cottage in time. But still the guilt has never left her, the belief that she could have done something, anything, to save them both. She should have protected her sister. She should have stopped Jack, somehow. After all, she'd been the only other person there.

As she parks and makes her way to the café, Viv considers phoning her mother to let her know she's thinking of her, but decides against it. Stella doesn't like to dwell on today's date, and that's understandable. After all, she has her own demons to fight; her own 'what ifs'. What if she hadn't gone to work that day? What if she'd fought harder to keep Jack Delaney away from Ruby? Now that Viv has her own child, she feels only too keenly how Stella must punish herself, even after all these years.

She thinks again of the dismal iris-strewn grave, the two names on the temporary wooden cross, and bites back her tears. She and her mother had never once returned to their old village to pay their respects in that crooked and crowded churchyard. Perhaps they should have: perhaps it might have given them some sort of closure. After all, her sister would have wanted her to be happy, to get on with her life. And Vivienne *was* happy. Yet thirty-two years on the nightmares persist, as if something is holding her back from moving on completely. She wonders if she ever will.

She's grateful when she opens the door of her café, soothed by its cosy familiarity. She takes in the mismatched wooden tables, the large yellow sofa, the box of children's toys and shelves full of books and board games, the paintings by a local artist on the wall, and feels her tension ease, glad of a day's work ahead to distract her. It's her new employee Agnes's first day today, and she spends time showing her the ropes. Agnes is eighteen with a nervous little face and round hazel eyes that seem perpetually baffled by the world, but proves herself a fast learner nonetheless, and after the morning rush, the café settles down to its usual steady stream of customers and bustling ordinariness.

It's heading towards lunchtime when she spots the middle-aged woman with streaks of blue in her hair and shiny orange DMs walking past the café's windows. She squints in consternation, not quite able to place her.

When it finally dawns on her she gives an excited shriek and runs out, calling after the woman's departing back, 'Hayley! Hey, Hayley, wait!'

The woman turns and with a shout of recognition retraces her steps and they meet together in a hug.

'Vivienne!' she cries. 'I don't believe it!' Her West Country accent is as strong as ever, and she has the same wide, gapped-tooth smile she'd known from when they'd lived together in the commune. They pull apart and look at each other in amazement. 'What the bloody hell are you doing here?' Hayley asks.

'This is my café!'

'Your . . . ? No way!'

'Come and have a coffee!' Vivienne says, dragging her into Ruby's.

Once they're seated, Vivienne drinks her in. The changes since she last knew Hayley as a twenty-something student are there – a few crow's feet, a few pounds extra weight – but apart from that there's barely any difference. She remembers how Hayley used to turn a blind eye when she and Samar pilfered weed from her stash, how they would hang out in her bedroom for hours listening to her talk about politics and feminism, how she'd give them books to read and lend them her Joni Mitchell albums.

'I've not long moved back to the area,' Hayley tells her. 'Went to live in Bristol for a bit, then got a job down here. Been in social work for a decade.' She beams at Viv. 'How's your mum doing? I often think of her.'

'She's well. Still running her refuge.'

Hayley nods. 'Heart of gold that woman, always had.'

'Do you ever see any of the others?' Viv asks.

'Well, Jo moved to Spain, as you know. Sometimes hear from Sandra and Christine, though they split up a few years ago.'

'Yeah, I think my mum mentioned it. But how about Rafferty Wolf? He must be in his thirties now – whatever happened to him?' Viv smiles in disbelief at the thought.

'He changed his name by deed poll to Martin, and works in data inputting I believe.' When Viv laughs she adds with a grin, 'I think Christine's just about over it, but it took a while.'

Next they talk about Kay. 'She – or rather, he – transitioned a few years ago,' Hayley tells her. 'Calls himself Kyle these days. And Soren sadly passed away some years ago, as you probably heard.'

Viv nods sombrely at this. She thinks about her years in the commune, the warmth and support of those women who'd made such an impression on her life and who, like Hayley, must be in their fifties or even sixties. Margo must be in her early eighties. Their eyes meet suddenly, then skitter away. Margo's is the only name that has remained unspoken by them both and Viv almost feels her there, a malevolent ghost sitting at the table with them. It goes without saying that none of the women kept in touch with the commune's founder, and Viv still feels the same tug of disgust and confusion as she did all those years before. She hesitates, debating whether to tell Hayley about the time she'd caught sight of Margo a few years back, then decides against it. Her exit from Unity House had been such a painful episode for them all – why dredge it up after all these years?

'God, you've done well for yourself,' Hayley says, glancing around the café admiringly. 'I'm so bloody proud of you.' She raises her eyebrows, 'And are you married? Kids?'

'One daughter, very much single. You? Any man in your life?'

'God no – can't stand the fuckers,' Hayley replies cheerfully, and Viv laughs.

The lunchtime rush is getting under way as Hayley leaves for her meeting, promising to keep in touch. Despite Agnes's help, Viv barely has time to surface before two thirty when things begin to calm down. She's about to make herself a coffee when she turns to see the doctor walking in.

She smiles. 'Hello again, did you have a nice weekend?'

He stops and nods. 'Yes, thank you. I had both days off, so . . .'

'Lovely! And did you get up to much?'

He hesitates before answering but then says, 'Not really, no. I met up with some friends.'

So perhaps no kids, and he doesn't wear a wedding ring . . . And then he asks politely, 'And you? How was your weekend? Not working either, I hope.'

'No, it was quiet; it's just me and my daughter, so you know . . . footie practice and so on.'

'Ah,' he says, nodding.

Sensing that he's about to move off, she blurts, 'Do you have kids yourself?'

Something passes across his face. 'A daughter, also. She lives with my ex-wife in Kosovo now.'

'Oh, I see. That must be hard.'

He nods and gives a slight shrug that seems to say, 'It is what it is.' And then with a final smile he goes to his usual table and pulls out his notepad and begins to write.

It's only half an hour later when a courier arrives to deliver a parcel. It's a plain cardboard box, long and slim with no business address label – unusual for deliveries to the café. When she opens it she gives a start. Inside is a large bunch of dying irises. There's no message or note, no indication from where it came, nothing but the flowers, petals beginning to wither, browning around the leaves. It's not the sort of bouquet sent by a florist – no card, no plant food, no pouch of water – and as she stares uncomprehendingly down at it her heart begins to beat faster. Who would send irises, Ruby's favourite flowers, on the anniversary of her death? She looks up and meets the doctor's gaze and, flustered, turns away.

'I'm just . . . I'll be back soon,' she tells a startled Agnes. When she runs outside it's to see the courier already speeding off on his motorbike. Wrapping her cardigan around her she crosses the road to the Rye, sits on a bench and, realizing that she's close to tears, pulls out her phone.

Samar answers on the third ring. 'Hello, love,' he says. 'What's up?'

'Sammy, did you send me flowers?'

'Nope. Why? Should I have?'

'I had a delivery of a box of half-dead irises.'

'Um . . . OK . . . ?'

'They were Ruby's favourite flower,' she says impatiently. 'We had them on her gravestone. Today's the anniversary . . .' she hears her voice rise in distress.

'Oh love. Oh God, I'm so sorry. But it's a coincidence, surely? Or . . . maybe Stella sent them?'

'No, definitely not, Mum would never do that. It's so weird.'

'Well, maybe you have a secret admirer . . .'

She sighs unhappily. 'Look, I have to get back to the café. I just wanted to check it wasn't you.'

'Viv, wait, are you OK?'

'I'm fine. I've got to go. I'll speak to you soon.'

As she hurries back across the road, she thinks about Samar's theory of a secret admirer and Shaun's face flashes across her mind. But why would *he* send her flowers? Half-dead ones at that?

Her unease lasts for the rest of the afternoon and she barely notices when the doctor says goodbye. Perhaps Shaun *was* responsible. After all, he'd been hanging around her house the night before – and God knows how long he'd been doing that for. Samar might be right: the date and choice of flowers were sheer coincidence. Who else, after all, knew they were Ruby's favourite flowers, apart from her mother and Samar? The answer trickles through her like icy water: Jack. Jack Delaney knows what Ruby's favourite flowers were. Same as he knows the anniversary of her death. It's a date he'd hardly be likely to forget. Nausea churns inside her. *It can't be him. It couldn't possibly be.* In one quick movement she picks up the box and throws it in the bin, then she leaves, locking the café door behind her with shaking fingers.

Her double French lesson finally over, the bell rings for lunch and Cleo rises with her classmates to head for the canteen. Surreptitiously, checking that no one's watching her, especially sharp-eyed Layla, she reaches into her bag to check her phone. Sure enough, 'What are you doing that for?' Layla asks. 'You'll get detention if they see you, you know.'

Cleo sighs and drops the phone back into her bag, but not before she's noticed there are no new messages from Daniel. Grumpily she rolls her eyes at her friend. 'You're such a bloody goody two shoes sometimes,' she says and walks off towards the girls' toilets, Layla staring after her in surprise.

Later, sitting in her history class, Cleo gazes distractedly out of the window. She's going to her gran's today after school, because her mum's breaking in some new girl at the café and can't leave early, and the thought does nothing to improve her mood. She used to love spending time at Stella's, but lately things have changed.

It was a few months ago that it happened. Stella had been busy with one of her guests and, feeling bored, Cleo had gone upstairs to her gran's bedroom to find a book to read.

For a few minutes she'd browsed through Stella's large, shell-covered jewellery box, something she used to love doing when she was little – her grandmother's bright and shiny pieces being far more exciting than the plain silver things her mum wore. But, tiring of this too, she'd moved to the bookshelf, running her eyes along the spines, hoping to find something as racy and eye-opening as *The Women's Room*, the last book she'd pilfered from her gran's collection. Spotting one called *The Female Eunuch* and thinking it sounded promising, she'd reached up and pulled it from its spot, a tightly bound bundle of envelopes falling out as she did so.

She'd picked the letters up and examined them with interest. Having recently watched *The Notebook* she was full of hope that she'd accidentally discovered evidence of a secret passion between her grandmother and a long-lost love akin to the one between Ryan Gosling and Rachel McAdams. She hesitated, listening out for signs that Stella might be nearby, but hearing nothing, opened one.

As her eyes scanned the words her tummy twisted in confusion. Quickly she put the first letter back in its envelope before pulling out another, and then another, her shock rising with each line she read. When she'd finished, she caught sight of her own stunned face in

Stella's dressing table mirror. Did her mother know about this? If she did, then she had been lying to Cleo her whole life. And if she didn't, then Stella had been lying to both of them. She sank onto her grandmother's bed, trying to make sense of it all. Her mum wouldn't lie to her, would she? But if she hadn't, then that made Stella the liar . . . and how could that be? Hearing footsteps on the stairs she hurriedly stuffed the letters back into their hiding place, but when she next saw her grandmother, she'd found it hard to meet her gaze.

After her history lesson, Cleo hurries to the girls' toilets and pulls her mobile out, her heart lifting when she sees a new message from Daniel. Hey gorgeous, it says. What u up to?

Hey, she replies. School, what about u?

Same, hiding in loo so I can text u, lol. She smiles but feels a jolt of surprise when she reads his next message. U have a boyfriend?

Cleo hesitates. No, why?

Would u like one?

Maybe. He can't see her, but still she goes red.

Would u be my girlfriend?

She hesitates again. OK.

U ever kissed a boy?

69

She stares at the question without answering. It feels as though the fairground ride she'd been enjoying has suddenly accelerated. No, she eventually types.

I'd like to kiss u.

She feels the heat in her cheeks. U don't know me . . .

No, but u seem really nice, from ur picture and the things u say. But that's OK, I no I'm not good looking, we can just be friends if u like, it's cool.

U are good looking. Ur really handsome.

As she leaves the toilets she finds she can't stop grinning, and the tiny flicker of doubt she'd felt has all but disappeared by the time she reaches her next class.

Viv drives the short distance to her mother's, still thinking about the flowers. Stella's street is almost in sight, but the traffic lights are out of order and she's caught in the resulting gridlock. Tapping her fingers on the steering wheel in frustration, she tries to lighten her mood by thinking about her encounter with Hayley earlier. Hearing about the other women – and poor Rafferty Wolf – had been so lovely, and idly she wonders if it

70

might be possible to organize some kind of reunion for them all, at Stella's place perhaps.

Reluctantly, her thoughts turn to Margo. In the twenty-two years since she left Unity House, Viv had seen her only once. It had been in a supermarket in Herne Hill that Viv happened to be passing and had dived into to escape the rain. She'd been browsing magazines when she'd looked up to see an elderly black woman walking with a stick. Viv had known instantly who she was; despite the intervening years her striking features were unmistakable. The older woman had turned her head and they had locked eyes. And it was the strangest thing. Viv wasn't sure what she'd expected: shame, perhaps – guilt, almost certainly. But the look on Margo's face had been something else entirely, an emotion she never thought she'd see in those beautiful brown eyes. Shocked and angry, Viv had turned and left without acknowledging her and never went back to that supermarket. Whenever she thought of it she'd bristled with disgust, her sense of betrayal visceral and raw once more. The traffic jam shifts at last and she turns into Stella's road, the memory of that unsettling meeting lingering.

Getting out of her car, she sees Shaun smoking a cigarette outside her mother's house and feels a sudden burst of fury.

'All right?' he leers, when he sees her.

'So it's not just my house you smoke your fags outside?' she snaps.

71

'Come again?'

His arrogant, handsome face is repulsive to her now. 'I saw you. Hanging around outside my house last night. What do you think you're playing at?'

'Free country, ain't it?'

'Was it you who sent me flowers?'

He bursts out laughing. 'Me, send you flowers? Off your head, you are!'

And all at once she knows with absolute certainty that the irises hadn't come from him. 'Leave me alone,' she says, turning away to hide her mortification. 'Next time I see you in my street, I'll call the police.'

'Yeah, you do that, love.' He blows out a long stream of smoke and laughs. 'Fucking nutjob.'

Her mother's in the kitchen when she goes in. 'Where's Cleo?' she asks, looking around for her daughter.

'Hmm? Oh, not sure. Maybe she went to the loo.'

She thinks of Cleo wandering around upstairs, where Shaun could happen by at any moment, and says crossly, 'For God's sake Mum, don't you know?'

Going out into the hall, she calls her daughter's name. 'I'm in the bathroom!' is the response, and Vivienne waits in the hall, trying to regain her composure. She shouldn't have spoken to her mother like that, today of all days.

When she goes back she touches Stella's shoulder. 'Sorry for snapping. How are you?'

'Oh . . . you know . . .' she replies with a sigh.

'Yeah.' Viv nods. 'I know.'

When Cleo comes back in, Stella says tartly, 'There you are. Thought you'd fallen in. Expect you took your phone up there, did you?'

'Oh, give it a rest, Gran,' Cleo says. 'Stop hassling me.'

Her voice is sharper than Viv has ever heard it and she looks at her daughter in surprise. 'Cleo!' she says. 'Don't speak to your gran like that!'

Her daughter sighs and shrugs, before flouncing out of the room.

Vivienne stands there, watching her mother stir something on the stove. And then, unable to keep it to herself any longer, says to her back, 'Someone sent a bunch of irises to the café today.' She waits anxiously for Stella's reaction.

Stella stops what she's doing, but doesn't look at her daughter.

'I don't know who sent them,' Viv goes on. 'It's freaked me out a bit, to be honest, especially today . . .'

Finally her mum turns to face her. 'It must be a coincidence. Who might have sent them to you?'

'That's just it – I have no idea. They were sent in a box, a courier dropped them off. They weren't from a florist or anything, in fact they were half dead. I threw them away.'

'How horrible.'

'Do you think I should tell the police? Do you think it's someone connected to Ruby?' She sees her mother's wince of pain and feels instantly guilty.

'What do you mean?' Stella asks quietly.

'Well, like . . .' Viv makes herself speak her fear out loud. 'Like Jack Delaney.'

'He emigrated,' Stella says, turning away. 'Years ago. Why would he be sending you flowers now?'

'I don't know.' After a silence, she says, 'Where do you even get irises in November, anyway? They're not in season, are they?'

'Florists can get hold of anything these days, I should imagine.'

Viv hesitates. 'Where did you get them for . . . for Ruby's funeral?'

Her mother carries on stirring, then glances over her shoulder at Viv. 'I didn't. Morris sorted them out. He knew how much she loved them.'

She stares at her. '*Morris?*'

Stella stops stirring and turns to face her. 'Yes, Morris Dryden. The butcher's son. He offered, he knew they were Ruby's favourites. He got hold of a florist in one of the big towns, I can't remember which. I expect his father helped him, you know Morris wasn't entirely all there.' She's silent for a beat or two, then adds, 'He loved your sister, would have done anything for her.'

'He did?'

'Yes. That's why he was always inventing reasons to come over, running pretend errands for his dad.'

A sudden memory of Morris comes to Vivienne. How on the village green her kite had landed in a tree and he'd shinned up to get it for her. How once he'd swung

74

her round and onto his shoulders when she was very little. She recalls Ruby, the sun glinting on her curls, aged about fourteen and wearing a white cotton top and jeans, her face tanned from summer, saying, 'Thank you, Morris, you're sweet,' and Morris's grin of delight.

She'd never remembered that before. 'He was nice,' she says to her mother. 'I liked him.' Then, 'What do you mean, "pretend errands"?'

'Look, Vivienne, I'm sorry, I don't want to talk about all this.' Stella turns back to her stirring. 'I just can't.'

'Of course, Mum, I'm so sorry.'

7

Living at the commune changed Stella. It happened so slowly that at first nobody noticed until one day it was plain to see that she was a very different person from the woman who had arrived lost and grief-stricken at Unity House all those months before. It was Sandra who started it, who said one day that Stella should go with her to the women's refuge she worked at, that she might find it interesting to hear the stories of the people there. And she was right. 'I think it helped her,' Viv heard Sandra murmur to Christine afterwards, 'to make her feel less alone in what she's been through.'

Another time, Hayley said to Stella, 'Why don't you come along to one of my Women's Lib meetings?' And gradually, Stella had found what to do with all the grief and shock and sadness of Ruby's death.

Vivienne went to one of the meetings once. On the

door of the community centre had been pinned a hand-written sign that said, 'Women Unite Against Domestic Violence'. Hayley was supposed to be looking after Viv in another room, because there was nobody at home that night to leave her with, and she'd sat in the draughty ante-room with a bag of Jelly Babies Sandra had given her. But when Hayley told her to stay where she was, slipping through the door into the main hall, Viv, curious, had followed her.

She saw a circle of women sitting on orange plastic chairs and then, to her amazement, her mother stood up and began to speak. The Jelly Babies never got eaten. As Stella talked about discovering her daughter's body, about how she lost her grandchild too that day, the hall was so silent you could have heard a pin drop, and the lump in Vivienne's throat was far too large to swallow anything. Afterwards, one by one, the women came to Stella and hugged her, each of them thanking her, telling her she was an inspiration, and asking her how she'd found the strength to carry on. Viv, who'd crept out of the shadows by this time, was near enough to hear her mother say, 'I carried on because I had no choice: I had my other daughter to think of. I couldn't allow that monster to ruin her life too.'

Slowly Stella began to drop the plain dark trousers and shirts she once wore, replacing them with the long, colourful garments of the type that Margo favoured. She grew her chin-length brown hair long and coloured it a rich red with henna. She began to go to more and more

77

meetings, was even asked to lead them sometimes. At Sandra's suggestion, she went on a course to learn how to become a life coach – 'I think you have a real talent for helping others,' Sandra said. It seemed to Viv that her mother even began to carry herself differently, adopting a dignified, straight-backed posture, her head held high. Every week at Unity House's Sunday meetings, which had always been led by Margo, the other women began to ask, 'What do you think, Stella?', 'What's your view on this?' and more and more frequently Stella would give her opinion while the others listened with silent respect.

When Stella got a job at an old people's home in Catford, if Viv wasn't at school she stayed at home with whomever happened to be about. She would hang out in the attic with Soren, watching her paint, organizing her brushes for her and listening to her stories about her childhood in South Africa. Or else she would go to Sandra and Christine's floor and play with Rafferty Wolf. She liked, too, to go down to the basement where Kay lived. She did this when she was feeling lonely but didn't really want to talk. Together they'd listen to music on Kay's portable cassette player; sad, mournful stuff so beautiful it made her want to cry, but in a good way. 'What is this music?' she asked Kay once. And when Kay told her she'd looked back at her perplexed. 'Bark? What, like what a dog does?' but Kay just smiled and taught her how to play four different kinds of Patience. They would sit, side by side, quiet but for the music and the slap of playing cards on the table.

Hayley's room was the most fun. They'd dance together to her David Bowie LPs and Hayley would tell her about Greenham Common and the rallies and marches she'd been on, and about Maggie Thatcher and the rest of the Tory scum. She taught her how to roll cigarettes for her and Viv would sit carefully with a pack of Rizla papers and a pouch of tobacco and diligently make one roll-up after another, which Hayley would either smoke or tuck behind her ears and say, 'Cheers, kiddo.'

But it was Margo who really captured Vivienne's heart, who she would seek out to spend time with when her mother was out. Margo never asked her questions, but there was something in the way she listened that made Vivienne tell her things she never told anyone else. Together they would tend the vegetables in the garden, or Margo would show her how to help her make an enormous chilli con carne for that evening's meal, and Viv would talk – about her old life in the village she'd grown up in, and about Ruby. She found she could talk to Margo about her sister in a way she didn't like to with her mother. Each time she tried to with Stella it was like a heavy weight pushing down on her, her words clogging her throat. But with Margo it was different. She didn't talk about the murder, just about things she and her sister used to do together, about how kind Ruby was, how she made her feel safe and loved. It made her feel better to talk about her; she didn't want to forget.

To Vivienne, Margo was the best thing about Unity

House. Which is why it was such a shock to discover how wrong she'd been about her, how terribly, terribly wrong. Her mother knew, though. She'd known it almost from the first day. She always had been so clever like that.

Cleo's waiting for a bus to take her home from school when a text arrives from Daniel asking for her email address. She sends it to him immediately and, feeling suddenly restless, decides to walk on to the next bus stop. As she avoids puddles and crowds of school kids, she thinks about the letters she'd found in her grandmother's room. An uneasy, anxious sort of feeling has been swilling around inside her ever since. It weighs heavily on her, the predicament of keeping such a huge secret from her mother. She should, she reasons, ask her grandmother about the letters . . . but always something stops her. For as long as she can remember, Stella has never talked about the past. Never ever. Cleo remembers the time, aged about ten and not long after she'd learned the truth about Ruby's death, she'd mentioned her aunt's name in front of Stella. She recalls her mum's urgent shake of the head, her silencing glance of warning.

Cleo scowls as she dodges a large puddle and sees her bus sail past. She hadn't been very nice to her grandmother since her discovery and feels bad about it. Stella senses something, she knows. Now there is this odd chill between them and she doesn't know what to do about it.

She thinks sometimes of telling Layla about the letters,

just to feel the relief of speaking it out loud, but some-thing stops her – as though it would be betraying her mum somehow, discussing something so private and painful. But as she walks the cold wet streets towards home, Cleo comes to a decision. She will tell her mother. She won't be able to stand it if she doesn't. But not yet. It's too soon after Ruby's anniversary, and her mum is so busy with the café . . . and before long it will be Christmas and she doesn't want to spoil that. She will tell her after Christmas, she decides. Definitely.

She feels better, having come to a decision. When her phone vibrates in her pocket and she sees that she has a new email from Daniel, she opens it eagerly, her worries instantly forgotten.

Hey Cleo, u OK? It's nice being able to email you, feels like we can talk properly now, she reads.

Me too. How are u?

Not good.

Why? What's happened?'

My dad. I was late coming home from school yesterday, he got angry. Sometimes he hits me and stuff.

Cleo stops at a bus shelter and sits down, staring at the words in dismay. That's terrible, I'm so sorry. Are u OK?

Yeah. I've got a black eye and a fat lip, could be worse.

Her fingers hover over the keypad, unsure how to respond, and a new message appears. I hate him. I always tell people I walked into a door or whatever, guess I'm ashamed that he does it.

It's not ur fault. Don't ever think that. Cleo hesitates, then writes, What does ur mum do when he does that?

My mum died when I was little.

Cleo catches her breath. I'm so sorry.

U ever had anyone close to u die?

No. I mean, my aunt died really young, but that was before I was born.

How did she die?

She was killed by her boyfriend. She was only sixteen.

That's awful.

I know 😢 Her name was Ruby. My mum says I look like her.

She must have been beautiful then.

Cleo smiles. I have a picture of her, she was way prettier than me.

U know how u could cheer me up? Take a selfie right now and send it to me.

After a second's hesitation, she does as he asks.

Ur so pretty.

Can I have one of u?

I have a fat lip, remember?! Hold on, I'll find one from the other day.

She waits, counting the seconds, and then there he is. He doesn't have the hat on in this one, and he's smiling shyly at the camera. He's so good-looking with such beautiful blue eyes that her heart flips. She can't bear the thought of anyone hurting him. Are u OK? she writes. After what ur dad did, I mean?

I am now I've talked to u.

She looks up and sees her bus approaching. I better go.

OK. I wish I could see u in real life.

Me too.

Maybe one day. X

The following Saturday, Viv waits at the foot of the stairs for her daughter to come down. When she appears she looks so pretty, her cheeks flushed and glowing, that Vivienne feels a surge of love and pride. 'Come on,' she says, 'we're going next door to visit Neil.'

Cleo rolls her eyes. 'Oh God, can't I stay here?'

'No. He's our neighbour and he invited us both. Come on, stop being so grumpy. It'll be half an hour, tops.'

Viv smiles enthusiastically when Neil opens the door, hoping to make up for Cleo's (and her own, if she's honest) reluctance. 'Come in, come in,' he cries excitedly as they follow him through to the kitchen.

Immediately he makes a big fuss about what Cleo might like to drink, 'Coke? Lemonade? Juice? Or I've got Dr Pepper, if you like? Water? Are you sure? Go on, treat yourself. No? Have a biscuit, then, here you are, take two. Not on a diet, are you? Lovely slim girl like you.'

At this point, Viv hurriedly butts in. 'Gosh, isn't it great in here, Neil? You must tell me which builders you use!' And thankfully Neil's attention is diverted once more.

In fact, the kitchen is pretty cold and sterile, but it's expensively done and she finds enough to compliment to keep him on the subject for several minutes. The room opens up on to a living room and, spotting a collection of games consoles, Cleo asks if she can take a look.

'Sure! Help yourself, you can come round any time and play with them, if you want,' Neil replies. 'Honestly, it'd be no trouble.' When she's out of earshot he murmurs, 'Lovely girl, your daughter.'

'Thanks, I'm very proud of her.'

'I see she inherited her mother's good looks.'

Viv sighs inwardly but manages to keep smiling. 'Cleo tells me you have a son?'

The expression in Neil's eyes alters a fraction. 'Yes,' he nods. 'Mark.'

Glancing around the room she notices there are no photographs on display and in the following silence she asks politely, 'Have you and his mother been apart long?'

But it's clear he doesn't want to talk about it and he answers almost curtly, 'Ten years, yes. But tell me about you,' he says, grinning once more. 'How's that little coffee shop of yours doing? I must drop by one day, sample your wares!'

For the following half hour Neil proudly shows her around his home, and while doing so, barely stops talking. He tells her about the holiday he's going on next year, the golf he likes to play, the car he's got his eye on. On the few occasions he does ask Viv about herself, it seems clear that he is merely waiting for her to finish so that he can turn the subject back to himself. The strange thing is that, despite this, Viv is left with very little sense of who he really is. There are no plants or pets or music, no books, no art on the walls. Everything is neat, expensive and bland. Forty minutes later, Viv is finally able to make their excuses and leave, by which time she can feel a tension headache forming between her eyes.

'He's a bit of a wally, isn't he?' Cleo mutters as Viv unlocks their own front door.

'Oh don't, he's harmless enough,' admonishes Vivienne, 'I'm sure he means well,' and then they catch each other's eye and smile.

The next Thursday, Viv calls into Sainsbury's and spies the doctor from her café wandering the vegetable aisle, basket in hand. She hesitates, wondering whether to approach him, but hearing again Samar's voice saying, '*Ask him out, for God's sake!*' she mutters, 'Bugger it,' and, going over to him, loudly exclaims, 'Oh, hi!'

He looks up, his preoccupied frown turning into a smile of recognition. 'Hello,' he says. 'How are you?'

'Yeah, I'm good, thanks. Listen, um, Aleksander, right?' At his look of surprise she says, 'I, erm, saw your name on your ID card the other day.'

He nods. 'Please, call me Alek.'

'I'm Viv.'

He smiles. 'Yes, I know. You told me at the café. How your name's not Ruby, but Vivienne.'

'Sorry, yes. Of course I did.'

They both stare down at Alek's shopping basket. A tin of artichoke hearts, some asparagus, a haddock and a punnet of mushrooms, and she wonders what he might be making, if it's some sort of Kosovan speciality, perhaps, and whether he's a good cook. She looks up and realizes that he's gazing at her quizzically.

She clears her throat, feeling the heat creep up her neck. 'Look, I don't usually do this sort of thing, but I'm going to anyway,' she blusters. She takes a breath then says, 'Would you like to go out for a drink one night? With me, I mean? Would you like to go to a pub or, well, yes, in fact, just a pub, and have a drink?' She can't remember the last time she asked a man out – it must be decades – and she listens to herself speak in shocked fascination.

He stares at her, then his eyes shift from left to right, as if seeking help from one of the passing shoppers, and she can tell with absolute certainty that the idea of going on a date with her has caught him completely off guard, that he'd never considered it before, and she feels herself die a little inside.

Almost immediately the polite smile is back in place and he says, 'Well, yes. OK. That would be nice. Perhaps I can take your number and we can work something out . . . I'm sorry but I don't know my shift pattern this week so . . .'

Awkwardly they do the getting their phones out thing and the confusion about who should give their number first and then it's done and Viv decides she can live without the courgettes and teabags she'd gone in there for and goes back out into the night and keeps walking until she's out of sight and exhales loudly and says, '*Shit!*'

As she approaches her road she phones Samar. 'You'll never, in a million years, guess what I've just done,' she says.

They're still chatting while she lets herself into her house and she doesn't think much of the envelope lying on her doormat, barely noticing it as she picks it up and carries it to the kitchen. It's only when she's said goodbye to Samar and hung up that she gives it her full attention. Frowning, because the envelope has no address or stamp, she opens it. And when she pulls out the neatly folded piece of A4 paper she can only stare down at it dumbly. In her hand is a photocopy of a news story, dated 9 November 1984, from the *Essex Enquirer*. Its headline reads: 'TEEN MUM-TO-BE SLAIN IN BEDROOM'. Alongside is a black-and-white photograph of her sister. Across the accompanying article someone has written in thick red pen, 'Who killed Ruby?'

Icy fingers close around her heart. *Jack*. She looks wildly around as though he might be somewhere near, might somehow be watching her even now. Jack has come to her house, has invaded her and Cleo's home with his threat and his madness and in that instant the last three decades melt away, she is eight years old again, shivering in her bed as she waits for the letter box to rattle. But this time it's not Jack's brothers or uncle who have come for her; it's Jack himself, she knows it is.

Dazedly she checks the time: three o'clock. Cleo will

be going straight to football practice after school, so won't be back until five. Scarcely breathing, still holding the piece of paper, she picks up her keys and hurries from the house.

8

When Viv arrives at Peckham police station and explains the reason for her visit she's taken to a small interview room where a Detective Sergeant Christopher Bennet listens to her story with polite attention.

'I think Jack Delaney's behind this,' she says after she's shown him the newspaper cutting and described the circumstances of her sister's murder.

Bennet has grey, very deep-set eyes, which he turns on her now. 'Because . . . ?'

'Because this is exactly the sort of thing sent to us by his family after he was found guilty. It was my evidence that put him in prison in the first place. They couldn't accept his conviction.'

There's a short silence while Bennet considers this. 'You said he moved to Canada after his release?' he asks.

'Apparently. But he must be back in the country. I don't know why he's started doing this. The flowers, then this . . .'

'And there's no one else you can think of who might want to upset you? No one you've fallen out with recently, or . . .'

Briefly a picture of Shaun's sullen face flashes into her mind, but she dismisses it at once. 'No, and even if I did, nobody apart from my mum knows about the flowers, the date Ruby died and so on.'

'Nobody?' he asks. 'No one else came to the funeral, or knew about her death?'

She sighs. 'Well, I mean, of course lots of people from the village did but—'

'So there could in fact be a number of people who would have known the relevance of the day's date, the type of flowers at your sister's funeral and so on.'

'But why would they want to, after all this time? Surely you can at least consider that this is Jack Delaney's doing? Look, he spent thirty years in prison, it was my evidence that put him there. I feel like he's . . . I don't know, trying to punish me or something . . .'

The officer's eyebrows shoot up. 'He got thirty years?'

'His original sentence was extended after he attacked his cellmate – who he half blinded and left in a coma, by the way. Look, this isn't some petty criminal we're talking about. He killed my sister and their unborn child, for God's sake.'

'Yes, I understand your concern.' Bennet gets to his

91

feet and looks at Viv expectantly until reluctantly she does the same. 'Leave it with me,' he says as he shows her out of the room.

'But what if something else happens?' Viv asks anxiously. 'I have a child. I'm terrified that he's going to do something worse, maybe even turn up in person.'

'If anything at all happens to concern you then do phone us immediately,' Bennet says. 'As things stand, we have no clear indication that it is Jack Delaney who's behind this. Nor have you received any actual threat of violence either to yourself or your child.' He smiles at her then, blandly reassuring. 'However, whoever did send that article to you clearly did so maliciously, and I can assure you that's something we take very seriously. I'll make some enquiries and see if I can ascertain Delaney's whereabouts to put your mind at rest. I'll be in touch.'

Once back in the street, Vivienne slowly makes her way towards her car. She has a sudden, desperate longing for her mother. Stella will know what to do, she always does. She glances at her watch: 4 p.m. An hour until Cleo gets home. Quickly she unlocks her car and gets in.

It had been Stella who first saw through Margo, of course. Vivienne was ten when the trouble began. It was a beautiful day in the long summer holidays before she started secondary school, and she and Margo were in the garden, picking runner beans for dinner. They knelt, side by side, a red colander between them, their arms occasionally brushing as they worked in companionable silence. She liked the way Margo smelled in this heat, her sun-soaked skin giving off a salty warmth, her long dreadlocks, bound up with a mustard-coloured scarf, emanating a sweet, earthy scent with a hint of rosemary.

'I heard you, last night,' Margo said quietly, her eyes on the vine she was stripping. 'I heard you shouting in your sleep.'

Viv stopped, and not looking at her said, 'I have nightmares sometimes.'

And Margo nodded.

There was a silence, as Viv looked down at the bean in her hand. 'I'm sorry if I woke you.'

Margo shook her head. 'You have nothing to be sorry for.' After a pause she said, 'You have them often?'

'Yeah.' She wanted to tell her that she had them almost every night, had done ever since Ruby died, that they were too dreadful and frightening to bear, but without a word she carried on picking the beans and dropping them into the colander, not even looking in Margo's direction.

'You know you can always talk to me, Vivienne, about anything at all,' Margo said after a while. 'We're friends, right?'

She nodded. 'I know.'

And Margo had reached over then and put her arm around her, and Viv had breathed in her warm sweet scent and felt comforted.

Later that day she'd been helping her mother make the evening meal when Stella said carefully, thoughtfully, 'You get on well with Margo, don't you? She's kind to spend so much time with you.'

Viv had smiled. 'Yeah, I do, she's ace.'

'Good,' Stella said, nodding thoughtfully. 'That's good.'

But Vivienne, always highly attuned to her mother's moods, had sensed something disconcerting in her voice. 'Why,' she said, 'don't you like her?'

Stella sighed. 'Oh, yes. I mean, she's clearly a remarkable woman to have set up all this,' she gestured at their surroundings. 'I just . . . I don't know . . . It's probably nothing. Something about her bothers me . . . I don't know why. I can't put it into words. I don't think she likes me very much.'

Viv had stared at her in surprise. Margo seemed so nice; surely Stella was mistaken? They'd continued preparing dinner together, but her mother's words had stayed with her, a troubling itch she couldn't quite reach.

Sure enough, at the next Sunday house meeting, she saw the first hint of what her mother meant. They'd been talking about the possibility of selling produce from their garden and Stella had been putting forward her idea to make jam from their plum tree when Margo had sighed deeply and said, 'Shall we give the others a chance to speak now, Stella?' The coolness in her tone had been unmistakable and Stella had dropped her head and fallen silent, but not before she'd met Viv's gaze with a look that said, 'You see?'

A week later, while they cleaned the bathroom together, Stella had spoken to her again about Margo. Vivienne liked how her mother had begun to talk to her recently as though she were another adult, whose opinion she respected. 'She always singles you out, always calling you away to spend time with her alone. Have you noticed that?' She frowned, 'Perhaps it's because she doesn't have children of her own.' She'd sighed, then, staring into space. 'I can't help feeling there's something a bit odd about it, though.' And right at that moment Margo had walked in.

'Vivienne,' she'd said, after giving a brief nod to her mother, 'I managed to get that book from the library we were discussing. Would you like to come and take a look?'

Viv had hesitated, feeling intensely awkward, and in the silence Stella had smiled and said quietly, nicely, 'I think she's happy here, Margo, for the time being.'

The two women stared at each other for a beat or two, until Margo nodded and said quietly, 'Another time then, Viv.'

'See how angry she is?' Stella had murmured when she'd gone. 'It's so strange, don't you think? I wonder what happened in her life to make her so angry.'

Viv stands on her mother's doorstep, wrestling with her panic. She needs to compose herself so as not to

95

alarm her, and she takes long deep breaths before she knocks on the door. But when Stella opens it she takes one look at her daughter and pulls her quickly inside, her eyes scanning her face, immediately alert to her daughter's mood. 'What is it?' she asks. 'What's happened?'

She should have known she could hide nothing from Stella. Any resolve Viv had tried to muster on the way over – to hide the true extent of her fear, to shield her from the memories Jack's name would dredge up – melts instantly away, and within minutes she's told her everything. Her mother's face is pale as she gazes back at her. 'But . . . it can't be him. It can't be Jack! Why would he do this? Why now?' She gets to her feet, her hands trembling as she grips the back of her chair.

'I don't know. I'm really scared, Mum. He came to my house and put it through my door, exactly like Jack's family did after Ruby died.'

'Do you think it might be one of them? One of his brothers, maybe?' Stella stares at Vivienne with frightened eyes. 'He was sentenced according to the law! He was found guilty!'

'I know.' Viv nods. 'I know he was.' For the first time, her mother looks older than her sixty-five years; frailer and more fearful than Viv's ever seen her. 'I'm sorry, Mum,' she says miserably. 'I'm so sorry for upsetting you like this.'

At that moment Shaun appears in the doorway and he glances in at them sullenly before sloping away, looking so much like a sulky teenager that Viv almost laughs.

The two of them sit in silence for a while before Stella sighs. 'I'll make us some tea,' she says.

'No,' Viv tells her, getting to her feet. 'I'll do it.' When she's brought their mugs to the table she sits down again and glances at her mother's anxious face. Trying to lighten the mood, she forces a smile. 'God, I was actually feeling pretty good before I found that bloody envelope. Typical, isn't it?' She passes Stella her mug and says, 'I asked someone out on a date, believe it or not. And he said yes.'

Stella looks at her. 'Did you? Who?'

'A guy called Alek. He comes to my café sometimes. We're going out for a drink.' When her mother doesn't respond she adds, 'I'm looking forward to it.'

Stella stirs her tea. 'Hmmm.'

Viv frowns. 'Well, what does that mean?'

'Oh . . . nothing, darling. Just . . . you know, be careful, that's all. Remember how men have treated you in the past, how fragile you can be. You don't want to become ill again.'

'Mum, that was a long time ago.'

'I'm only saying it because I care. I don't want you to be hurt.'

Viv sighs. She should have known better than to broach the subject of her love life with her mother. Stella has always been odd about her having boyfriends. An overprotectiveness born of what happened to Ruby, no

97

doubt, but aggravating nonetheless. 'I know, Mum,' she says. 'I know you do.'

That evening, Viv is at home with Cleo making their evening meal when DS Bennet calls her. She hurriedly closes the kitchen door, anxious that Cleo shouldn't overhear their conversation.

'You were right in thinking that Jack Delaney went to Canada,' Bennet tells her. 'He arrived there with an electronic travel visa, ostensibly as a tourist, and he didn't apply for residency.'

She holds the phone more tightly. 'And . . . ?'

There's a pause. 'We haven't been able to trace his whereabouts since then.'

'So he could have come back to Britain?'

'There's no record of a Jack Delaney re-entering the country.'

'I'm sure someone who's been in prison for thirty years would know how to get a false passport!' she says.

Bennet's reply is guarded. 'Look, it's possible, but we have no way of telling whether Delaney's responsible for the newspaper article and flowers.'

Viv exhales in disbelief. 'So what now? I'm supposed to wait until he does something else? What if he – I don't know – breaks in, attacks me or my daughter? What then? He's a convicted murderer, for Christ's sake!'

There's a short silence. 'I'm sorry, Vivienne, I can only advise you that, if anything happens, or if anything else concerns you, you should call us straight away.'

'Is that it?' Vivienne cuts in. 'Seriously?'

'I understand your frustration. But—'

She doesn't let him finish. 'OK. Thanks for your time,' she mutters, before hanging up.

For the next few days Viv exists in a state of tense watchfulness. She begins driving Cleo to the bus stop each morning, parking across the road so she can see her safely on her way. Even so, she worries. 'Cleo, darling,' she says cautiously over breakfast one morning. 'You know never, ever, to talk to strangers, don't you? Or accept lifts, or anything like that. Even if they tell you they're . . . I don't know, a friend's dad or something . . . You never would, would you?'

Cleo looks up from her cornflakes and stares at her in disbelief. 'What are you on about, Mum? Of course I know that. I'm not six.' She rolls her eyes and turns back to her book.

'Yes, I know. Of course you're not. Sorry.' She bites her lip, 'But promise me, won't you, if anything odd happens, you'll tell me straight away . . .'

Cleo puts her spoon down. 'Mum, why are you being weird? What's going on?'

'Nothing!' She makes herself smile. 'You're right. I am being weird. I worry about you, that's all.'

At night her dreams are filled with threat, at work she jumps at slamming doors, sirens wailing, shouts from the street, and she eyes every man who walks through the café's door with suspicion. But the days pass uneventfully and when Bennet eventually calls her to check there have been 'no more incidents', she has to admit that all has been quiet.

'Good,' he replies. 'Perhaps that will be an end to it then.'

When she puts the phone down, for the first time since receiving the newspaper cutting she dares to allow herself to hope that he might be right.

It's a day later that she receives a text from Alek saying that he's free the following Tuesday. She stares down at the message blankly then phones Samar. 'He wants to meet up. I think I'll tell him I'm busy,' she says. 'I'm not really in the mood any—'

'Don't you bloody dare,' Samar interrupts. 'Text him back immediately and say yes.'

'But—'

'Viv, go on the date. It's only a date. You need to think about something other than Jack Delaney. Seriously. If you don't text him back, I will come over there and do it for you.'

'All right, all right! Jesus.' She hangs up and does as Samar says, arranging to meet Alek in a pub overlooking the Rye at 8 p.m. the following Tuesday. And after that, just as Samar said, she barely thinks of Jack Delaney at all.

9

When Tuesday arrives, Samar comes to Viv's house at seven thirty, ready to keep Cleo company. 'We'll watch *Saw II* and smoke crack,' he promises loudly as Viv leaves the room to get ready.

Upstairs, she stands in front of her mirror and wonders what to wear. She pulls out a dress and holds it against herself before discarding it for another, then rifles through her wardrobe once more, trying not to panic. Eventually she decides on a silky blouse, black jeans and heels, with lots of eye make-up and red lipstick, and considers her reflection again. Jesus. When did she get so old? She stands up straighter, sucking her tummy in, examining her crow's feet. She thinks of Alek, of his look of confusion when she'd suggested this date, and feels a fresh flurry of nerves.

Samar whistles obligingly when she finally comes

downstairs. 'You look hot,' he tells her cheerfully. 'He'd be a total fool not to fancy you in that.'

Viv turns to Cleo. 'What do you think? Too much? Too boring? Oh God, I'm so nervous.'

'You look really pretty, Mum, I hope he's nice. I hope you like him.'

She gives her a hug. 'Me too. Wish me luck!'

As she hurries from the house she thinks how out of practice she is – she's barely dated anyone over the past thirteen years. She's been too busy – with work, with Cleo; too determined not to fall back into the self-destructive cycle of her teens and early twenties, when one bad man had followed another, and then another. Her heels click against the pavement and she wraps her coat around her as she tries not to think about how thrown Alek had been when she'd suggested this date. She sees the pub ahead and inhales deeply. *Oh God oh God oh God.*

Alek is there already, sitting at a corner table when she arrives, and he stands up as she approaches. They dip and weave, making a clumsy fudge of kissing on both cheeks before he hurries off to the bar.

When they're both seated with their drinks they smile self-consciously. 'So,' he says.

'So.' She raises her eyebrows and gives a half-laugh. 'How was your day?'

The conversation flows easily enough; she asks about his job and he tells her that he's an anaesthetist, and that he recently transferred to King's College Hospital from St Thomas's. In return she tells him about her café, and they then discuss the pros and cons of life in London, how the area he now lives in compares to the one he just left. He wears a pale blue cotton shirt, open at the neck, the sleeves rolled up to show the smooth olive skin of his forearms, lightly downed in dark brown hair. She notices that the material on his collar is frayed, worn and pale with age, and when he gets up to return to the bar she sees that one of his shoes is coming apart at the sole.

'So you're from Kosovo,' she says when he returns.

He nods. 'I'm Kosovar Albanian. My ex-wife and I came over in ninety-eight. Our daughter turned fourteen this year.'

'And you said they returned there?'

'To Pristina, yes.'

'You didn't want to go?'

He shakes his head. 'No, I do not wish to return there.' He drains his drink. 'It is . . . I guess . . . defiled for me. I can never go back . . .' He trails off, shrugging. 'The war . . .'

She nods, the following silence holding the weight of his last two words, alluding to an experience she can have no hope of understanding, of horrors she can't begin to imagine.

'But tell me about your café,' he says, brightening. 'You have had it a long time?'

'Since my mid-twenties. I inherited some money when I was eighteen, a real windfall, so I spent it on buying a house and getting Ruby's off the ground.'

He looks impressed. 'Quite an achievement, so young.'

She smiles, thinking about that time. How, after she'd moved back to live with her mother and slowly begun to heal, she had discovered her love for cooking. Instead of getting high, staying out all night, and sleeping with random strangers, she'd put her energy into experimenting in the kitchen, eventually realizing what she really wanted to do with her life. At twenty-five she'd invested some of her grandparents' money into buying the café and spent months studying how to run a business before finally opening its doors a year later.

After a few moments she says, 'I see you writing a lot, in the café. What are you working on? A novel?'

He smiles, 'No, I'm writing to my daughter, I send her letters every week.' He hesitates, 'Things are not simple between us.'

He shifts in his seat and she catches his scent, smells the sharpness of lemons, the weight of musk. He is almost laughably attractive, despite his slightly shabby appearance. She thinks about how she'd got dressed up for tonight, how it seems ridiculous now, the idea that he might be interested in her when the polite distance between them seems so impassable. Yet when they reach for their drinks and their hands accidentally brush he does not instantly pull his fingers away and electricity crackles between them as their eyes meet. She feels a jolt of surprise. Had she imagined it?

'It gave you a shock when I asked you out for a drink,' she says at last, deciding to be bold.

He shrugs. 'Yes.'

'You didn't want to?'

'No, I did. I did. I just . . . it has been a long time, for me.'

She nods. 'Yeah, me too.'

They smile, the awkwardness dissipating a fraction as her eyes search his. But too soon, even though it is barely ten thirty, there is the sense that the evening has come to a close and they both rise and shrug on their coats.

'So,' Alek says when they are standing in the street. 'I'm going this way. And you . . . ?'

She nods and they set off together, along the edges of the dark and silent Rye, its treetops stirring restlessly in the wind.

Samar and Cleo are playing Gin Rummy and watching *Gossip Girl*, and as Cleo deals the cards she thinks about her mum and wonders if she's having a nice time. Lately she's been acting kind of odd – on edge and jumpy, staring into space a lot. Sometimes in the mornings she looks as though she's hardly slept the night before. Cleo wonders about the man she's meeting and what he's like. Her mother never goes on dates, or hardly ever, and when she was younger Cleo had been fine with that, had found the idea of sharing her kind of horrible. But things are different now.

A change has come over Cleo lately. So slow and vague at first it has crept up on her almost without her knowing. She can feel herself for the first time separating from Viv, feel herself wanting to break free from the ties that have always bound them so tightly. That safe little world consisting of her, her mum and grandmother doesn't feel as satisfying as it once did. Sometimes she finds herself looking at older girls – at school, on the street, at the shopping precinct – observing their make-up and their confidence and their fast way of talking, how they flirt with boys, how they laugh and toss their hair and move through the world with such certainty, and she feels drawn to them in a way she hadn't before. It makes her feel both thrilled and fearful, pulled between the world they represent, and the one she's always known. Talking to Daniel feels a safe bridge between the two.

She sighs. 'Wonder how Mum's getting on,' she says.

'I guess we'll find out soon enough,' Samar shrugs.

She picks up a card from the pack and says, 'Rummy. Can I stay up and wait for her?'

'Nope. She might not be back for ages yet.' He nods at the playing cards. 'Another game?'

She's about to agree when her mobile bleeps. Snatching it up eagerly, she jumps to her feet. 'I'm just going to the loo,' she says.

'Who's that?' Samar asks, then laughs. 'You got a boyfriend, Cleo?'

She glances at him crossly. 'Don't be stupid. It's Layla.' She rolls her eyes and heads for the door.

'OK, sorry I asked.' Samar stares thoughtfully after her as she hurtles up the stairs.

Once safely in the bathroom, Cleo clicks on her new text message. **Hello beautiful,** it says.

106

Smiling, she types her reply. Hey! How are u? U OK?

No, my dad's being an arsehole again.

She bites her lip. He didn't hit u, did he?

Just a shove this time, but I tripped and knocked my head. I'm OK, though.

She reads the words in horror. Look, maybe I should tell my mum. She's really nice, she'll be able to help u. She'll know what to do.

His reply is almost instant. Please don't do that. My dad would kill me if he finds out I've told anyone.

She stares down at his message, feeling his panic. I wish I could help u.

Maybe I could come to London to see u soon? I could tell my dad I'm at my friend Adam's house. I've got some savings so I could get a train down. What do u think? U could come and meet me and we could spend the day together.

Her eyes widen with excitement. How amazing would that be! Yes, I'd love that.

Don't tell ur mum though.

She thinks of how odd her mother's been acting recently, how distracted she's been. I won't, she writes. I promise.

Viv and Alek walk together, the street almost empty. A silence has opened up between them; whatever brief spark of chemistry there'd been in the pub entirely absent now. She feels her spirits sink with every step. She had tried, but it hadn't worked out, and now the evening she'd so looked forward to had come to an end, and she feels sadder than she thought she would, knowing that she would have to go home to Samar and paste on a cheerful smile and say, 'Oh well, another one bites the dust,' and drink a glass of wine or two.

But then Alek comes to an abrupt halt and turns to her and says, 'Vivienne, forgive me, I am not good at these things, I have spent too much time . . .' but his voice trails away, and he doesn't tell her what it is he's spent too much time doing.

'No, it's fine,' she falters.

He continues to look at her, the expression in his eyes indecipherable, and it strikes her in that moment that she is not happy, despite the café, despite her love for Cleo. She is not happy with her life – not really. And she is so surprised, so blindsided when he steps forward and kisses her that at first her mouth won't react. It is a brief, cautious kiss, over before it's begun, but when they pull apart she looks up at his face, at the brown depths of his eyes, the curve of his mouth and, suddenly unlike herself, she reaches up to put her hand against his cheek. They stand like that as a car passes, its tyres slick against the wet tarmac, and he gently takes her hand and kisses the heel of it before he lets it fall, and when she says goodbye she thinks how, though she knows him not at all, a small part of her that had always felt empty feels a little less so, just a bit.

At her gate she pauses, wanting to savour the last ten minutes before she's cross-examined by Samar. Just then a movement catches her eye and she looks up to see Neil standing at an upstairs window. She raises her hand in a wave but he turns as though he hadn't seen her and, shrugging, she lets herself in.

Samar touches his wine glass with hers. 'I have a very good feeling about this,' he tells her.

She thinks about Alek, their sudden, unexpected kiss, and leans back against the sofa cushion. 'Maybe,' she says. 'But I'm not getting my hopes up.' She looks at Samar and says anxiously. 'Everything was all right here, wasn't it?'

'Yep. Everything was fine, don't worry.' When she nods unhappily, he asks, 'That dickhead Shaun hasn't been hanging around again, has he?'

'No,' she says. 'Nothing like that. I just . . . I feel like I'm waiting all the time for Jack to come up with something new to scare me with.'

Samar squeezes her hand. 'You know you and Cleo

can always come and stay with me and Ted, don't you? I mean it, Viv, you're welcome anytime.'

'I know. Thank you, Sammy.'

It's as she's seeing Samar to the door that her phone bleeps. She frowns at it in surprise when she sees that it's from Alek. Will you come to lunch at my flat? it says.

Samar reads it over her shoulder. 'Blimey. He's keen.'

'Maybe they don't believe in beating around the bush in Kosovo,' she replies.

'Well, go on then,' he prompts. 'Text him back.'

She thinks about it, then types, When?

His reply is instant. I have a day off on Friday.

'He's totally asking you round for sex,' Samar says.

'It's a perfectly innocent lunch date,' she says primly. 'Why shouldn't he cook for me at his place? It's all totally normal. You've just got a squalid mind.'

'It's a sex date and you know it. But so what? Fill your boots, it's been a while, after all – well, apart from Shaun, but the least said about that the better.'

She laughs and pushes him towards the door.

Upstairs in the bathroom, Cleo washes her hands and listens to the sound of voices drifting up from the living room. Samar's low rumble, her mother's occasional light burst of laughter. She stares at her reflection in the mirror, at the specks of grey and hazel in her green eyes. Her hair is growing longer, the curls almost to her chin. Last month her mother had watched her playing football, and afterwards she'd said, 'We need to buy you some

110

bras, sweetheart.' And though she'd smiled as she said it, there'd been a look in her eye, the same one she'd had when Cleo had started her periods earlier in the year – just the smallest trace of sadness, of fear. In five months she will be fourteen, only two years from being the age Ruby was when she died.

Occasionally, when she watches her mum and grandmother together, she sees how careful her mother is with Stella, how unthinkingly she jumps in to please her, to protect her. It is because of what happened to Ruby, she knows. That long-ago explosion of violence that reverberates to this day. And she feels her mother loves her differently because of Ruby's murder, loves her in a fearful sort of way that weighs her down, constricts her. She's never talked about this with anyone – these are things she'd be hard pressed to articulate, but nevertheless she feels them, understands that they are true.

The following days pass without incident and a cautious sort of hope begins to bloom inside Vivienne. When Friday morning rolls around she feels a mounting anticipation as she drives to the address Alek had texted her. Her satnav leads her to an area of Herne Hill where the rapid spread of gentrification clearly has not yet reached. His flat is in a rather shabby street above a chicken shop, its paintwork peeling, its guttering broken, black bags full of rubbish on the street outside, the smell of marijuana wafting from a next-door neighbour's open window. She presses the doorbell and waits.

111

After a few seconds she hears his footsteps and when he opens the door they kiss each other lightly on both cheeks, before he leads her up the narrow stairway. When he pushes open the door to his flat she follows him in and looks around at the cramped, low-ceilinged rooms, the stained carpet and peeling wallpaper and feels a small jolt of confusion. She's not entirely sure what an anaesthetist earns, but even taking into consideration NHS wages, she's more than a little taken aback.

But, 'This is nice,' she says, as enthusiastically as she can. When he doesn't reply she turns awkwardly to the mantelpiece and picks up a small framed photograph, 'Is this your daughter?' she asks.

He comes to where she's standing. 'Yes, this is Elira.'

'She's lovely,' Viv murmurs. The picture shows a sweet-looking girl of around ten, with long dark hair and olive skin, a wide smile and Alek's dark soulful eyes. 'Elira? That's a pretty name.'

'It's Albanian, it means "the free one". The last time I saw her was when this picture was taken.'

There's such sadness in his voice that Viv puts the picture back where she found it, casting around for something else to comment on, but she can feel the heat of his nearness, smell the musk of his skin, and the words die on her lips. 'Come and sit down,' he says, nodding at a small table in the corner, which she now sees is laden with dishes of food. But when neither of them moves he bows his head and brushes her mouth with his.

Desire winds itself around her as they kiss and when he lifts his head and looks at her, a question in his eyes, she nods, once, and lets him lead her to his bed. Although she'd told herself this wouldn't happen, she had known from the moment he opened the door that it would, that she would not be able to help it. Not just because her fear of Jack has made her feel more alone than she has for a long time but because some previously frozen part of her responds to the indefinable pull of him, this quiet, serious man, this stranger, so that she hardly knows herself.

Rain batters against the bus's window and Cleo sits on the top deck, phone in hand, trying to decide what to write. Eventually she opens a new message and types, Hey Daniel, haven't heard from u for a while. Hope ur OK. She hesitates before adding an X, then a heart, and presses Send. She stares down at her mobile for a while, before sighing and throwing it back into her school bag. She hasn't heard from him for three days.

When, a few minutes later, she hears her phone ping from somewhere in the depths of her bag, her heart leaps with fresh hope as she reaches for it, only to sink again when she sees it's a text from her dad. He's sent her a picture of Max, wearing a yellow Babygro that has a hood with eyes and an orange beak. Underneath it is written Our little duckling. She smiles. He is the cutest baby she's ever seen, her baby brother. She thinks about texting, Would it be OK if I came to see you soon, but remembering her last visit she puts her phone back in her bag, the text going unanswered.

Her mum had once said that her dad had been too young when she'd got pregnant, that at twenty-four he hadn't been ready for fatherhood. A mutual shyness has always existed between them. It had been something of a relief when Sonia – friendly, talkative – had come on the scene; her cheerful presence a natural buffer to their awkwardness. She thinks of Christmas approaching. Last year he'd bought her an enormous pink unicorn, the sort a five-year-old might dream of. When she was ten he'd sent her a bottle of Coco Channel. She'd overheard her mother complaining to Samar – 'How old does he think she is, exactly? Thirty-two?' – but she had loved it. It had pride of place on her chest of drawers, she couldn't stop opening it to smell it, admiring its lovely box, so sophisticated and glamorous. Even the unicorn gets to occupy the pillow next to her own.

Her stop approaches and as she rises to get off she becomes aware of a teenage lad staring at her, his gaze hot against her skin. When they get off the bus he is ahead of her, but he turns to look at her again, and suddenly she is conscious of her body within its uniform, her breasts, her legs, in a way she has only begun to be conscious of them. She has noticed boys, sometimes men, have the same glint in their eyes when they look at her lately. Is that how Daniel would look at her too, if they met? She is both excited and repelled by the idea. She checks her phone, but there is no reply.

* * *

Vivienne and Alek lie entwined, the sheet draped across them, their skin only now beginning to cool. Her ear pressed against his chest, she listens to his heart beating. 'We didn't eat,' she says at last, then smiles. 'You went to so much trouble.'

He strokes her arm. 'I can bring the food to us. We'll have a picnic, here in bed.'

He gets up, and pads naked from the room and she takes in the muscular dips and hollows of his back, the curves of his buttocks, savouring the taste of him on her lips, the touch of his hands upon her body.

He returns a few minutes later with a tray laden with dishes which he sets out between them on the sheets. 'Some Albanian food,' he says, laying the plates before her one by one. 'This is burek . . . and suxhuk, and tave kosi . . .'

She looks at the offerings of sausage, filo parcels, olives, and cheese, and smiles. 'God, this feels so decadent, eating in bed while the rest of the world works.'

He smiles and, picking up a tomato, begins to slice it in two, the tip of his knife puckering the taut skin before piercing the flesh, juice dripping over his fingers and onto the plate.

They eat in silence for a while, then, 'What was it like, growing up in Albania?' she asks.

And Alek tells her about his parents' farm, an idyllic rural childhood spent climbing trees and swimming in lakes with friends. 'Were you born here in London?' he asks.

'No, Essex. My mum and I moved here when I was eight, after my sister died.'

He considers this, brow furrowed. 'She was young when she died? A child?'

Viv nods. 'She was murdered when she was sixteen.'

His eyes widen. 'My God. Vivienne, I am so sorry.' He shakes his head in disbelief. 'Who . . . ?'

She pushes her plate away and lies down. 'Her boyfriend. She was due to give birth to their son a few days later.'

'Vivienne,' he says sorrowfully, 'that is so terrible.'

'I like the way you say my name.' She traces the curve of his ribcage with her finger, feeling the softness of his dark skin. He is the most beautiful man she has ever seen, she thinks, and when a small, spiteful voice says, *So what the fuck is he doing with you?* she ignores it.

He moves the plates from the bed and lies down next to her. And as he strokes her hair, she tells him about Ruby, about how the police had found her in her mother's wardrobe, saying only Jack's name, that her evidence had put him in prison. 'I remember very little about it. I have nightmares, bad ones, all the time. I think about it far too much. Sometimes I feel like I'll be stuck there forever, the day it all happened.' She gives a small embarrassed laugh. 'Sorry, this probably isn't the sexiest pillow talk you've ever heard.'

But he doesn't smile. His gaze rests on her thoughtfully as he says, 'Perhaps the only way of getting over it is by confronting what happened.'

116

'Maybe.' She shrugs. 'But, I mean, I start to panic whenever I think about it, so . . . I guess I try not to think about it at all.'

'And so the nightmares continue,' he says.

'Yeah.' She wishes they could change the subject and wonders how to lighten the mood.

'A friend of mine, an ex-colleague, is a therapist, a trauma specialist,' Alek says. 'Maybe she could help you.'

'Right,' she says unenthusiastically. 'You think?'

He nods. 'She practises something called EMDR therapy. I believe it's very effective in helping people overcome their experiences.'

'Hmm.' She sighs, 'Look, Alek, I appreciate you trying to help, I really do, but to be honest I don't want to confront what happened, I want to forget it, I want to leave it all in the past, that's the whole point.'

'But you're not leaving it in the past. Not if you're dreaming about it every night.' He glances at her and, seeing her expression, smiles. 'Sorry, I'm a doctor, I don't believe that anyone should suffer if there's a way to fix the problem.'

She turns so that she's lying on her back. 'I've never been one for therapy, the idea makes me uncomfortable, it always has, I don't know why.'

He nods and bends his head to kiss her and the moment passes. After a while she props herself up on her arm and says, 'And how about you?'

'How about me?'

'Escaping the war . . . I mean . . . Christ, I can't even imagine.'

For a long time she thinks he's not going to answer, and then he says quietly, 'I was one of the lucky ones. We came here and were granted refugee status. At the time the British Medical Association ran an initiative that enabled refugee doctors to work for the NHS. But you are right, it wasn't easy.' He lies back, staring at the ceiling. 'War changes you. It turns you into someone you never thought you'd become. Makes you do things you never thought you'd have to do . . .'

'What sort of thing?' she asks, struck by the heaviness of his tone. But instead of replying he reaches out and pulls her towards him, kisses her, and her question goes unanswered.

10

In the days that follow, Vivienne returns to those brief few hours with Alek again and again, turning them over in her mind like playing cards. His hands on her skin, the taste of his kiss. Suddenly, unbidden, his image will appear to her and she will feel again the slow creep of desire.

When they'd said goodbye they'd made vague plans to meet again, but the days pass one after another and she does not hear from him. She is glad in a way that he occupies her thoughts so fully, maddening though it is, because at least they are a distraction from the constant nagging fear of Jack, the nightmares that have returned to plague her dreams with fresh urgency.

Last night's dream had been particularly bad. In this one she had opened the door to her sister's bedroom to find a figure standing over Ruby's body as usual. But this time the figure had half turned, and she'd been certain that she was about to see his face, but her terror had been so intense that she'd screamed herself awake before she did so. She'd lain awake for hours after that and in the morning had to drag herself from bed exhausted.

Over breakfast she finds herself thinking back to the conversation she'd had with Alek about his therapist friend who he said could help her. What had he said she practised? EMDR? She'd vaguely heard of it before. Perhaps Alek was right that it might put a stop to her nightmares – the broken sleep was beginning to drive her insane. Tiredly she looks it up on her phone and begins to read, discovering that EMDR stands for Eye Movement Desensitization and Reprocessing, involving something called 'bilateral stimulation' that gradually helps the patient deal with past trauma.

She keeps scrolling, skim-reading an article about how the therapy changes neurological pathways, how it works by stimulating both hemispheres of the brain, before pausing when she gets to a passage about buried memories, a doctor talking about how the recalling of a 'touchstone memory' can lead to accessing other, previously suppressed ones, how one patient had even remembered murdering someone in their past. Viv puts her phone down with a shudder. It definitely doesn't sound like something she wants to get involved in. In fact she's pretty sure she'd rather just live with the nightmares.

The next day she's in her café checking through some invoices when she looks up to see Alek walking through the door. He comes to where she's standing behind the till, her hands resting on the counter, and briefly strokes one of her fingers with his own as he says her name. And it's such a small, such an inconsequential thing, but that one light touch is charged with such electricity that she feels her blood crackle in response.

'Hello,' she says, smiling. 'Coffee?'

He nods and goes to his usual table, pulling from his bag his notepad and pen as he takes his seat and it is as if nothing at all has changed between them, as though they are to each other as they'd always been, before the moment she'd walked through his door and into his bed. But as she goes about her work, clearing tables, chatting to customers, she feels his eyes upon her. Once, when she meets his gaze he lets his own slowly and deliberately traverse her body, and she shivers as though he were reaching out and touching her, and it's almost more than she can bear not to chase her customers away, pull down the blinds and lock them both inside awhile.

He sits and writes for half an hour, and when a sudden influx of customers arrives he leaves, giving only a brief wave. A few minutes later, however, a text message arrives. When can I see you?

Whenever you want.

Tomorrow? My place?

She glances at Agnes, busy filling sugar bowls. Calling over to her she asks, 'Can you work tomorrow?'

'Yep, no probs.'

Vivienne thinks of how she'd felt when he had touched her hand earlier and types, **What time?**

And so it goes over the next two weeks. When Alek's working late shifts and has his daytimes free, they meet at his flat, spending their time talking, making love, or eating the small Albanian delicacies he brings to his bed. He tells her about his boyhood in Pristina, holidays with his grandparents in their village, days spent fishing, or building dams, and she talks to him about Unity House and the women who lived there, or about her adventures with Samar. They are both careful to stick to happy memories, their separate sorrows left unspoken. She likes that when his steady gaze is upon her it feels as though he truly sees her; how when he asks her how she is it's like he genuinely wants to know.

Only once does she tentatively question him about his daughter. 'Does she reply to the letters you send?' she asks, watching him with curiosity.

'No. But I will never stop sending them. I don't like emails, they are too easy to ignore – or she could change her address, block my name. I prefer her to have something physical, that she must hold in her hand, must tear up or throw in the bin if she wants. I send them to my sister, and she passes them on in person, every week, without fail, but I don't know what Elira does with them, or what she says. I prefer not to ask.'

'What happened between you?' she asks. 'Why won't she speak to you?'

He gives a slight shrug. 'She believes something about me that isn't true.'

'Really? What's that?'

But he only shakes his head. 'It doesn't matter now. I cannot change how she feels, not yet. All I can do is remind her of how much I love her.'

In the days when she doesn't see him she goes about her life as usual, working, seeing friends, spending time with Cleo, though all the while she's aware that she's waiting for when she can see him next – the moment they can close the door of his flat behind them.

'I'm not sure this is entirely normal,' Samar tells her. 'It all sounds rather obsessive to me.'

She laughs. 'I don't care, Sam. I can't help it.'

'Go easy, though, won't you? I don't want you to be hurt. Try not to let things get too intense.'

She shrugs. 'It *is* intense, it's incredible.'

But her mother, too, is dubious. 'Things are moving fast,' she comments disapprovingly, when Viv sits in her kitchen one afternoon.

'Mum, I'm forty years old. I know what I'm doing.'

Stella looks pointedly at her. 'Do you, darling?'

'Yes, of course I do.' She looks away, irritated. 'Mum,' she says, 'you don't have to worry about me, honestly.'

But before Stella can reply, Shaun walks in. He studiously ignores Viv, directing his greeting at her mother, who smiles affectionately back at him and doesn't notice her daughter's sudden tension. Instead, Stella turns back to Viv and, lowering her voice only a fraction, says, 'What do you even know about this man? I mean, I'm sure the sex is wonderful, darling, but—'

'Mum!' Viv hisses. 'For God's sake!' She widens her eyes and jerks her head in the direction of Shaun, who's making himself a sandwich on the other side of the room.

'Don't be silly, Vivienne. He can't hear, and why should he be interested in your love life anyway?'

'Just . . . keep your voice down, would you? It's nobody else's business.'

Stella raises her eyes to the ceiling but waits until he leaves the room.

'When's he going, anyway?' Viv asks irritably. 'He's been here for months.'

Stella shrugs. 'I've let him stay a bit longer while he sorts something out. He's had such a difficult life, and he's so incredibly helpful around the house. Did I tell you what a wonderful baker he's become? Apparently he could scarcely boil an egg before he came here and started helping me in the kitchen. He made some wonderful walnut bread the other day.' She looks at her daughter crossly. 'Why are you sneering? There's more to that man than meets the eye.' She gets up. 'Anyway, darling it's been lovely to see you, but I'm afraid I really need to get on. There are some bulbs I want to plant in the garden. You can see yourself out, can't you?'

Once Stella has left through the garden door, Vivienne heads upstairs to the bathroom, creeping quietly along the landing so as not to alert Shaun to her presence. But as she passes his room, he suddenly appears. 'Got yourself a new fuck buddy have you?' he asks, leaning against the door frame and staring at her insolently. 'Put it about a bit, don't you?'

She shoots him a look of disgust. 'Leave me alone.' She begins to move away but he crosses the landing in three quick strides and she shrinks from him as he looms so suddenly close. Before she can escape he pushes her roughly against the wall, trapping her between his arms and thrusting his face towards hers until it's only centimetres away. 'True though, ain't it? Who's the mug this time, then?'

'Get your hands off me.' Her words are hissed, furious, but though she struggles he holds her fast, and her heart begins to pound. Are they alone up here? Are the other guests all out?

He grins then, and very slowly, very deliberately reaches below her skirt, sliding his hand upwards until he gropes her buttocks. She gasps, struggling fiercely, but his grip is firm. A white-hot rage rises inside her until with one almighty jerk she manages to push him away then hits him hard across the face. 'You fucking arsehole,' she shouts, panting with fear and indignation.

He backs away, mock innocent, his left cheek red

from where she struck him. 'You didn't seem to mind last time. Seemed to fucking love it, in fact.'

She looks at him with loathing. 'I don't want anything to do with you. Can't you get that into your thick head? Last time was a mistake.' She pulls out her phone. 'I'm calling the police. You might have my mother fooled but you won't fool them.' She's no sooner finished speaking than she hears her mother coming in from the garden. Not wanting to face her, she shoots one more disgusted look at Shaun then runs down the stairs and out of the house. For a long time she sits in her car, hot with fury and humiliation. She looks down at her phone, still clasped in her hand. She should carry out her threat, she knows, but that would mean telling Stella the whole story and she's not sure she can face that. *Shit*, she thinks, thumping the steering wheel. *Shit shit shit*. Shaun will have to wait.

The next day, Cleo is sitting at the kitchen table, her school textbooks laid out in front of her, while her mother makes dinner. It's as if Daniel's completely disappeared – he doesn't even turn up on the gaming forum where they met. What if his dad has really hurt him this time? He could be badly injured and she'd never know. She doesn't have an address for him and she hasn't wanted to risk phoning him because he'd said his dad didn't like him taking calls. Finally, however, last night in desperation she'd tried his number anyway, to be greeted with total silence – it didn't even ring.

'Lovey, can you move your school stuff, please? Dinner's almost ready.'

Cleo blinks out of her reverie. 'Yeah. Sorry.' Her mother smiles at her, then turns back to the pan she'd been stirring, and Cleo watches her, realizing suddenly that there's been something a bit different about her lately: a sort of distracted, dreamy air, a different sort of energy radiating from her. She frowns, something occurring to her that she'd let slip from her mind. 'What happened with that guy you went on a date with a while ago?' she asks. 'Are you going to see him again?'

Her mum hesitates before turning back to her. 'I have seen him, actually, a few times. Just for lunch, though.'

'Oh, right. Do you like him then?'

She smiles. 'Yeah, I do. I really do.'

Cleo thinks this over. 'Am I going to meet him? What's he like?'

Viv begins to lay the table. 'Oh . . . would you like to? I mean, I don't even know if it's going anywhere yet . . . might be a bit soon.'

Cleo shrugs, her attention already drifting back to Daniel. 'Whatever, I don't mind.'

A few days later, Viv and Alek lie in his bed, listening to the pounding bass emanating from the flat next door. A siren wails somewhere in the direction of Brockwell park and a man on the street shouts, 'Stop your crying, you miserable little shit!' They turn to each other and laugh. She has been surprised to find that he laughs

127

often, a grin suddenly breaking over his usually serious face, his eyes crinkling with amusement. She kisses him then lies on her back and they lapse into a sleepy silence.

She's staring at a patch of damp in the left-hand corner of the ceiling, trying to decide whether it looks more like a whale or a rabbit, when Alek, who had been absent-mindedly stroking her wrist, turns to her, his eyes searching her face and says, 'You look tired.'

'I didn't sleep well last night.'

'No? Why not?'

'Oh, another nightmare.' She thinks about last night's dream, which had been a particularly disturbing one. Declan had made an appearance, this time sitting on the old leather armchair in the living room with her, his pale blue gaze on her face while she'd listened to Ruby and Jack arguing upstairs. As before, there'd been that strange, creeping disgust and confusion that his presence seemed to instil in her. After she'd woken, breathless and soaked in sweat, she'd lain awake for hours. There was something she needed to remember about her neighbour; something that hovered at the periphery of her consciousness, but whenever she tried to focus on what it might be the panic and fear hit her, derailing her efforts.

Alek is considering her thoughtfully. 'The colleague I told you about, who can help you, let me give you her number . . .' He gets to his feet, prowling naked around the flat until he finds his phone. 'Her name's Miranda Auerbach,' he says, tapping away at the keypad. 'She

128

has a private practice . . .' Viv's mobile bleeps from her handbag and Alek glances at her. 'I've texted you her details. She will help you.'

'Thanks.' Viv smiles gratefully, though she knows she won't be calling the therapist. Reluctantly, she gets up and begins searching for her clothes, her mind already on the café, realizing guiltily that she's left Agnes rather in the lurch again. But as she starts to dress, Alek goes to her. Kissing her, he slowly shrugs the blouse back off her shoulders. She laughs, pulling away. 'Alek, I have to go.'

He shakes his head. 'No,' he says. 'You don't.'

'I do,' she murmurs, even as the heat climbs inside her. 'I need to get back to work.' With a sigh of defeat, he watches her finish dressing.

As she picks up her coat she says with a half-smile, 'My mother and Samar think you've bewitched me. They're starting to worry.'

He looks at her, brow furrowed. 'Why?'

She laughs, 'Oh, nothing, I'm only joking. I mean, they've never met you, so you could be a mad axe murderer for all they know . . .' She feels herself blush. They have not spoken yet about where this thing between them is going.

But he pulls on his T-shirt and shrugs. 'Then I shall meet them. If that is what you want?'

She's surprised. 'Oh! Really? I mean, yeah, maybe.'

'And your daughter?' he asks. 'I will meet her too?'

'Well . . .' she mulls it over. 'I mean, I don't see why

not.' Perhaps it *would* be a good idea. A low-key dinner around at hers, no big deal. It wasn't as if he'd be staying the night. Just an easy, friendly, casual introduction over supper. After all, Cleo *had* shown an interest in meeting him. And it would be good to see Alek somewhere other than this strange little flat, to see how he transfers to her real life, to observe him amongst her family and friends. Maybe then he wouldn't seem so unknowable to her. 'I'll think about it,' she says lightly.

He smiles. 'Good.'

Cleo trudges along the wet pavement. Last night she'd gone through all of Daniel's emails and text messages, trying to find a clue as to why he'd disappeared with no warning. Perhaps he'd got tired of her, she thinks dejectedly; perhaps he'd found another girl who was prettier, or funnier, more intelligent. But she had liked him, and he had liked her, she was sure of it, and she can't help feeling worried about him. With every step she feels sadder, and then, just as she reaches her house she hears a car engine growling behind her and turns to see her mother pulling up to the kerb.

'You OK, love?' Viv asks, getting out and gazing at her in concern. 'You look upset.'

Cleo shrugs. 'I'm all right.'

'Sure?' Her mother puts her hand on her shoulder, eyes searching her face.

Cleo hesitates. Suddenly she has had enough of it all. Enough of worrying about Daniel and whether his dad

130

has hurt him, about the letters she found in Stella's room and keeping them secret from her mum, of the gap that has grown between her mother and her without Viv even knowing, the gap between the person she was and the person she is now. In a sudden rush she blurts, 'It's just . . .'

But they're interrupted by Neil crossing the road towards them. 'Hello, ladies,' he says.

'Hi, Neil,' her mother says vaguely, her gaze still focused on Cleo. 'How are you?'

'Actually, I'm glad I caught you both.' He turns to Cleo, fixing her with his eager little eyes. 'Was wondering when you wanted to come round and use my Xbox, Cleo. Seems a shame to have it sitting there gathering dust. Why don't you come over some time and see if you can beat me at Mario Cart?'

Before her mum can speak, Cleo mumbles, 'I'm not into gaming much any more.' She turns away and walks on towards the house, letting herself in with her key without saying goodbye.

Viv looks at her departing back in surprise. There's no way she'd have allowed her thirteen-year-old daughter to spend time alone with a man who, all said and done, she barely knows, but there were nicer ways to decline an invitation. 'I'm so sorry, Neil,' she says, turning back to him. 'It's so kind of you to offer, I think Cleo's feeling a bit out of sorts today . . .'

He waves her words away. 'Quite all right, no need to apologize. The offer's there if she wants it.'

'We must have you round for a coffee sometime though and let us return your hospitality.' She smiles as she moves away.

'As a matter of fact, I'm glad to have a moment alone with you,' he says quickly. 'I've been meaning to say this for a while . . .' he breaks off and smiles broadly at her. 'Look, Viv, I think you and I should bite the bullet and go out for dinner, don't you?'

'Bite the . . . ?' She stares back at him, lost for words.

He rolls his eyes indulgently. 'Let's be grown-ups about this and take the plunge, shall we? Don't get me wrong, the flirting's been good fun, but I think it's time we acknowledged what's going on between us and did something about it.'

She holds up a hand. 'Neil, please. I think there's been a misunderstanding.'

'Nope – not on my part, anyway. You're still a very attractive lady you know, Vivienne.'

She lets out a gasp of shocked laughter.

'What I mean is, I usually go for younger women, but on this occasion I'm more than happy to make you the exception.'

She presses her lips together in silence. 'Well, that's very kind of you, Neil,' she manages at last. 'Thank you. I think I should tell you though that I've recently started seeing someone. So, um . . .'

'Have you?' He stares at her in amazement. 'Oh, right. OK, fair enough. I mean, I won't tell if you won't.'

'Right. The thing is, while I'm flattered, I'm afraid I'm not interested in you in that way.'

'Oh.' He looks at her in stunned disbelief.

'Anyway, I'd better go in now, get dinner started . . .' Viv gives a final apologetic smile before gently closing the door in Neil's bewildered face.

Once safely in her kitchen, she slams around irritably for a while, throwing the ingredients for dinner on to worktops, tugging saucepans from cupboards. 'More than happy to make me the exception,' she mutters. 'Bloody cheek!'

She goes to the foot of the stairs and calls her daughter down.

'What is it?' Cleo asks when she appears in the door.

'Nothing . . . I just wondered if you'd like to have a chat. You looked like you wanted to say something earlier.'

But Cleo shakes her head and turns away. 'It's nothing. I'm fine. I've got to call Layla about our maths homework.' And with that she disappears, her mother staring thoughtfully after her.

Later, Vivienne phones Stella. 'I was wondering if you would like to come round for dinner next Saturday,' she says.

Her mother's voice is distracted, Radio 4 babbling loudly in the background. 'How lovely. What's the occasion?'

'Oh, nothing special . . . I thought I'd invite Samar and Ted, and . . . maybe Alek too.'

133

'Alek? So you're introducing him to Cleo already, are you?'

'Well, I've been seeing him a while. Cleo said she'd like to meet him, so I thought, why not?'

When this is met with a disapproving silence, Viv sighs, 'Mum, I don't know what your problem is, but I like him a lot. Things are going well between us, can't you just be happy for me? Are you going to come for dinner or not?'

'Yes, yes, of course I am, don't be so uppity, darling. I'll see you on Saturday.'

At least Samar's reaction is more positive. 'Of course we'll come,' he says excitedly when she calls him. 'Ted's dying to meet him too. Can't wait.'

11

The following Saturday, Vivienne pours herself a glass of cold white wine and begins to prep her ingredients for that evening's meal. From the moment she got up that morning, everything had seemed to go wrong. First Stella had called to ask if she could bring Shaun, taking huge offence when Viv had told her no, then her supermarket delivery had arrived incomplete, forcing her to make a panicked last-minute dash to the shops. To top it all, Cleo had been sulky and odd all day, with no sign that she was going to cheer up before their guests arrived. Grumpily she begins to season and chop the fillets of haddock and salmon for the fish pie she's planning to make, wishing that she could just cancel the whole damn thing.

At last she puts the finishing touches to the pie and slides it into the oven. She sighs and checks her watch:

7.52 p.m. She has exactly eight minutes to get ready. A fresh wave of nerves hits her and, glancing at her empty wine glass, she pours herself another helping before hurrying upstairs.

Alek arrives first. He's dressed in his shabby coat and threadbare shirt, but looks, she thinks, extraordinarily handsome standing there on her step, a bottle of wine in his hand. They kiss, briefly, before she ushers him in. As she leads him through to the kitchen she waits for the usual effusive compliments about how lovely her home is, before realizing with a smile that Alek is not the sort of guy to even notice, let alone be at all impressed by such things. Instead he's standing in her kitchen, looking decidedly ill at ease.

'You OK?' she asks, going over to him.

'Of course,' he nods. 'Certainly.'

She gazes at him with concern, feeling his tension, and wonders once again whether this had all been a very bad idea. 'OK, I'll get Cleo,' she says lightly. 'I warn you though, she's in a bit of a mood today. Hormones, I guess. She's really very sweet though, so don't hold it against her.'

He reaches over and rubs her shoulder and smiles at last. 'It is OK, Vivienne. Everything will be fine.'

'I know, sorry.' She exhales and returns his smile. 'I'm sure it'll be OK. I'll go and call her down.'

To her relief, Cleo is polite and chatty when she meets Alek, immediately firing questions at him about his job. 'What's it like anaesthetizing someone? Aren't you worried you'll accidentally give them too much and they'll never wake up? What's the goriest operation you've seen? Have they ever put the wrong bit back in the wrong place?'

Viv laughs. 'Cleo! Give him a chance to answer, and stop being so morbid!'

But though Alek smiles, and answers her questions with good humour, Viv can't shake the feeling that his mind is elsewhere, and she feels a tug of disappointment that her mother might not see the best of him. Stella has always been so pessimistic about her having boyfriends she's keen to prove her wrong. When she hears Samar and Ted ring the doorbell five minutes later she answers it hoping that their arrival might loosen him up a bit, and, to her relief, it seems to do the trick at first. Her two friends walk into the kitchen on a wave of good-natured energy, shaking Alek's hand with enthusiasm, and as Cleo entertains them all with a story about how her drama teacher was caught snogging her football coach, Viv at last begins to relax.

She goes back to her cooking, then begins to lay the table before realizing that she's forgotten to offer her guests a drink. She glances over at Alek. 'Would you like a . . .' but she breaks off when she sees the expression on his face. Her daughter is sorting through a stack of CDs and Alek is staring at her with a look of such intensity that he appears utterly oblivious to the world around him. 'Alek?' she says, her voice faltering, then has to repeat his name more loudly before he turns around.

'Sorry,' he says, his smile in place once more. 'What did you say?'

She stares at him a beat or two, before replying, 'I just wondered what you'd like to drink.' She turns away to fiddle with something on the stove, trying to still the disquiet that has bloomed in her chest.

'I'll sort the drinks out, if you like?' Ted offers.

She nods gratefully. 'Thanks, love, there's a nice Sancerre already open in the fridge, or there's some red on the side.' Perhaps Alek is feeling nervous, she tells herself while she seasons the soup she's made. Perhaps he's missing his own daughter. But she's uneasy that he should have been looking at Cleo in such a peculiar manner.

The doorbell rings again and Cleo hurries off to answer it, reappearing almost immediately with Stella. Her mother sails in wearing a voluminous coral-coloured dress, her hair freshly dyed a rich hennaed red, her many bangles clanking together on her arms, injecting the air with her distinctive spice-and-floral scent. 'Hello!' she cries, hugging Samar and then saying to Ted, 'How lovely to meet you at last! Isn't this nice!'

'Mum, this is Alek,' Vivienne says, feeling unaccountably nervous.

Alek steps forward and offers his hand, saying politely, 'It's very nice to meet you, Stella.'

Viv looks at her mother, expecting her to be as charming as she usually is when meeting new people, but Stella merely gives a brief 'Hello,' with a small, tight smile, before dropping Alek's hand and turning back to the others.

Viv stares at her, astonished, then glances back to Alek apologetically. 'I guess she's a bit distracted,' she says.

'Of course,' he murmurs. 'Please do not worry.'

Stella is busy talking to Cleo. 'And how are you, Cleo?' she asks.

'Fine,' is the response, her frosty tone not lost on Viv. There is definitely something up between them – she resolves to ask Cleo about it later.

She sighs. The evening seems to stretch out before her interminably, but she makes herself smile brightly and says, 'Let's all sit down to eat, shall we?'

'Darling, before we do, I want to tell you about the fabulous idea I've had,' Stella says.

'Oh?' Viv says, 'What's that?'

'It's such a shame you didn't feel able to include Shaun tonight, because he's become such a good friend and he's leaving us tomorrow.'

'Is he?' Vivienne tries to keep the delight from her voice.

'Yes. It's terribly sudden and sad, though thankfully he's staying in the area. The main thing is, he's looking for work.'

'Right . . .' Viv looks at her mother warily.

Stella's fishing around in her bag for something. 'Yes, and I had such a wonderful thought. You know I told you what a brilliant baker he is? I thought you could use his help in the café! He could make cakes for you and so on.'

'Um . . . I already have a great—'

But Stella pulls out a Tupperware box and thrusts it at her. 'He's made a sample for you. It's apple turnover. He said he hopes you enjoy it.'

Viv takes it reluctantly. 'Mum, I—'

'Go on, try it. He made it specially for you.' She looks at Viv expectantly.

Sighing, Viv obediently opens it to find a slice of something grey and crumbly inside. Gingerly she picks off a small portion.

'Oh, don't be silly, darling,' Stella tuts. 'Have more than that!'

Resignedly Viv takes a large bite. It has a texture that manages to be simultaneously slimy and dry, horrendously sweet but with a lasting bitter aftertaste. She swallows it, but can't help grimacing. 'Oh good God that's vile!' she says. 'Ted, pass me my wine.' She takes a large gulp.

'Don't be ridiculous, darling,' Stella says crossly. 'It's delicious.'

Viv catches Samar's eye and they both laugh. 'It really isn't, Mum, sorry.' She puts the box down on the counter. 'Come on, everyone, let's eat.'

Twenty minutes later things seem to be going well. Ted is telling Alek all about his job in town planning, and Alek is making a good fist of showing polite interest. Cleo and Stella are laughing at Samar's incredibly bad impression of Kim Kardashian, and they've all asked for

140

second helpings of her pie. But she can't help feeling slightly aggrieved that Stella has made no attempt to talk to Alek, and she sees how distracted and on edge he seems. She leans over and brushes his hand with hers. 'You OK?' she whispers.

'Of course,' he replies, frowning slightly. 'Why not?'

Noticing that the others are watching, she smiles brightly. 'Samar,' she begins, 'you must tell Alek about the—' but before she can finish, Alek has reached for her empty wine glass.

'I brought some Albanian wine for you to try,' he says, abruptly cutting across her. 'It's in the fridge, let me get you some.'

'Oh,' she says, taken aback. 'OK, thanks . . .' she looks at the others, trying to hide her embarrassment. 'Perhaps everyone else would like to try some too?' she asks. 'Why don't you bring it to the table, Alek?'

But Alek is busy looking in the fridge and appears not to hear. 'That's OK,' Ted says. 'We've still got some of your delicious Sancerre. We can try some later.' He smiles warmly, as if to overcompensate for Alek's abruptness and she feels a sting of embarrassment. Aware her mother is watching her, she doesn't meet her gaze.

The doorbell rings. 'I'll get it,' Stella says, jumping to her feet. They listen to her talking animatedly to someone in the hall, and a moment later she returns with, of all people, Neil.

Viv's heart sinks. 'Hello, everything all right?' she asks unenthusiastically.

141

'Your poor neighbour has had a power cut,' Stella tells them, adding dramatically, 'his house is in complete darkness.'

'I wondered if you were having the same problem,' Neil says, apparently surprised to find himself in a room full of people. 'But I, er, see you're not.'

'I said he should come in and join us for dessert and coffee!' Stella tells her. 'Come on, Neil, take a seat, there's plenty of room.'

'Er . . . I'm not really . . .' Viv begins, horrified.

To his credit, Neil has the grace to look embarrassed. He starts to back out of the room. 'Oh, no, no, I couldn't possibly intrude. If I could just borrow some candles or a torch, I'll be on my way . . .'

'Nonsense!' Stella says, pulling out a chair for him. She turns to Viv. 'We can't have the poor man sitting alone in a cold dark house, can we, darling?'

'No, of course not,' Viv agrees through gritted teeth. 'Please do join us, Neil. I'm afraid we've finished dinner, though.'

Neil, still standing, says, 'Oh, well, if you're sure, I've got a cheesecake in the fridge, why don't I fetch it? It's the least I can do.' Ignoring Viv's remonstrations, he says, 'It's no bother! I won't be a tick!'

'I've made a bloody pavlova,' Viv mutters under her breath, ignoring Samar's snigger.

Neil returns a minute later. 'Who's for a slice?' he asks. 'It's a good one, Waitrose!'

'I'll get some bowls,' Viv says resignedly, standing up.

'No, no. You sit down Vivienne.' He presses his hand on her shoulder until she's forced back into her seat. 'I'll sort it. Bowls in here, are they?'

They all watch as he starts dishing up, Samar barely able to contain his laughter as he fusses busily about.

Neil passes the first bowl to Viv. 'Eat up, enjoy!'

When he's served everyone else he sits down next to Stella and the two are soon deep in conversation, Stella laughing merrily, apparently oblivious to Viv's attempts to direct her attention towards Alek, who has grown quieter as the evening has progressed.

When Alek excuses himself to go to the bathroom, Viv looks at Ted, who raises his eyebrows. 'Bloody hell,' he says. 'He's ridiculously attractive, isn't he?'

She laughs. 'I know.' And then she says in a low voice, 'But what do you think? Do you like him?'

There's the briefest silence, before Ted says, 'Well . . . he's got that whole smouldering mysterious thing down pat, hasn't he? I mean, he doesn't give much away.'

Viv nods. 'Yeah, he's a bit quiet tonight. I don't know why. Maybe he's nervous.'

'Well, I think he seems great, Viv,' he says reassuringly. 'Really nice chap.'

'I think so too, Mum,' Cleo says. 'I like him.' Viv shoots her a grateful smile.

When she turns back to Ted she watches him finish his cheesecake with a swell of affection. He seems chattier, more relaxed tonight, and it strikes her that she'd been wrong about him before. He is a kind man, she

143

realizes now; just a little shy, that's all: her fears that he might disapprove of her appear to have been groundless, and she feels a surge of relief.

'Well,' she says, looking around at their empty bowls and getting to her feet. 'Why don't we all go through to the living room? I'll make some coffee.'

Cleo stretches and yawns. 'Actually, I'm a bit tired, Mum, think I'll just go up, read in bed for a bit.' She kisses them all goodnight and heads for the stairs.

'I'll be off, too,' says Neil.

'Oh?' Viv says drily. 'So soon?'

'Afraid so, better see what's going on with my electrics.'

'Let me see you out,' says Stella warmly. 'It's been so lovely to meet you.'

Viv ushers the others into the living room, then returns to the kitchen to find Alek standing by the window, staring out at the garden. He turns around when he hears her come in.

'Everything OK?' she asks.

'Of course,' he says, passing over her glass. 'Here, I poured more wine for you.'

She takes it from him and he waits until she's had a sip before coming over and kissing her, his arms holding her tightly. She's startled at this sudden show of affection after how quiet he's been all evening, and after a moment or two she pulls away. 'They'll be wondering where we are,' she says. 'You go on through. I'll make the coffee.' When he leaves she picks up her wine glass and drains it, staring thoughtfully after him.

A few minutes later, Viv brings the coffees through to the living room and takes a seat. 'Did I tell you that Alek's an anaesthetist at King's?' she says pointedly to her mother.

Stella breaks off from her conversation with Samar and says, 'Oh yes, I think you did.' She looks at Alek. 'That must be very interesting?'

'Yes,' he says. 'It is.'

There's an uncomfortable silence until Ted says politely, 'Viv tells me you have a daughter, Alek?'

'Yes, but she lives in Kosovo. I haven't seen her for four years.'

Stella frowns. 'Why not?'

There's an accusatory edge to her voice, prompting Viv to cut in: 'Mum, that's none of—'

But Alek looks at Stella, his expression neutral, and replies, 'It's a long story.'

There's another silence, and again Ted comes to the rescue. 'Well,' he says, 'Samar and I have been talking about adopting one day.'

Viv gasps. 'No! Oh, Sammy, you never said, how fantastic!'

Samar looks a little taken aback but quickly recovers. 'Well, it's only hypothetical. I mean, we don't even live together properly yet, but yeah, maybe in the future. It's something each of us has felt we wanted for some time, even before we met, so possibly . . .'

He's trying to play it cool, but Viv can see that he's excited. Before she can reply, however, Alek says, 'But priority will be given to heterosexual couples, no? It won't be easy for the two of you to adopt?'

'It's become a bit easier the last few years,' Ted tells him. 'Samar and I will need to get married, and obviously we're talking a bit further down the line, but . . .'

'Yes, but it is better for the child if one parent is a woman, no?' Alek persists.

This time Samar breaks the awkward silence. 'Not necessarily,' he says coolly. 'A child just needs love, surely?'

Alek shrugs. 'I think a child needs a mother, where at all possible. I mean, that is the ideal.'

Hurriedly Viv cuts in with, 'Alek, I don't think that's necessarily true . . .' but the damage is done.

'Why?' says Samar. He's sitting forward, his expression frosty as he stares at Alek. 'Why is that the ideal?'

'I completely agree, Samar, it's ridiculous to say two men can't make good parents,' Stella says stoutly, shooting Alek a disapproving look.

Before Alek can reply, Ted says, 'Oh God, come on, everyone, let's not get into this debate. Viv, did I tell you that Samar and I are thinking of Barcelona for our next trip? You've been there, haven't you?'

But despite Ted's valiant attempts, the atmosphere remains flat. Silently Viv curses Alek. She'd been so pleased to see Ted finally come out of his shell tonight, so touched at his efforts to put Alek at ease. His talk of adoption should have been cause for happiness – she was thrilled for Samar – but now Alek had put a dampener on it all. To make matters worse, Viv has begun to feel decidedly peculiar. 'God, I feel like I've been run over with a steamroller,' she tells them, her head in her hands.

Ted looks at her in concern. 'Are you OK?'

'You haven't drunk that much, have you?' Samar asks.

'I didn't think so, but . . .'

'Oh, Vivienne!' says Stella, despairingly.

'Mum, I'm fine. I've hardly drunk anything. I must be coming down with some bug.' She gets to her feet, and, picking up an empty bottle, says, 'I'm going to take this out to the bin. I could do with some fresh air.'

But even outside in the crisp evening breeze the world continues to pitch and roll, and she begins to feel far worse. As she walks towards the bins she staggers a little. What on earth's going on? She tries to remember how much she's drunk, but even including the two glasses she had before everyone arrived, she's sure she hasn't had enough to be feeling quite so ropey. After all, she's drunk far more in the past without any ill effects. She's holding on to the bin, trying to steady her dizziness, when she hears the sound of Neil's front door opening. 'Vivienne?' he says, coming out. 'I saw you from my window. Are you ill?'

'I'm fine,' she says faintly as the world continues to slide first one way, then the other.

He comes closer, and when he clocks the bottle of wine in her hand, his tone alters. 'Oh. Had a bit too much to drink, have we?'

'I suppose I must have.' She can hear her words

slurring. She glances at his house, sees the living room light shining brightly. 'Electricity come back, has it?'

His eyes flick away from hers. 'Oh. Yes, a few minutes ago, actually.'

'Well,' she says, turning to go back into the house, 'I'd better . . .'

But before she can move very far Neil comes and puts an arm around her. 'Let me help you in. Can't have you keeling over, can we?'

Viv pulls away. 'I'm fine.'

'Come on,' he says cajolingly, his grip tightening. 'Let me help you.'

'Neil. Stop it, I'm all right . . .'

She's interrupted by a voice behind her saying, 'Vivienne? Is there a problem?'

Alek is at the front door, staring coldly at Neil.

Beneath Alek's glare, Neil releases Viv and pulls himself up to his full height, which is at least three inches shorter than Alek's. He gives a quick, uncertain laugh. 'No. There's no problem.'

'Why are you touching her?' Alek goes on.

Neil puts up a placating hand. 'Look, there's no need for that tone. I saw that Viv was feeling ill and I tried to help, that's all.'

Viv says weakly, 'I'm fine, Alek, honestly.' She turns to go back in but stumbles and hears Neil make a disapproving tutting sound.

'She doesn't need your help,' Alek says, staring coldly at Neil.

148

'Alek,' Viv says. 'I said I'm fine, can you leave it now, please?'

At first Alek seems intent on standing his ground, but eventually he shrugs and goes back inside the house.

'The new boyfriend, I take it,' Neil remarks. 'I hope your daughter doesn't have to see you carrying on like this.'

'Oh piss off, Neil.'

'Charming!'

Tiredness weighs down on her so heavily that it takes everything she has just to stand upright, and anything else she might have said to him drifts away from her. Her mouth feels thick and slow. Without bothering to reply, she too goes inside.

Upstairs in her room, Cleo gets ready for bed. She can hear the low rumble of the adults' voices downstairs, the occasional sound of doors opening and closing, and hopes that her mum is having a good time. It strikes her that, though she'd wanted to the other day, she still hasn't told Viv about the letters she'd found in her grandmother's bedroom. In fact, it seems ages since she confided in her mum about anything and the thought makes her feel a little lonely. She used to tell her mother everything. She will do it tomorrow, she resolves – and while she's at it she will tell her about Daniel, too. It would be good to get it all off her chest. Feeling a little happier already, Cleo gets into bed and checks her watch: 10.40 p.m. Reaching over to turn her bedside light off, she closes her eyes and tries to sleep.

It's ten minutes later when her mobile bleeps. Groping around for it on her bedside table she wonders if it's perhaps a text from Layla – though it's unusual for her to send one so late. Bringing it closer she blinks in confusion; it's a message from a number she doesn't recognize. And then she clicks it open.

Cleo, u there? she reads. It's Daniel.

Her heart flips, and hurriedly she texts back. OMG r u OK? I've been so worried.

I need ur help. I've run away from home. I'm on the train coming to London.

She stares at her phone in shock. Right now? she asks.

Will u help me? I don't no where to go. I had to get away from him. I really thought he was going to kill me today. I'm so scared, Cleo.

She sits up in bed. Of course I'll help u. What should I do?

Can I come to ur house?

She hesitates. I'd have to ask my mum.

No! Don't do that! She might say she has to speak to

my dad first or something. He'll come after me and kill me. Can't u sneak me in for one night? I could sleep on ur floor. I promise I'll be quiet.

She stares at the phone uncertainly. There's no way she could explain everything to her mum now – she'd completely freak. But if Daniel's dad has hurt him so badly he's had to run away, then shouldn't the police be involved? Again she hesitates, torn, but eventually writes, OK. She looks at the clock: almost eleven. The adults are still talking downstairs. What time will u be here?

I'll text u when I get 2 ur street.

Hurriedly she gets dressed again and lies on her bed to wait for him, her phone on the pillow beside her, her heart thumping with worry, and it fails to register that he hadn't even asked for her address.

When Viv follows Alek back inside the house, she finds her mother, Samar and Ted standing by the window, looking at her with concern.

'Where's Alek?' she asks.

'I think he went to the kitchen,' Ted tells her. 'You OK? What was all that about with Neil?'

Viv sits down heavily and drops her head to her hands. 'God, I feel wrecked. I really must be coming down with something.' And it is the strangest feeling, she reflects;

151

as though the world is slowing down, moving sluggishly around her. Even sound has begun to be a bit distorted.

Samar comes over to her. 'Why don't we stay and help clear up? You pop up to bed and we'll bring you a cup of tea. You actually do look terrible.'

'Yes,' says Stella. 'Good idea. I'll tell Alek to go home.'

At this Vivienne looks at her mother. 'What is it with you and Alek?'

Stella bristles. 'Don't be ridiculous, Vivienne.' She sniffs then says, sotto voce, 'There's just something about him that I don't like. Sorry, I don't know what it is. I can't put my finger on it.'

And at that moment Alek walks back into the room. He stands staring at them, his hands in his pockets.

'We were just saying, Alek,' Ted says pleasantly, 'that as Viv's feeling rough, we'll stay here to see her into bed. Why don't you head off?'

Alek walks over to Viv and looks down at her carefully. 'I will stay and look after her. I think maybe you had too much to drink, yes?'

Samar clears his throat. 'Listen, mate, she probably needs to sleep it off. Might be best to call it a night.' The two men stare silently at each other for a beat or two.

'Why don't all of you go home, and I'll stay here with her,' Stella says decisively.

Viv gives an exasperated sigh. 'Oh for God's sake, everyone. I'm not some poor little flower who needs looking after. Mum, Ted, Samar, I appreciate the offer, but please, you can all get off. I'm tired, and a bit pissed. I must have drunk more than I thought.' She manages a smile. 'Honestly, I'm fine. I'll give you a ring in the morning.'

Reluctantly they nod and after saying their goodbyes to Alek rather stiffly, they see themselves to the door.

'Call me tomorrow when you wake up,' Stella says. 'I'll bring over some ginger and fennel powder.' She shoots Alek one final look of disapproval, before closing the door behind them all.

Viv lies back on the sofa. 'God, I'm sorry, Alek. I don't know what the hell is wrong with me tonight. I must be coming down with the flu.'

He nods thoughtfully and disappears off to the kitchen, returning with a glass of water. 'Here,' he says. 'Drink this.'

Cleo wakes to the sound of her phone bleeping and she blinks in confusion. What time is it? She glances at her clock: 12.30 a.m. She stares down at herself. Why is she wearing all her clothes? Then realization hits her and she snatches up her phone in panic and reads the text on her screen. At the end of ur street. Can u meet me outside ur house? it says. Hurriedly she types OK before stuffing the phone in her back pocket and creeping from her room. Glancing at her mother's bedroom door as she passes she sees that it's slightly ajar, and scarcely breathing in case she wakes her she tiptoes down the stairs. The house is dark and silent as she grabs her coat from where it hangs on the end of the bannister. Then, very slowly, she reaches for the front door's handle and turns it. She waits for a few seconds to check that there's no sound from upstairs, then lets herself out.

On the pavement she shivers as she glances from left to right. The street's completely empty. She looks down at her phone in confusion but there's no further text from Daniel. 'Where is he?' she murmurs. But just then she sees a figure approaching from the far end of the street. She wraps her arms around herself for warmth as she squints at his approach. It looks, she realizes, like a grown man, not a fourteen-year-old boy, and, standing alone in the dark she experiences a small ripple of doubt. A minute later, however, when the figure passes beneath a street lamp twenty yards or so away, her face clears with recognition and she smiles in relief. 'Oh! It's you!' she says as he draws near. 'What are you doing here?' When he doesn't reply she falters in confusion, 'Why are you . . . have you come to see Mum?'

He smiles then, and it is only as he walks the last few feet towards her that she sees in his face something that makes her freeze. The person who is approaching her is entirely different from the man she'd met; the eyes that look back at her utterly devoid of warmth. As he reaches her, she understands somewhere deep inside herself that it was only a mask he wore before and she just has time to cry out once for her mother before a folded wedge of fabric is forced over her nose and mouth, and as soon as she breathes in its sharp chemical smell she falls backwards into darkness.

Viv opens her eyes. She's not sure what woke her. For a minute or two she lies there, drifting in and out of sleep, dimly aware of her headache, her parched mouth. It's only when she turns over, groping around for her duvet, that she realizes something's wrong. Fully awake now, she sits up. There is no duvet. She is lying on the living room sofa, still wearing her clothes from yesterday. What is she doing here? Looking around herself in confusion she sees the glow of the buttons on her Sky box, moonlight trickling in through a gap in the curtains.

She squints at her watch. Almost 3 a.m. Her mind's groggy, her headache sharpening into stabbing knives of pain, her throat so dry she can barely swallow. Slowly the evening comes back to her. The dinner party. She remembers standing outside by the wheelie bin, feeling very ill. She rubs her head and tries to recall what happened after that. Through the fog in her brain she remembers her mother, Ted and Samar putting on their coats and going home. Then . . . what? Alek handing her a glass of water . . . but beyond that everything's blank. She shivers and stumbles to her feet, turning on the lights as she goes into the kitchen where she sees the table, covered in plates. Running the cold tap, she drinks directly from its stream, then splashes some more water on her face. What happened to Alek? Did he simply let himself out when she fell asleep? Embarrassment mingles with her confusion.

Exhausted, she fills a glass with water and goes upstairs to bed. On the landing she pauses outside Cleo's bedroom and, seeing that her door is slightly ajar, tiptoes over and glances in. Moonlight streams through the open curtains falling in two bars across Cleo's bed. Cleo's empty bed. She feels a bolt of shock, walking further into the room, looking around in confusion. Her daughter isn't there. She switches on the light, then calls her name. 'Cleo? Where are you?' but there's no reply. It takes less than a minute to search the house, running stupidly from room to room, panic building until she can scarcely breathe. 'Cleo!' she cries, 'Cleo, where are you?' But there's no answer.

12

A police car's engine growls outside Vivienne's house, blue lights flashing silently. Another, unmarked, vehicle waits further down the street, two officers standing next to it conferring quietly. Neighbours peer from bedroom windows, awoken by the commotion. A Detective Sergeant Ian Marshall and Detective Constable Giovanna Spilleti sit at her kitchen table, regarding Vivienne seriously.

'I'd like you to tell me again from the beginning,' says DS Marshall.

She wants to scream with frustration. 'I've been through this with your colleagues already. This is Jack Delaney's doing. I know it is. I reported last month that he'd made contact, but I was pretty much dismissed. And now he's got my daughter! Why aren't you out looking for her? You have to find her, she's only thirteen!'

Her voice is shrill and desperate, but Marshall merely

nods calmly. 'Please rest assured that we are doing everything we possibly can to find her.'

Viv stares back at him. DS Marshall is in his early forties, a thin, redheaded man, with tired eyes drooping at the corners, large freckles covering his pale skin. The woman sitting next to him, DC Spilleti, is in her late twenties, with the sort of Mediterranean looks that make one think of olive groves and dappled sunshine, though when she speaks her accent is more Lewisham than Tuscany.

Above their heads another officer searches Cleo's bedroom, though for what she has no idea, and they listen to his tread on the ceiling before Marshall speaks again. 'As I said, we need to be absolutely sure of the events leading up to Cleo's disappearance last night. If you could go through the details one more time.'

Viv sighs and closes her eyes, gathering herself before she repeats her account. 'We had some friends around for dinner . . .'

Spilleti glances at her notepad. 'That would be your mother Stella Swift, Dr Aleksander Petri, Ted Johnson and Samar Basra?' she says.

'Yes. My neighbour Neil joined us for an hour or so. My daughter ate with us then went upstairs to bed around ten.'

'And how did she seem?' asks Marshall.

She shakes her head helplessly. 'Normal. Like I've said. She just seemed normal.' She has already called every one of Cleo's friends, dragging them from their beds only to be told they'd neither seen nor heard from Cleo since school on Friday. She has told the police that to disappear in the middle of the night is entirely out of character for her not-at-all-streetwise child. And yet they persist with the possibility that Cleo has gone of her own volition, making Viv feel trapped in a nightmare where she's screaming into a vacuum, everyone around her apparently deaf to her panic. She wishes that her mother was here to take control, to make them see, but Stella, herself frantic with worry, has been told to stay at home in case Cleo should turn up there.

At that moment a male officer comes in holding something in his hand. 'Found this in the gutter, Sarge,' he says to Marshall.

Viv's heart stiffens as she recognizes the pink and blue stripy case of Cleo's mobile. 'That's my daughter's phone! That's Cleo's!' She rises and tries to take it from him, but the officer holds it back. DC Spilleti gets up and indicates that the officer should follow her from the room.

The detective sergeant continues to stare at Viv expectantly. 'And you didn't see or hear Cleo after she went up to bed?' he presses.

'What?' Dazedly she turns her attention back to him. 'No. My neighbour Neil left shortly afterwards, my mother, Samar and Ted left about eleven, I think, and . . .'

'And what about Dr Petri? Did he leave too?'

'No. I . . . I fell asleep. I had started to feel unwell. I guess I crashed out, and he must have seen himself out.'

Marshall considers this. 'And what is your relationship to Dr Petri?'

'We were . . . seeing each other. He was a customer at my café, but we had begun dating.'

DS Marshall nods. 'And it was a sexual relationship?'

She holds his gaze. 'What has that . . .' she sighs. 'Yes, it was.'

'OK, so tell me how you discovered that Cleo was missing. You said you woke up on the sofa?'

'Yes, like I said, I'd been feeling ill. I guess I'd had too much to drink, although . . .' she pauses, reflecting on the quantity of wine she'd consumed – it hadn't been that much, she was sure – nowhere near as much as she has drunk on other occasions when she'd barely been affected at all. 'But anyway,' she continues. 'When I woke up at about three a.m., Alek was gone. I went upstairs to bed and looked in on Cleo, but she wasn't there. And then I phoned the police.' Tears spring to her eyes and impatiently she swipes them away.

Marshall waits until she's composed herself. 'We have officers interviewing your dinner guests at their homes now and we'll also be talking to your neighbours to see if anyone in the street happened to see anything,' he says. 'We've also called Cleo's father to tell him to be alert for her turning up at his place, and we'll be keeping him abreast of the situation as it continues.'

She looks at him imploringly. 'You have to find Jack Delaney. You have to trace him. He's behind this, I'm certain he's taken her.'

'And why do you think he'd want to do that?'

She shakes her head helplessly. 'Revenge? Punishment? I don't know! Like I've told you, my evidence put him in prison. He's always said that he's innocent . . .'

She breaks off as Spilleti appears at the door once more and beckons Marshall into the hall. He glances apologetically at Viv as he rises and leaves the room, closing the door behind him. For some minutes Viv sits alone, staring unseeingly into space. She checks her watch: 6.02 a.m. Cleo has been missing for between three to seven hours already.

It had taken a long time for the police to arrive – almost forty-five agonizing minutes, due, she was told, to a double stabbing on Peckham High Street. While she'd waited, after calling Cleo's friends and then Stella, she'd tried to contact Alek to see if he'd noticed anything strange when he'd left earlier. Unsurprisingly at three thirty in the morning it had gone straight to voicemail, so she'd left a brief, panicked message telling him the police were on their way. After that she'd paced restlessly until, wanting to keep herself occupied, she'd cleared up the kitchen, mechanically picking up every plate and bowl and glass and depositing them in the dishwasher. She'd moved as if in a dream, the work soothing her, barely noticing as she scraped Neil's cheesecake from bowls, emptied wine and water glasses, even the Tupperware pot holding the remains of Shaun's disgusting apple turnover, until the room had been entirely spotless.

She goes to stand at the window. It's starting to get

light and as she peers out she sees some of her neighbours on their doorsteps staring over at her house and
the police cars outside it, or else standing in groups,
deep in conversation. The woman who lives opposite
appears, holding her toddler on her hip; she makes eye
contact with Viv and gives her a cautious, concerned
smile before turning away.

One thought, sickening but insistent, runs on a
constant loop inside her head. *When you went to sleep,
Alek and Cleo were here in this house. When you woke
up, both were gone.* She thinks about the Albanian wine
Alek had been so insistent that she drank; she thinks
about how edgy and odd he'd been all evening, how
she'd caught him staring so intently at Cleo, and then
she thinks about how the last thing she remembers was
him handing her a glass of water, how uncharacteristic
it was of her to sleep so deeply without her sleeping
pills. So deeply in fact that she didn't even wake when
Cleo left the house, despite the fact she was lying only
feet away from the front door. A sickening possibility
occurs to her like a cold hard punch and she runs into
the hall.

'DS Marshall!' she calls, coming to a halt when she
sees him. 'I think Alek—'

But before she can finish, he asks, 'What can you tell
me about your daughter's friend Daniel?'

She stares at him blankly. 'Cleo doesn't have a friend
named Daniel.'

'Cleo has been in regular contact with someone of

that name, purporting to be a fourteen-year-old boy. He texted her at twelve thirty a.m. to ask her to meet him outside this house. Whoever Daniel is, it seems likely that Cleo is with him.'

She shakes her head in confusion. 'But I don't understand . . . she doesn't know any Daniels!'

Marshall considers this, before saying, 'From what we can tell, they have been talking via text and email for several weeks.'

'*What?* But she would have told me! We don't have secrets from each other—' She's interrupted by the appearance of Spilleti and it's then that she remembers her fears about Alek. 'Listen,' she says desperately. 'I think Aleksander Petri has something to do with Cleo's disappearance.'

The two officers exchange a glance. 'And why do you think that?'

'Because he was acting so strangely all evening. I think he drugged me. He kept getting me to drink this wine he'd brought over. He was behaving so oddly; jumpy, barely talking . . . ask Samar and Ted, they'll tell you the same. And he's a doctor, so he would know what drugs to use.' The more she talks, the more certain she becomes. 'Oh God!' she says, frantic now. 'You have to find him!'

'But why would Aleksander want to kidnap your daughter?' Spilleti asks.

She thinks about his grubby flat, his obvious lack of money despite what must be a relatively decent wage.

'I don't know. Maybe . . . maybe Jack Delaney paid him.' And as soon as she's said this, she knows that it's true, that it is exactly what has happened. And she feels shame and fear and misery like she's never known before. Alek led Jack to Cleo, gave her to him like a gift, and she, her mother, had allowed it to happen. 'You have to find Alek,' she tells Marshall, her voice rising in desperation.

He nods. 'We have officers heading to his address. Do you have the wine glass you drank from last night?'

Viv closes her eyes in despair. 'No,' she says. 'I put everything in the dishwasher. Oh God, I didn't think. I didn't realize. I just wanted to keep busy.'

When the officers have left her alone, though it's a form of self-torture, Vivienne tries to call Alek's phone over and over, but every attempt results in the same cold silence: no ringtone, no voicemail message, nothing. She closes her eyes in despair when she thinks how she'd left a message on his phone telling him that the police were on their way, unwittingly warning him they'd be knocking on his door soon enough. He'd be long gone by now. She thinks about how he'd come to her café, how easily she'd fallen for him, how effortlessly he'd sucked her in. He and Jack must have planned their deception from the beginning and she – desperate, foolish, gullible – had fallen for his lies.

Seeing a movement outside on the street she goes to the window where she watches Marshall and Spilleti emerging from Neil's house before pausing to confer quietly at his front gate, their expressions giving nothing away. She checks her watch: almost eight a.m., the winter sky turning gradually paler as it slowly shakes off the night. People have begun to emerge along the pavement, heading for buses and trains, and she watches as they stride obliviously towards her house before slowing, a look of astonishment and curiosity on their faces when they spot the police and their cars. They turn to peer through her window, looking guiltily away when they see her standing there. Finally, Viv moves to the sofa where she sits motionless, her daughter's name pulsing through her like a heartbeat. *Come back to me, come back to me, please, Cleo, be safe.*

When DS Marshall returns ten minutes later she can tell that there's been a development. She waits, her heart in her mouth, as he takes the seat next to hers. 'Mr Basra and Mr Johnson have been questioned by our officers, and their stories concur with yours; that you were taken ill and Alek Petri was with you when they left.'

'And Alek?' she says urgently, searching his face.

Marshall looks at her gravely, confirming her worst fears even before he speaks. 'I'm afraid that we have, as yet, been unable to locate Dr Petri. He was not at his address when our officers called and after they forced entry it was clear that he'd left in something of a hurry. We're trying to ascertain his whereabouts.'

So she'd been right. The realization lodges in her

throat, hard and bitter. She wonders how much of his life had been a lie. 'What does the hospital say? Does he even work there?' she asks quietly.

To her surprise, Marshall nods. 'King's College has confirmed that Mr Petri is employed by them. He's due to start a shift there this afternoon, in fact, so we'll have officers waiting for him.'

She nods mutely, already knowing it will be pointless.

'Vivienne,' Marshall says, 'since your mother lives nearby, perhaps it would be a good idea for you to go and wait with her. We need to conduct a thorough search here, so it might be easier for you to . . .'

'Why do you need to search this house?' she asks dully.

'It's standard procedure. I really do think it would be best if you go to your mother's. An officer can drive you round there.'

'No. I need to stay here in case Cleo comes back.'

'There will be police here at all times, and we'll tell you as soon as we have news.'

His tone is polite but authoritative and she thinks about her house being filled with strangers, searching through her and Cleo's things. She's hit with a sudden longing to see Stella and at last she nods and allows herself to be guided to one of the waiting police cars. She sits in the back, a cold emptiness filling her as the engine starts and they pull away.

Cleo cannot move. She's lying on the floor of what seems to be a transit van, her arms and legs bound tightly, her mouth taped shut. It's very cold, and she has cried so much that snot and tears have dried itchy and sticky on her face. Her eyes are two raw slits. She doesn't know how long she's been lying here, only that when she woke with a pounding head and racing heart the van was in motion. About ten minutes later they'd come to a halt and after that there'd been silence. She doesn't know what she's most scared of: the thought of him returning or the thought of him leaving her here forever in the dark.

She wants her mum, she wants her mum so badly; to curl up on her lap like she did when she was little and breathe in her smell and feel her warmth and tell her how sorry she is – for believing that Daniel was real, for bringing this on herself, for the worry she must be feeling. She's so frightened of her kidnapper, of the hatred and violence that radiated from him before he knocked her out, that when something thumps against the side of the van she screams against her gag, her heart nearly bursting from her chest. But still he doesn't come. And as she lies there, cold and frightened, she thinks about the danger her mum is in, of how Viv doesn't realize that the man she thinks she knows is someone else entirely.

As soon as she sees Stella, Vivienne begins to cry. 'He's got her, Mum,' she says. 'Jack, he's got Cleo.'

'We don't know that,' Stella replies, her face pale. 'We don't know Jack was involved.'

'It's him! I know it is. She would never ever run off like this.' Viv's eyes search her mother's face. 'Why is he doing this, what is it for? Revenge? He always said he was innocent. What if he didn't kill Ruby? What if I got it wrong back then and he's going to hurt Cleo to punish me?'

'Of course he killed Ruby! He was found guilty!' Stella's voice rises in distress.

'But that's exactly it. What if we were wrong?' Viv sits at the kitchen table and puts her head in her hands.

'Vivienne,' Stella says firmly, 'the police agreed he was guilty and so did the jury. He was there in the house when she died! And what about the other witnesses? Declan from up the lane, and that Morris boy? They both saw him running from the house after she'd been killed.' She takes hold of Viv's hands and holds them tightly. 'You know what Jack was like, what a horrible violent bully he was. Surely you remember how he treated your sister! Nobody but Jack was responsible for her death.'

Viv stares mutely back at her, knowing that she's right. *And now he's got my daughter too*, she thinks.

There is nothing left to say and so the two sit silently together, through minutes that feel like hours, until Vivienne tells her quietly, 'I think Alek was involved.'

Stella looks at her aghast. 'What?' she says. 'Why?'

'I think he drugged me. He was behaving so strangely last night. I think Jack paid him to get Cleo away from me. And it's all my fault. Alek used me to get to Cleo. Oh God, Mum, what have I done? What the hell have I done?'

13

Cleo hears the doors to the van open and suddenly there he is, towering over her as she blinks in the sudden shock of sunlight. Panic-stricken, she shrinks from him, but he takes hold of her arms and pulls her roughly up to a sitting position. He doesn't speak until he rips the tape painfully from her mouth and passes her a bottle of water. 'Drink,' he says.

'Please,' she begs, her voice a croak, 'please let me go home.'

But he only pushes the bottle closer to her mouth. 'Drink.'

She shakes her head, whimpering in fear.

When he hits her across the face it is so sudden and violent that she falls backwards with a cry, smacking her head on the side of the van. He hauls her back up and forces the bottle painfully into her mouth until at last she drinks. She's crying so hard that the water spills down her chin but his eyes are expressionless as he watches her. When she's finished he stoops to put the bottle down and she catches a glimpse over his shoulder of the world beyond the van's door. It looks as if they are in some sort of vacant lot or builder's yard, with high corrugated-iron fences, two cranes in the distance. She has no idea how far from home she is; how long they were travelling before she woke.

'Why are you doing this?' she asks and almost chokes with terror when he grabs her by the throat.

'You open your mouth one more time, you spoilt little cunt, and I will slice your face off,' he says. 'Do you understand?'

She nods and he puts the gag back on her, then tightens the rope that binds her arms and legs, before pushing her backwards into the van. Slamming the doors shut, he leaves her alone.

Vivienne stands at Stella's kitchen window staring unseeingly out at the street for a while, before noticing Shaun loading a box into a large red van. 'So he's going, then?' she asks without much interest.

Stella comes to stand beside her. 'Yes. It was all very sudden.'

They continue to watch him as he throws in a bin bag after the box. 'Why does he need such a big van?' Viv asks, remembering the sparseness of his room.

Her mother shrugs, 'He borrowed it from a friend, it was the only vehicle he could get hold of.'

Shaun shuts the van door and pauses to light a cigarette. It strikes Vivienne then that he must know about Cleo's disappearance, after all he could hardly have missed the police coming to question Stella earlier, or the car that dropped her outside an hour or so ago. And right at that moment he glances around and sees them watching him and for a second or two his eyes meet hers, his expression unreadable, before he turns and gets into the driver's seat, starts the engine and drives away.

The hours pass. Again and again Viv tries Alek's number, but she's met with silence. No matter how hard she tries to banish them from her mind, memories keep appearing; the two of them in bed together, the touch of his hands, the expression in his eyes as he'd undressed her, the taste of his skin, and she feels a piercing shame.

She remembers too how he'd said, 'War changes you, it turns you into someone you never thought you'd become.' She thinks about his daughter, her refusal to see him, and how he'd once said, 'She is angry because she believes something about me that isn't true.' What had he meant by that? Viv's thoughts jump from one possibility to the next, but each time draw a blank. She wonders if he's given Cleo to Jack yet, and horror courses through her.

How could she have missed Cleo talking to strangers

online? What sort of mother lets that happen to their thirteen-year-old child? When she had bought Cleo her first phone, aged twelve, it had been with the strict caveat that Viv would check her internet use at regular intervals. She would not be allowed to take it up to bed with her, and she wasn't allowed to use social media. At first she had upheld these rules. But gradually, bit by bit, as Cleo had grown older, she'd taken her eye off the ball. Cleo was so sensible, so honest and innocent, more interested in sports and computer games than Snapchat or boys. When Viv had talked to her about online safety, her daughter had been more clued up about it than she had. Each of her spot checks had proven entirely unnecessary. And so, over the past six months or so, she'd let her attention slide. And as a result her daughter had been groomed and lured from her home right under her nose. Self-hatred spills through her, biting and acidic.

When the doorbell rings, Stella and Viv stare at each other fearfully before Vivienne rushes to answer it, certain that it must be the police. *Please*, she thinks to herself, *please, please have good news*.

But it's Samar and Ted who she finds at the door. 'Oh love,' Samar says as he hugs her. 'I'm so sorry, darling. How are you holding up?' He releases her and gazes back at her. 'I can't believe it. I just can't fucking believe it.'

Wordlessly she turns and they follow her into the house. 'What have the police said?' Ted asks her when they're sitting down.

'I think Alek had something to do with taking Cleo,' Viv says. 'I think he drugged the wine and the water he gave me.'

'What?' Samar stares back at her, horrified.

'But . . . why on earth would he . . . ?' Ted asks.

She shrugs helplessly. 'I think Jack paid him. Remember how strange and quiet he was last night? I thought there was something weird going on with him. Who else could it have been? Someone drugged me, I'm certain of it. Let's be honest, I barely knew him. Oh God!' she pounds her forehead with her fist. 'Oh God, what have I done?'

'Jesus,' says Ted, staring back at her, aghast, and even through her panic it strikes Viv how incongruous he looks here, mild and stolid amidst such gut-wrenching chaos, dressed in his brown, freshly pressed chinos, his plain, metal-rimmed glasses perched upon his shiny round face. 'But, I mean . . . that can't be . . . what do the police think? Have they talked to him?' he asks.

'He's completely disappeared. They searched his flat and said it looks like he left in a hurry.'

Samar gapes at her. 'Shit.'

'The last thing I remember is him handing me a drink of water, then I just . . . fell asleep. I usually wake up at anything without my pills, but I didn't even hear Cleo leave the house.' She presses the heels of her hands to her eyes to try to stem her tears. 'I'm such an idiot! I'm such a fucking stupid idiot! My little girl, my poor little girl.'

'No, sweetheart. No. They'll find her,' Samar says,

reaching across and taking her hand. 'They'll find her, I know they will.'

'But what if they don't?' she cries. 'What if they don't, Samar?'

Over the following hours Ted and Samar stay with Viv and Stella, picking over the lunch Stella makes them without enthusiasm, the four of them waiting in tense silence for news. It's not until three p.m. that they get a visit from DS Marshall.

'What's happened?' Viv says anxiously as he walks into the kitchen. 'Is there any news?'

Marshall takes the seat Stella offers him. 'Aleksander Petri didn't arrive at work today. He left a voicemail with his department secretary saying he'd had a family bereavement and would need time off.'

Vivienne's heart sinks: even though she knew she was right about Alek, a small part of her had clung to the hope that she wasn't. 'You haven't found out anything else?'

'I'm afraid we've been unable to locate Cleo on any local CCTV, nor on any bus or train station security cameras,' Marshall tells her. 'Which indicates that Cleo was probably taken away by car or some other vehicle.' He pauses. 'Unfortunately, the messages from "Daniel" were sent from a pre-paid phone and are untraceable, as are his log-ins to the gaming forum where he and Cleo first made contact. The photos he sent of himself are from a stock photo library, easily found from a Google image search.'

At this Vivienne puts her head in her hands. 'Oh Cleo.'

'I want to assure you,' Marshall continues evenly, 'that we're doing everything in our power to find her. We've issued a high-risk missing person report, circulated her picture to every force around the country and we're watching every station and port. We've issued a child rescue alert across social media and passed Cleo's picture on to national news agencies. We'll be organizing a television appeal later today.'

As Vivienne listens to him talk, she desperately tries to derive some comfort from his words, some sense that through his efforts her daughter will be brought home to her, but the seriousness with which they're treating Cleo's disappearance only makes her terror keener. Jack has got her, of that she's sure. The man who killed her sister has taken her child.

When Marshall has gone, promising that a family liaison officer will be in touch, Samar puts his hand on hers. 'Vivienne?' he says, looking at her with concern, and it's only then that she realizes he'd been talking to her for some time.

She stares at him. 'Sorry, what?'

'I was just saying that they'll find her, I'm sure they will. She'll be back home in no time . . .'

'Sammy's right,' Ted says. 'They'll catch this bastard, no question.'

Though she smiles dully at their attempts at comfort, she feels an overwhelming exhaustion roll over her, a desperation to be alone, and she gets to her feet. 'I'm sorry,' she says. 'I need to lie down for a bit.' She looks at her mother. 'Is it OK if I . . . ?'

Stella nods. 'Of course. Use my room.'

And when she sinks onto Stella's bed, though she's sure that she won't sleep, her tiredness nevertheless gets the better of her and oblivion falls like a heavy cloak.

She wakes an hour or so later to the sound of her name being called and groggily she gets up and goes down to the living room to find Stella, Samar and Ted sitting in front of the TV. On the screen a newsreader is speaking in a voice of urgent gravitas. 'Police have launched a high-risk missing person's report following the disappearance of thirteen-year-old Cleo Swift from her home in Peckham, south-east London.' The newsreader's face is replaced with a picture of Cleo; she looks so pretty and happy it makes Viv's heart hurt. 'Cleo went missing from her house sometime between eleven last night and three thirty this morning. There was, according to her neighbour, a dinner party held at the address last night and we understand that police are talking to guests to try to ascertain when she was last seen. Police say that her disappearance is out of character and they are very concerned for her welfare. They are urging anyone with information to phone the number at the bottom of the screen.'

The report ends and Stella switches off the television to absolute silence. Vivienne finds she has scarcely breathed throughout the newsreader's words and takes a gulp of air. They are not talking about her girl, her child; they can't be. They are talking about an unloved, unnoticed girl, surely, because that is the type who might go missing. A child whose mother doesn't notice that she's in danger, a child so uncared for that she's groomed and taken from under her nose. It doesn't matter if Vivienne herself was drugged. She had put Cleo in this position, she had not protected her. Instead she had let a man into her house who had planned all along to give her to a murderer, and she had been so blinded and giddy with sex and flattery that she'd let him.

'Viv?' Samar says. 'Are you OK?'

'What time is it?' she asks, registering that it's already dark outside.

Ted checks his watch. 'Five thirty.'

Which means that, if Cleo went out to meet 'Daniel' after his text at 12.30 a.m., she has been missing for seventeen hours. 'I want to go home,' she says.

Stella looks at her anxiously. 'I think you should stay here. The police said they'll contact you if there's—'

'No.' Stubbornly she shakes her head and gets to her feet, desperate to be surrounded by her daughter's belongings once more, to be able to smell and touch her things.

Sam and Ted exchange a glance. 'Well, at least let us drive you,' Ted says.

She shrugs, already putting on her coat. 'Fine.'

* * *

She sits next to Ted as he drives the short journey home, Samar in the back, the three of them staring grimly ahead, lost in their own thoughts. She thinks about when Cleo was first born, how, when she cried in the night, Viv would wake from her own violent nightmares of Ruby and Noah to tend to her. As she held Cleo in her arms during those long, lonely midnight hours it was as much to gain comfort as to give it, her own baby a reminder of what had been lost, and what should have been. Now she clenches her hands into hard fists. She cannot let Jack take Cleo from her too.

When they arrive at the house it's to find a small crowd of reporters outside who surge forward as they pull up. 'Vivienne?' they call. 'How are you bearing up? What do you think has happened to Cleo? Is it true that she had an online boyfriend? Is there anything you'd like to say?'

Viv freezes, struck dumb by this sudden assault, but Ted and a police officer firmly hold the reporters back while Samar takes her elbow and leads her to the door. 'Is it OK to go in?' he asks the policewoman standing there, and when she nods he steers Viv inside.

'Let me make you something to eat,' Ted says when they're standing in the eerily still and silent kitchen, the curtains drawn against the melee outside. 'You hardly touched your lunch. How about some eggs or something?' When she doesn't answer, he murmurs to Samar, 'I'll make her some anyway.'

After she's pushed her food listlessly around her plate,

Samar and Ted sit with her for an hour, but she barely notices they're there, their attempts at comfort or distraction falling on deaf ears. Instead she stares out at the police and reporters, holding one of Cleo's jumpers on her lap, the same questions running endlessly through her mind. What does Jack want? What will he do next?

'You should go,' she says dully, when she sees Samar glance at his watch.

'No way. Or if we do, you're coming with us.'

'Yes, good idea,' says Ted. 'Come and stay with us.'

'Or how about I spend the night here with you?' Samar suggests when she makes no response.

But Viv shakes her head. 'I want to be by myself.' She needs to think, and having people in the house, even Samar and Ted, makes her more on edge. She wants to do nothing, to sit quietly without anyone telling her that she should eat or sleep, or trying to make her feel better: she doesn't deserve to feel better.

When she's finally persuaded them to leave she goes upstairs to Cleo's room and stands in the doorway, surveying the untidiness the police have left behind. Taking a seat on Cleo's chair, she picks up a framed photo from the windowsill and gazes down at it. It's of Cleo and Layla, their arms around each other's shoulders, each grinning widely at the camera. They must have been about eleven and look so joyful and innocent it pierces her heart. When her phone bleeps she pulls it hurriedly from her pocket, but seeing that it's only a text from the

179

gas board lets it drop to her lap, leans back and closes her eyes.

Some hours later she blinks awake with a start and gazes around in confusion. What had woken her? She's still clutching her mobile and she notices that it's illuminated, showing that she has a new text. Feeling stiff and cold, she wipes the sleep from her eyes then clicks it open, and then as she stares down at the image on the screen, her eyes widen in horror. The picture is of Cleo, lying on the floor of what looks like a van, her arms and legs tightly bound. She's staring up at whoever's taking the photo in pure terror. Horror courses through Viv as she tries to take it in. Beneath the photo is a message. Tell the truth about Ruby or your daughter will die. You have two days.

'No,' she whispers, 'no no no no.' Frantically she types her reply. I don't know, I swear. She sends it, then immediately starts typing again. I thought I was telling the truth. I believed that you killed her. If I'm wrong I'm sorry. I'm so sorry. She hesitates then adds. I'll put it right. I'll tell them it wasn't you. Please. Please don't hurt her, she's just a little girl.

She sits staring at her phone, willing him to answer. At last it comes. You have twenty-four hours to tell the truth. If you don't, she will lose a finger. After that you have one more day. If you still don't say who killed Ruby, Cleo will die. Call the police and I'll kill her anyway.

Instantly she begins to search for DS Marshall's number, then stops to re-read the threat. Call the police

180

and I'll kill her anyway. She thinks about what Jack did to his fellow inmate, how he'd left him in a coma, blinded in one eye. She remembers his cold, malevolent presence in their house. Jack was not someone who made empty threats; he was not someone whose bluff you called.

Her mind races. Wouldn't the police be able to find him by tracking his mobile via phone masts or something? She dimly remembers reading that they could trace a phone to within a few miles. But that was still too wide an area for them to find Jack instantly. Could she take that risk? What if during that time Jack somehow knew she'd told them? What if he retaliated by harming Cleo – or worse? Her dealings with the police since she'd first reported the flowers and newspaper article hadn't filled her with faith in their efficiency. Her longstanding fear of Jack, of what he might be capable of was too deeply ingrained and far more powerful than her trust in the police. Her mouth floods unpleasantly as though she's going to be sick. She can't take the risk, she just can't.

She gets up to pace the room. If Jack didn't kill her sister, then who did? '*Think*,' she whispers. Through her panic she forces herself to focus. If she's going to get her daughter back she needs to work on the assumption that Jack is telling the truth about his innocence. So who did kill Ruby? Who else had been in the cottage that day? There must be something, some vital clue that she's forgotten.

She sinks onto Cleo's bed, her head in her hands. Two other people had seen Jack shortly before and after Ruby was killed: their neighbour Declan Fairbanks and Morris Dryden. Morris had said that after he'd dropped off his delivery he'd gone back up the lane towards the village, passing Jack who was on his way to see Ruby. He'd turned to look over his shoulder and seen Jack knocking on their door. Another key part of the evidence had been the television programme Viv had been watching when she heard Ruby answer the door to Jack. This had been 1984, long before the days of TV on demand; they hadn't even owned a VCR. The time of the television programme had matched that given by Morris when he said he saw Jack entering the house.

Then there was Declan Fairbanks' evidence. In his early fifties at the time of the murder, Declan lived with his wife at the top of the lane. He'd testified that he'd been looking out of his window when he'd noticed Jack running towards the village from the direction of their cottage. Again, the timing of this had coincided with the programme Viv had been watching shortly before she went upstairs and found her sister's body.

But if Jack was innocent, did that mean Declan, or Morris, or indeed both of them, had been lying?

The thought that Jack *hadn't* killed Ruby seems preposterous . . . except, even as she thinks this, she is aware of a small shift inside her, as though a quiet voice whispers *But is it? Is it so ridiculous after all?* A vocalization of that strange nagging doubt that had always been there. Nausea rises inside her.

She closes her eyes and tries to remember Declan. A tall, well-built man in a suit, with greying hair and pale blue eyes. She has one solid memory of him – the time he shouted at her for accidentally kicking a ball at his window – and she remembers how he'd scared her, how he hadn't appeared to like children much. She closes her eyes tighter, trying to focus. His wife had been a quiet, shy woman who rarely left the house.

Most of her childhood memories had, for more than thirty years, been locked behind a wall of panic. It had always been easier, safer, not to think about any of it. But now, though the anxiety rolls through her in sickening waves, she clenches her fists and forces herself to push through it.

And then, fleetingly, a new memory appears, a recollection of being very small, of opening a door to a room to find Declan on the other side of it, of standing stock still with shock to see him there. Viv opens her eyes in surprise. Where had that been? Which room? Each time she tries to grasp the memory, it slips out of reach. But it is the accompanying emotion that this memory triggers that makes her heart jump to her throat, the same creeping, sickening disgust that she experienced before in her dreams of him. What is she remembering? What had she seen? Not Ruby's murder, she's certain of that, but what? It's no use: the memory has faded, and the more she tries to retrieve it, the vaguer it becomes.

She gets up. If Declan Fairbanks was in his fifties back then he would be quite elderly, possibly even dead by now. Even if he is still alive, would he provide any answers? She has to at least try to track him down. Her thoughts turn next to Morris Dryden. Had *he* lied about what he'd seen back then? If so, what part had he played in it? He'd been barely twenty then, so that would put him in his early fifties. His image is clearer than Declan's; in her mind's eye she sees a sweet, eager face with smiling eyes and curly brown hair, the red knitted vest he always wore. Stella has said recently he'd been in love with Ruby, that he'd invented errands just to see her. But he'd been a kind and gentle man – hadn't he? At any rate, if Declan *is* dead, Morris might be her only hope of finding out the truth. She has to track them down. She has to find Declan and she has to find Morris.

Going to the window she peers out at the dark street below and checks her watch: 5.45 a.m., Monday morning. The police cars and reporters have gone; nothing stirs on the pavement below. Her mind made up, she hurries to the bathroom and splashes water on her face, then runs down the stairs, grabs her coat from the banister and leaves the house. Once in the street she glances quickly around before going to her car. She sits motionless behind the wheel, unable to shift the image of her daughter, bound and gagged, a look of terror on her face.

At last with shaking fingers she puts her key in the

ignition, forcing herself to take long, even breaths. '*You have twenty-four hours to tell the truth,*' Jack's text had said. Starting the engine, she sets off for Essex.

14

The motorway when she hits it is almost empty and Viv speeds along, her Fiat 500 doing the best it can with her foot pressed to the pedal. She's barely conscious of her surroundings and it's only the cheery 'ding' and warning light on her dash to show she's nearly out of fuel that makes her grudgingly slow down and turn off at a service station.

After she's filled her tank she returns to her car, eager to get going, but when she glances at her watch she hesitates. It's barely seven a.m. She would be in Essex in less than half an hour. Even if Morris still lives above the butcher's, what is she going to do – drag him out of bed, demand he talks about events of over thirty years ago while in his pyjamas? Reluctantly she parks up then gets out and makes her way to the service station café.

Sitting at a corner table she sips her coffee and tries to get her thoughts into some sort of order. If Morris or Declan had lied about seeing Jack before or after Ruby had died, then what had been their motive? She starts with Morris: what reason would he have had to send an innocent man to prison? Or had he simply been mistaken, got the timings confused because, as Stella had recently put it, he wasn't 'all there'. She thinks of Declan, the odd, sickly disgust that had struck her a few hours earlier when she'd tried to picture his face, but which she still can't tie to any concrete memory.

She rubs her eyes, wishing she could turn to her mother, fearful that if she did Stella might try to talk her out of what she's about to do, would probably insist that she go to the police instead. In her heart she's certain that the only way to get her daughter back is to do exactly what Jack says. She looks at her watch. She has twenty-two hours before he carries out his first disgusting threat; forty-six to save her daughter's life.

The sun has begun its steady climb to shine on another cold, bright winter's day when she gets back in her car. Grimly she starts the engine and prepares to drive the remaining miles to her childhood home, in a village she hasn't clapped eyes on for thirty-two years. As the countryside flashes past her, she remembers a time when Cleo was around five and had pointed at her framed photograph of Ruby. 'Who's she, Mummy?' she'd asked.

'She was my sister, your auntie,' Viv had replied

cautiously. She'd always known that the subject of Ruby would come up one day, but had hoped that Cleo would be a bit older before she had to explain such a sad and complicated tale.

'My auntie? Like Layla's Auntie Patience?' Cleo had said excitedly. 'Where is she?'

'I'm afraid she's dead, my love.'

Cleo's green eyes had searched her face. 'Why?'

Viv had hesitated. She would have to tell Cleo the truth one day, but not yet, not quite yet, she couldn't bear to. 'She . . . got sick, sweetheart.'

Cleo's face had been full of confusion as she'd gazed at the photo of the pretty teenager in her hand. 'I don't want her to be dead,' she said, and then, 'will I die, too?'

And Viv had pulled her on to her lap and whispered, 'Not until you're very, very old. I will never let anyone hurt you, my darling. I promise.' But she hadn't kept that promise. She had failed, just as she had once failed Ruby and Noah.

Putting her foot to the pedal, she drives on until at last she comes to the exit for the village. Twenty minutes later, after following several twisting B roads, she approaches a brown sign which bears a name so familiar and evocative that it makes her throat catch. She progresses slowly, wonderingly, through street after unfamiliar street of new-build estates that must have sprung up in the three decades of her absence, more than doubling the size of the village she once knew. But as she nears the centre her surroundings become increasingly recognizable and she drinks it all in, everything her eyes fall on triggering memory after memory, snapshots steeped in colour and texture and emotion entirely buried until now beneath the weight of the intervening years.

There is the corner shop where she would go to buy her Sunday sweets; there is the laundrette that once nearly burned down in a fire, and there is the post office where her best friend's mother worked. She passes her old primary school, her car almost slowing to a halt as she gazes in through the playground's gates, every glimpse of Victorian brick wall, drinking fountain and climbing frame heart-stoppingly unchanged. Eventually, she comes to the village green where she and the other local kids used to play. She stops the car and gazes out, bombarded with memories of feeling hot and breathlessly happy, engrossed in a game of tag. A long-ago sensation returns to her of playing out far too late, knowing her mother will be angry with her but not wanting to go back home, longing instead to remain in the exciting freedom of the game, hoping when she returned to the cottage that Ruby would jump to her defence, the way she always did.

She sits and gazes at the daisy-speckled expanse of grass, the duck pond, the wooden bench, the huge oak tree where her kite once got stuck and Morris climbed up to retrieve it. She starts her car, driving slowly, gazing out wide-eyed, but when she passes the churchyard she instinctively looks away until she reaches the beginning of the high street. She isn't ready to face her sister's final resting place yet.

Getting out of the car she's surprised at how much smaller and shabbier everything seems compared to the village of her memories. Some of the shops have changed – the Woolworths and dressmakers and hardware store are long gone – but many are still recognizable from thirty years before: the baker's, the florist's, the chemist. She passes the old tea shop that's now a Gregg's bakery and with each step feels the weight of sadness press more heavily upon her. When she spies ahead the Bird's Nest pub her heart tightens: this was where Ruby had worked on Saturdays; where she'd first met Jack. Her unease deepens as a thought occurs to her. Are the Delaney family still in the area? They lived, she remembers, outside the village on the Colchester Road and she shudders at the thought that they might be living here still, that she might even happen upon them in the street. She would not know them if she did.

She keeps walking until she sees it: the shop that used to be Dryden's Butchers. She stops and gazes at it for a while, remembering how it used to look. A sign with mustard yellow lettering, two square bay windows where the meat was displayed. She remembers a sandwich board outside with a pig in a butcher's white hat and coat, the sudden chill and smell of fresh blood when you entered, sawdust on the floor. Morris's dad, red-cheeked and white-jacketed, a tall, ruddy-faced man;

Morris's mum, a neat, blond-haired woman, motherly and quick to smile. And Morris himself, working behind the counter, running errands for his dad.

But Dryden's is long gone. The sign is still there above the door, faded and almost illegible, but instead of sausages and chops the bay windows are filled with bric-a-brac and second-hand furniture; an umbrella stand, a parrot cage, a jumble of dusty books. She gazes in through the dirty windows but the place is closed and in darkness, a homemade sign on the door that says, *Judy's Junk. Back Soon*, though it doesn't look like it's been opened in months. What happened to the Drydens? Are Morris's parents dead? Has Morris moved away? She turns to gaze up and down the street, at what is so familiar but so changed, and wonders who to ask.

Cleo freezes in fear at the sound of the van doors opening. She's been lying here for hours. The cord that binds her wrists is cutting into her skin, but she is so cold and frightened she barely notices. Her legs and arms ache with stiffness and she keeps drifting in and out of sleep; whatever he'd drugged her with earlier is not ready to let go of her yet. Suddenly the van doors open and there he is looming over her, shocking and terrifying in the blinding light. Though she recoils in fear he reaches down and hoists her out, letting her fall heavily, painfully, onto the ground.

Through her panic she sees plainly the builder's yard he's brought her to. Her eyes scan high fences, stacks of bricks, piles of scaffolding poles and mounds of sand. At the furthest end are two small old-fashioned caravans, hardboard nailed over their windows. There's nobody around but she hears the sound of distant traffic. Next he unties the rope that binds her ankles and pulls her roughly in the direction of the caravans. When he unlocks the first one's padlocked door, he gives her a hard push, following closely behind as she stumbles up its step.

Inside there's a table, a bench that's covered in the same orange scratchy fabric that also hangs as curtains at the boarded-up windows. It's horribly cold and stinks of stale cigarette smoke, and something else, acrid and unpleasant; gasoline or turps, perhaps. 'Sit down,' he says, and it's terrifying how different he is from the man she thought she knew, every cell of him altered beyond recognition. She starts to cry. 'Please,' she begs, 'please let me go home.'

He makes no response but unties her wrists and from the wide pockets of his jacket he pulls out a greasy paper bag and tosses it onto the table in front of her. From his other pocket he pulls out the bottle of water. 'Eat,' he says, and then he leaves. She hears him locking the padlock once more, but though she waits for it, she doesn't hear the van's engine start. He's still out there somewhere and fear courses through her as she waits for his return.

As Vivienne stands in the street trying to decide who to ask for help, her phone rings. It's DS Marshall, his voice tense on the other end of the line. 'Vivienne?' he says, 'Where are you? We have officers at your door but you don't appear to be—'

'Have you any news?' she interrupts. 'Have you found Cleo? Or Jack or Alek?'

There's a pause.

'No? You've found out nothing?' She closes her eyes in frustration.

'Vivienne—'

'I see,' she says, cutting him off with a flash of white-hot anger. If they'd only taken her seriously when she first told them about Jack, they might have stopped him before he'd had a chance to get to Cleo.

'Where are you, Vivienne?' Marshall asks again.

'I'm looking for answers,' she tells him. 'I'll be back later.'

'Vivienne, it's important that—' but she hangs up before he can finish, and when her phone immediately starts ringing she doesn't pick up. She has little more than forty-five hours to save Cleo's life; there's no time to lose.

She crosses the road towards the newsagent's shop. The bell rings when she enters and an Asian woman dressed in a sari and a neon yellow puffa jacket nods hello to her. 'Can I help you, babes?' she says, her Essex accent broad.

'I hope so.' Viv approaches the counter. 'I used to live here a long time ago and I was wondering what happened to the Drydens?'

The woman stares back at her blankly. 'The who, love?'

'They owned the butcher's across the road. They had a son named Morris.'

'Oh right.' She nods vaguely. 'I've only been here five years or so, they'd long gone by then. That junk shop's been there the whole time, though it's hardly ever open. Waste of good retail space, if you ask me.' She jerks her head in the direction of the Bird's Nest. 'You should try the pub, sweetheart, the landlord's been here donkey's years, though it's run by his son now.'

Viv nods gratefully. 'Thanks. When does it open?'

'About eleven, but he lives above it. Carl's his name. Go and knock on his door, he won't mind.'

When she reaches the pub she peers through the window at its dark interior. There's a narrow front door next to its entrance which looks as though it might belong to the flat above. She presses the bell and waits. She's about to press it a second time when an upper window opens and a middle-aged man sticks out his bald head. 'You looking for me, love?' he asks.

She peers up at him, shielding her eyes from the bright winter sun. 'I'm sorry to bother you. My name's Viv, Vivienne Swift. I used to live in the village. I'm looking for the Drydens. The lady in the newsagents said you might be able to help.'

'Hold on a tick.' The head disappears and a minute or so later the door of the pub opens. He's a large man with a pleasant round face and smiling eyes, a belly so protruding she wonders how he stays upright. 'Come in,' he says. 'I'm Carl.' She follows him into the pub where sunlight shines through the windows to pool on the richly patterned carpet and the air is thick with the scent of stale beer and furniture polish. The chairs are stacked on each of the waggon wheel tables but he takes a couple down and gestures for her to sit. Then he tilts his head, considering her. 'Bloody hell,' he says wonderingly. 'Vivienne Swift. I remember you.'

She blinks at him. 'Really?'

'Yeah, I was in your sister's class at primary school.'

She feels a surge of emotion at this. There's something very moving about meeting someone who knew Ruby as a child, who actually remembers her from the days before Jack destroyed their lives.

Before she can reply, he adds, 'I remember what happened. Terribly sad. We all loved Ruby. She used to work here, as you probably know. Such a shock to us all.' He shakes his head. 'Bastard should have got life. Should never have been released.'

'Do you remember him then? Jack Delaney?' she asks.

He grimaces. 'Not much, enough to know he was a nasty piece of work, him and his brothers – though apparently they've gone straight. Model citizens, so I hear.' He raises his eyebrows sceptically.

'Do they . . . do the Delaneys still live near the village?'

'His brothers do. The mother and uncle are both dead. In fact Jack's mum died earlier this year. Had the funeral in the church over there.'

'Did Jack go to it?'

Carl shakes his head. 'No, love. Probably knew what sort of reception he'd get if he showed his face round here. As far as I know, only his brothers turned up.'

She takes this in silently. 'I'm trying to find Morris. Morris Dryden. Do you remember him?'

'Morris?' He frowns. 'Yeah, his dad had the butcher's.'

She nods eagerly. 'Do you know where he is?'

He looks at her strangely. 'I'm afraid he's dead too, love.'

Her stomach drops. 'Dead?' she says faintly. 'How? He can't have been that old?'

'Hung himself,' is the blunt response and Viv stares at him in shock. 'Yeah, 'fraid so.' Carl folds his arms. 'Can't have been that long after you and your mum left the area. Awful business. He was only twenty-one. His parents never recovered. Goes against all nature, don't it, having to bury your own child.' His face alters. 'Oh God, sorry, I wasn't thinking.'

She waves his apology away and asks, 'Did anyone know why? Why he killed himself, I mean?'

'Who can say? We were all very shocked – he didn't seem the type. Lovely bloke, he was. Had a good heart.'

She nods, trying to take it in. 'Are his parents both dead too?'

At this Carl feels around in his jacket pocket, then pulls out an elaborate vaping machine. He inhales deeply before blowing out a billowing strawberry-scented cloud into the air. 'Ned is,' he says. 'Had a stroke about ten years ago, but Val, she's alive, though only just, love her. She's in the old folks home up on Wellbeck Road. My auntie pops up to see her every so often.'

Viv considers this silently. After a while she says despondently, 'I don't suppose you know what happened to the Fairbanks, do you? The couple who lived a few houses up from us on Ambrose Lane?'

Carl screws up his face, trying to remember. 'God, I'd forgotten about them.' He pauses, thinking hard. 'The Cockles have lived there for so long it's hard to remember, but now you mention it I've an idea the Fairbanks moved away around the same time you did.'

She nods, trying not to let her hope evaporate. 'I don't suppose you'd know of anyone who might have kept in touch with them or have any idea where they might have moved to?' she says. 'It's very important.'

He shrugs. 'I can ask around. Seem to remember he was a bit of an awkward sod. Don't think he was too popular around here, though I can't recall why. But I'll ask my aunt. If anyone will know, she will.' He grins, 'Bit of a busy-body, my Auntie Sue. Likes to keep tabs on the comings and goings of the village.'

She remembers Declan Fairbanks' cold gaze, the squirming feeling of disgust and confusion that grows stronger every time she thinks of him, and nods. 'Thank you, I'd really appreciate it.' She finds a pen in her handbag and scribbles down her number on an old receipt. 'If you do hear anything about where he might be now, please give me a call. Like I said, it's very important.'

He takes the number and studies her intently. 'Bloody hell, Viv Swift! I can't believe it! You keeping well, are you? I've thought of you and your mum often over the years, it was such a bloody terrible thing. I don't think any of us in the village ever quite got over it, to be honest.' He shakes his head. 'But you're keeping all right, are you? You look well, I must say,' he adds encouragingly, clearly hoping for a happy ending to the tragedy.

She looks back at his round, cheerful face and thanks God that, if he's watched the news in the last twenty-four hours, he hasn't made the connection between the missing south-east London girl with the woman who sits in front of him. 'I'm fine,' she says with all the reassurance she can muster. 'I'm doing OK. Thank you.' She gets to her feet. 'And thanks for your help, I really do appreciate it.'

'No problem!' He walks her to the door. 'I'll see what I can find out about the Fairbanks and give you a bell.' As she turns to leave, he surprises her by wrapping her in a bear hug. 'Little Vivi Swift. It's lovely to see you after all this time,' he says, clearly emotional.

When she's safely back in her car she sits in stupefied silence, thinking over Carl's words. Morris, dead. She slams her palms on the steering wheel. 'Fuck!' But why did he kill himself, she wonders. Because he had something to do with Ruby's death and couldn't live with the guilt? Because he let an innocent man – no matter how awful – go to prison? But what would have been

Morris's motive for killing Ruby? Because he loved her and she didn't love him back? As hard as she tries, she can find no answers. She checks her watch: 9 a.m. Turning the key in the ignition she follows her satnav to Wellbeck Road.

15

Meadow View Retirement Home is a modern, yellow-brick building situated amongst nicely kept lawns. When Viv presses the buzzer she's let in by a short black woman with a Jamaican accent, wearing a neat lavender-coloured uniform and a name badge on her chest that says Yolanda Evans, Deputy Manager. As Viv follows her white squeaking pumps towards reception, she inhales the institutionalized smell of school dinners and disinfectant. The building is so unbearably overheated after the freezing cold air outside that she feels quite sick. 'Are you related?' Yolanda Evans asks cheerfully when she hears Viv's request to see Valerie Dryden.

'No, I'm an old friend of the family's. I was passing through and thought I'd come and say hi.' She makes herself hold the other woman's gaze, smiling brightly through her lie.

Apparently satisfied, Yolanda nods. 'OK. Well, she'll be happy to see you I'm sure. Better not stay too long though, she gets very tired.' And with that she motions for Viv to follow her.

Valerie's room is small but pretty with mint-green flocked wallpaper and a view of the garden. She's sitting in an armchair watching television when Viv walks in and Viv pauses at the door, taking in the frail figure in her pink dressing gown, her hair in white wisps around her face.

When Valerie looks up and notices her, she smiles uncertainly. 'Hello, dear.'

'Hello, Mrs Dryden.' Viv returns her smile as she approaches. 'I don't know if you remember me, but I used to live in the village. My name's Vivienne Swift and my mum was Stella Swift. I had a sister named Ruby.'

Unexpectedly, recognition shines in the pale, rheumy eyes and she points her remote control at the TV screen and turns it off. 'Yes, I know. Vivienne Swift, from Ambrose Lane.' Her head bobs constantly on her fragile neck as she reaches out a trembling hand. Viv takes it in her own, the fingers like twigs wrapped in tissue paper. 'Sit down, dear, sit down,' Valerie says, indicating the armchair next to hers.

'How are you?' Viv asks when she's seated. 'It's lovely to see you.' As she gazes at Morris's frail, tiny mother a memory surfaces of Valerie as a much younger woman, blonde and smiling, full of energy and fierce protectiveness of her son.

'I remember you,' Valerie says again, still holding Viv's hand. 'Such a sweet girl. And your sister too, so pretty. I always felt so sorry for you, you didn't deserve it, but what could anyone do?' She pulls her fingers from Viv's and they flutter to her throat.

'Mrs Dryden,' Viv says gently, leaning forward. 'I don't want to upset you, but I wondered if I could talk to you about Morris.'

The old woman looks back at her, stricken. 'My Morris? He's dead, dear. Morris died. Didn't you know?'

Vivienne nods. 'I did know, yes and I'm so sorry for your loss.' She swallows. Every scrap of decency in her tells her to leave Mrs Dryden in peace, to not dredge up such painful memories, but Cleo needs her to find the truth and so she says, 'I'm sorry, Mrs Dryden, but I need your help. I'm trying to find answers about my sister Ruby's death, and . . .' She reaches over and takes Valerie's fluttering hand in her own. 'Mrs Dryden, I'm so sorry to ask you this, but why did Morris kill himself? Do you know why he did it?'

Valerie stares at her, her pale eyes searching Viv's until Viv continues, 'Was it because of something he did that was bad, something he couldn't live with, do you think?'

At this Valerie nods. 'Yes, dear,' she says. 'That's right. He did it because he lied.'

Viv can scarcely breathe. 'About what?'

But Valerie is straining to look around Vivienne to the door. 'Would you like a cup of tea? Can I get you something? A biscuit maybe? If you call for Yolanda, I think she'd get you one . . .'

'No.' Viv shakes her head. 'I'm fine. Please, Valerie, Mrs Dryden, I'm so sorry to have to ask you this, but you were talking about Morris, about how he lied. Can you remember what it was he lied about?'

The old woman turns her face away to gaze out of the window. 'The night before he died, he came to me before bed and he seemed so sad. He could get like that sometimes. I asked him what the matter was and he said he had a secret, and that the secret had been eating him up and he couldn't live with it no more. I didn't know what he meant.' She pauses, considering this, nodding continuously. 'Well, I gave him a cuddle and he went up to bed. We were very close, you see, me and Morris. Next day we found him.' She looks stricken. 'Poor little Morris, we loved him so much, his dad and me.'

Vivienne nods and urges her on. 'Who did he lie to, Mrs Dryden? Was it about Ruby?'

Valerie turns her face back to her and her frail voice is full of anger. 'They wouldn't leave him alone, those Delaneys! Wish we'd moved away, wish we'd protected him from them. But Ned, my husband, he didn't want us to. We had our business, you see. We thought when Jack went to prison, that'd be the end of it.' Tears brim in her eyes. 'We found him, my poor little boy. He was just a little boy, underneath. He'd never hurt a fly.'

Viv leans forward and touches Valerie's arm, tears in her own eyes now. 'I'm so sorry for upsetting you,' she says. 'I really am so sorry. But this is so important. What do you think he meant when he said he'd lied, do you know?'

Valerie doesn't answer, just continues to stare ahead, nodding to herself, her fingers plucking at her dressing gown.

'Please,' Vivienne begs, 'please, please tell me. My little girl . . .' her voice catches and she swallows hard. 'My daughter's only thirteen, and she's in terrible danger. I need to find out what happened to Ruby. I think Morris might have known who killed her. I think he lied about seeing Jack Delaney that day. If there's anything you can remember, anything that Morris said that might help me . . .'

But Valerie only glances at her, and her eyes are glazed and unreadable. A flash of confusion passes through them, then she smiles tenderly at her. And Vivienne can't tell whether the old woman's silence is due to incomprehension or deliberate obtuseness, but she grips Valerie's arm more firmly and pleads, 'Valerie, it's so important, tell me what Morris lied about. Please tell me!'

Valerie looks past her, to the door and Viv turns to see that Yolanda has appeared, and she's looking at them both in alarm. 'Valerie, are you all right?' She crosses the room and peers at her, then turns to Viv, her voice firm. 'I think you'd better go. Mrs Dryden is clearly very tired and needs to rest.' She waits expectantly, her arms folded.

For a moment Viv continues to look imploringly at Valerie. But when Yolanda clears her throat meaningfully, she reluctantly, and with crushing disappointment, gets to her feet. And then, just as she's about to move away Valerie reaches over and lightly touches her hand. 'I'm sorry we didn't help you back then,' she says. 'We wanted to. We did.' Her eyes flutter shut as she adds, 'Thank you so much for coming, Ruby, but I'm rather tired now.'

Viv stares down at her in silence, a nameless longing spreading through her. She has a sudden, overwhelming desire to kneel down and lay her head on this elderly woman's lap, feel those frail, delicate hands stroke her hair, breathe in her smell of skin lotion and tea rose shampoo, and the longing is so strong that she has to force herself to turn around and walk away. *Ruby*, she thinks as she leaves, *she called me Ruby*, and this feels like the saddest thing of all.

Vivienne sits in her car, motionless. She feels as if all the layers of her have been peeled off, one by one, until she is just the pain that rages in the centre of her. The car is stuffy, the winter sun burning through the windscreen making her nauseous, a dull ache pulsing behind her eyes. The vomit rises in her throat without warning and she barely has time to fling open the car door before she throws up into the gutter.

Afterwards she sits back and closes her eyes and thinks about how Valerie had called her son her 'poor little

Morris, my poor little boy', as though he'd been but a small child, not a grown man of twenty-one when he died. And it strikes her that whenever she has thought of Cleo in the terrifying hours since she disappeared, that she, too, has felt as though it is the infant Cleo who has been wrenched from her arms, not the sturdy teenager she has grown into. Perhaps that's the essence of a mother's love, she thinks; an instinctive protectiveness that burns from the first second of your child's life, reigniting just as fiercely whenever that child is in danger, no matter what their age, or however many years have passed.

When she drives back to the village she doesn't stop until she reaches Ambrose Lane. She parks at the top and stands looking apprehensively down the familiar narrow track, the two clusters of cottages with the fields stretching out behind them, first numbers one and two then a gap before three and four, and finally their own, number five.

Steeling herself, she begins to make her way towards the first two cottages. When she reaches number two, the Fairbanks' home, she sees a neat and tidy red-brick cottage that as far as she can tell has barely changed in the years since she last saw it. She gazes at it, waiting to see if that same eerie feeling she'd experienced the night before might return, but in fact it triggers no reaction at all. She has no memory of entering it, no recollection of its interior and is as certain as she can be that whatever she had half remembered before had not taken place within its walls.

She walks on until she reaches the next three cottages and the one that used to be theirs. It's both the same and entirely different; the once grubby whitewashed bricks are now painted a fresh pale yellow, the casement windows replaced with double-glazed glass and PVC. A modest extension has been added to the side. It is pretty, well cared for, and the sight of it fills her with a creeping dread that begins at her scalp and prickles down her spine.

At that moment a woman comes out holding a baby on her hip. She's in her early thirties, slender and blonde and looks a little tired and sad. 'Can I help you?' she asks.

'Hi, sorry . . . I'm . . .' Viv tries to catch her breath and holds out her hand. 'I'm Vivienne, I used to live here.'

The woman's youthful face brightens. 'Oh! Did you? When was that?'

'About thirty years ago. I was only a kid at the time.'

'Well . . .' the woman shrugs, 'did you want to come in? You can if you want. Probably changed quite a bit.'

Though every inch of her longs to turn around and run as far away from the house as she can, Vivienne nods gratefully. 'Thank you, I'd love to.'

It's the strangest feeling being back there. She stands in the kitchen and remembers her mother sitting at the table, silently drinking bottle after bottle of wine – the horrible emptiness, the coldness after Ruby died. The woman shows her all the changes she and her husband have made, proudly pointing out the kitchen extension and conservatory, the newly landscaped garden, while Viv smiles and nods. She is lonely, Viv senses, and pleased for the company, but Viv wishes that she would be quiet so she could focus, allow the memories to flood back in. She turns to her and smiles. 'It's lovely,' she says. 'You've done wonders with the place.'

Then, as though it's just occurred to her, 'By the way, were the Fairbanks living at number two when you moved in?'

She shakes her head. 'No, the Cockles – that's the family who live there now – they'd already been here a while before we came.'

Viv nods. 'And how about the people at number one? Did they ever talk about the Fairbanks?'

She shrugs. 'Not that I can remember. Think the Fairbanks must have moved out a long time ago, like you.'

'I see,' Vivienne says, swallowing her disappointment. After a pause, she asks as casually as she can, 'Would you mind if I used your loo?'

'Of course, it's up the stairs, first on the—' She stops and laughs. 'What am I saying? I don't need to tell you that, do I?'

Once she's upstairs, Viv creeps quietly past the bathroom before taking the narrow steps to the two bedrooms in the eaves. With each step the feeling of dread builds, every instinct telling her to turn around and leave, because this is almost every nightmare she's had over the past thirty years made real. In her dreams she has seen herself so many times climb these same narrow steps, standing outside her sister's bedroom door, pushing it open to find the faceless figure towering over her sister. It's at that point that she always wakes, senseless with fear.

Now, standing outside Ruby's old room for the first time in over three decades, she closes her eyes, willing herself to focus as she casts her mind back to the day her sister died. She had been downstairs watching television when she heard Ruby and Jack arguing. After that she'd heard his footsteps descending the stairs before he ran out of the house, slamming the door behind him. Then, as she'd told the police at the time, she had gone up to Ruby's room, opened the door and found her lying dead and alone on the floor.

She raises her hand to the door handle, willing herself back to that moment when she'd stood in this exact spot as a child, and tells herself to push it open. But she can't. As soon as her fingers touch the handle the panic becomes so unbearable that she can't physically do it, and barely aware of her surroundings she begins to cry. 'No,' she moans. 'No, no, no.' She drops to her knees and she's hardly aware of her distress, of the sound that she's making, until she feels a hand on her arm and looks around in confusion to see the woman whose house she's in gazing at her in horror.

'I want you to go, now,' she says, shielding her baby protectively as though Viv's lunacy might harm him.

'I'm sorry. I'm so sorry,' Viv stammers, and she doesn't bother to explain, only stumbles to her feet and runs past the woman, back down the stairs and out of the house, not stopping until she reaches the end of the lane where she stands gasping for breath, waiting for the feeling of dread to subside. But even as her heart begins to calm, she's increasingly certain of one thing: the account she'd given to the police when she was a child had been wrong. Someone else had been on the other side of that door when she'd pushed it open. Ruby hadn't been alone.

Dazed, she checks her watch and seeing that it's almost eleven o'clock, she goes back to her car. She needs to return to London, to work out what to do next. But instead of taking the road to the motorway, she finds herself driving in the opposite direction until she reaches the village church. Her mother had never wanted to go back to see Ruby's grave but now that she's here, Viv feels its pull, the need to see her sister's final resting place one more time.

Like everything else in this village the churchyard is smaller and more dilapidated than she remembers, its crooked slopes more crowded, the graves squashed together with barely room to walk between them. Only the cherry tree in the corner is bigger, though its branches are empty of leaves. She walks to the far corner and it doesn't take her long to find the headstone that replaced

210

the temporary wooden cross she remembers from Ruby's funeral. She recalls the small mound of earth covered in irises and feels the familiar onslaught of grief. Crouching down, she brushes away the dirt and weeds and reads: *In loving memory of Ruby Swift, 1969–1984 and her unborn son Noah Swift. Two angels taken far too soon.*

She sits there looking at it for a long time until finally she pulls out her mobile and begins to type a message to Jack. I think Morris Dryden killed my sister, she types. He committed suicide out of guilt. I will tell the police that I was wrong and clear your name. Please let Cleo go now. Please.

His message comes back almost instantly, Not Morris. Can't have been. You have until tomorrow.

16

As she drives back to London, Viv scarcely notices the winding country roads, green fields and motorway that flash past her window. Instead, staring straight ahead, she thinks about when she and Stella had fled Essex for the capital all those years before, the train journey they'd taken, still senseless with grief and shock, towards a future they could scarcely imagine. She thinks about those first weeks and months of aimless drifting before they'd finally, miraculously, stumbled upon the sanctuary of Unity House. She thinks about the women living there; of Hayley, Soren, Jo, Kay, Christine and Sandra, their kindness and their love. And then she thinks of Margo.

At first the commune's founder had seemed to Vivienne like a sort of movie star, certainly like no one she'd ever met in their tiny corner of Essex, with her huge brown eyes and rich, melodious voice, her long dreadlocks and colourful, flowing clothes, her charisma and stately beauty. The fact that she singled Viv out and wanted to spend time with her had made her feel special in a way she never had before. For the first time since Ruby died, Vivienne had felt as though she wasn't defined by the tragedy, but instead that she might one day become someone interesting and special in her own right in spite of it.

It was only after her mother voiced her concerns about Margo that her own small doubts began to set in. It didn't happen often, but occasionally Viv would see what Stella meant – the subtle putdowns, the chilly glances, the curt way in which Margo would sometimes address Stella – and Viv's admiration had been tempered with confusion, that the person she so respected could be so cold to the person whom she loved best.

She noticed too how Stella would become quiet and withdrawn in Margo's presence, almost as though she were frightened of her. When Vivienne asked her mother about this Stella had brushed it off. 'Not frightened, darling, no. Of course not.' And then she'd sighed and said, 'But you must admit, she can be a bit intimidating.'

And yet, whenever her mum was at work, or at a Women's Lib meeting, or doing her life-coach training, Viv would find herself seeking Margo out, drawn to her attention, to the way Margo made her feel, even though she knew that her mother was right: Margo did indeed seem to prefer it when the two of them were alone together, often inviting her to her room or some other secluded spot in the house or garden where they could talk in private.

One of the things she liked to do best was to try on Margo's charm bracelet. It was a beautiful, heavy piece of silver jewellery, which Margo said she'd had all her life, adding to it throughout the years. Some of the charms were animals, others denoted good luck, and some were tiny discs with Aztec symbols engraved on them. Vivienne would sit on Margo's bed, feeling the weight of it in her hands, admiring each tiny charm as Margo told her what each one meant: Love, Hope, Courage, Friendship and so on. Afterwards she would describe it to her mother and tell her how much she would love to have a charm bracelet of her own one day.

Vivienne had been fourteen when the awful truth had been revealed. It had started with a disagreement between Stella and Margo about the meal Stella was cooking for dinner. Vivienne hadn't been in the room when it had begun, had only walked in, accompanied by Jo and Hayley, once the argument was in full swing, but they were in time to hear Margo hiss, 'If it wasn't for your daughter you'd be out of here. It's only for that child's sake that I let you stay.'

'Margo!' Jo had said, and Margo had turned to face them, her face puce.

'What is it with you and my daughter?' Stella had exploded then. 'Your strange obsession with her? It's creepy, the way you behave!'

At this, Margo had recoiled. 'What the hell are you

suggesting?' Her eyes bright with anger, she'd spat, 'My God, you're a disgusting human being!'

Hayley had intervened, trying her best to calm the situation, but Margo had stalked out, leaving the four of them staring after her in shocked silence.

For the rest of the afternoon Margo had stayed in her room, not showing her face when they congregated for dinner in the evening. She had gone out early the following morning and remained alone in her room when she returned. Vivienne had stayed close to her mother, feeling obscurely responsible for the bad atmosphere that hung in the air. And then things had taken an even worse turn.

Stella had been helping Viv with her homework when Margo had come storming into the kitchen. 'Where is it?' she asked them, her face tight with anger. 'My bracelet. Where is it?'

Stella and Viv had glanced at each other in confusion, until Viv had asked, 'What do you mean? Has it gone missing?'

But Margo was staring at Stella. 'You took it. I know you did. I'd like to have it back.'

'Why on earth would I do that?' Stella had asked in amazement.

'As some sort of petty revenge for our argument yesterday, I expect,' Margo had replied.

By this time Sandra and Rafferty Wolf had walked in. 'Sisters, please,' Sandra remonstrated, 'this has gone on long enough.'

It was then that Stella lost her temper, slamming the cup she was holding onto the table. 'How would I know where it is?' she'd shouted. 'Why do you persist in persecuting me like this? I won't stand for it.' And then something had altered in her eyes. 'I bet it's in your room!' she said. 'I bet you're making this up!' And with that she'd stormed from the kitchen, the rest of them following.

'Don't you dare,' Margo had called, running after her. 'You have no right to go in there!'

'Mum . . .' Viv had pleaded when she'd caught up with Stella. 'Maybe you shouldn't—'

Ignoring her pleas, Stella had run to Margo's room and begun to go through her things, rooting through drawers and shelves while the others crowded in the doorway looking on, Stella's anger making her reckless as she tossed things here and there. At last she opened a drawer and gasped in surprise. In the shocked silence that followed, one by one she had pulled out a succession of items belonging to each of the other women in the house. Soren's silver hair comb. Christine's wallet containing three ten-pound notes. A small gold picture frame passed on to Kay by her mother. Stella's bank card, and worst of all, a necklace that had once belonged to Ruby and had been Vivienne's most treasured possession since she was eight. She had lost it months ago, had been inconsolable when she realized, had even cried in Margo's arms about it. All of the possessions were things that the women had lost in the past year or two.

216

Money had also gone missing, in small enough amounts for the women to reluctantly shrug off, but when Stella pulled out a tin of notes and coins, it was easy to guess where it had come from.

Each of the women standing in that room had been struck dumb with shock, but Viv would never forget the raw, visceral horror she'd felt. Margo knew how much the necklace meant to her. She'd seen her devastation when it went missing, and yet she'd said nothing. And it seemed that Margo had nothing to say now, for she just stared back at each of them, her own face ashen. And when Vivienne whispered, 'You took it? You had it all along?' Margo had held her gaze but not replied.

Vivienne ran from the room, but not before she'd spotted by Margo's bed, half-hidden by a sock, the lost charm bracelet lying on the floor.

Margo had moved out soon after, signing all responsibility for the commune over to Sandra and Christine. Vivienne had hidden upstairs with Hayley while she packed up, and when Margo had gone she wandered down to her empty room to find lying on her chest of drawers a small package addressed to her. Inside had been a silver chain attached to one of the Aztec symbol pendants from Margo's bracelet. She'd looked at it, resting in her palm, unable to remember what that specific symbol meant, before dropping it in the bin and leaving the room with a shudder of disgust. And in that instant all of Margo's warmth and friendship, her belief in Vivienne, was lost, mingling with her disappointment to create a sense of betrayal so deep that it never really left her.

It's midday when Viv draws up outside her house in Peckham. The rain has stopped, but the colourless sky remains heavy with moisture. The cluster of reporters at her gate has grown larger and when she gets out of her car they surge forward, pushing microphones in her face, shouting questions, a new excitement in their voices.

'Would you like to answer any of the stories in the papers today, Vivienne?' one asks. 'Is it true you'd passed out drunk when your daughter went missing?' 'Did you have any idea Cleo was being groomed online?' 'Can you tell us where your boyfriend Aleksander Petri is?'

She looks at them in dismay until a policeman who'd been standing nearby waves them back. Keeping her head bowed, she dashes into her house, slamming the door behind her. What had they been talking about? With shaking hands, she pulls out her phone and googles her daughter's name. Sure enough, a bunch of tabloid headlines leap out at her. 'Schoolgirl snatched while mum partied' reads one; 'Kidnapper groomed missing teen for weeks' says another.

The first article she clicks on is from the Mail Online:

Neighbour Neil Francis, 49, says, 'She was very drunk that night. She had her new boyfriend over. I don't like to judge but I'm not surprised that she passed out. Just so sad that she didn't wake to save

218

her daughter.' Mr Francis goes on to say, 'Cleo's a lovely girl, much more gentle than her mother, who can be a bit abrasive. I tried to tell her to sober up the night Cleo went missing and got sworn at for my trouble.'

'Bastard,' Viv mutters. 'You bloody bastard.' She picks up a mug from the coffee table and throws it at their adjoining wall. It bounces off with a thud, falling to the floor. Next she picks up her phone and, ignoring the missed calls from Cleo's father, Stella and DS Marshall, she tries Alek's number again, only to be met with the same deathly silence.

In despair she scrolls through more articles about Cleo. 'Police are increasingly worried . . .' she reads. 'No new leads in missing teen case . . .' She opens Facebook and searches for her daughter's name and sees that an appeal for information about her has been shared and liked hundreds of thousands of times already. 'Where are you?' she whispers, staring at the accompanying picture of her daughter's face. 'Where are you, my love?'

Her phone drops to her lap, nausea rising inside her as she remembers Jack's threat to cut off Cleo's finger. Time is running out. She puts her head in her hands and wants to scream with desperation. Her mobile bleeps, the noise making her jump violently and she snatches it up to find a message from Carl. Accompanying his message is a picture.

Hi Viv, not got hold of my auntie yet, soz, she reads.

Remembered we had this picture on the pub wall from years ago. My Dad must have taken it. That's Declan Fairbanks in the centre, isn't it? Dimly Viv remembers the pinboard of photos she'd seen on the Bird's Nest wall by the bar, similar to one she'd seen in many other pubs, displaying a selection of their customers over the years. Hurriedly she clicks on the image and stares down at it. Carl had obviously taken a photo of the picture with his phone, and it showed what must have been some sort of party at the Bird's Nest, Carl's lens focusing on a few drinkers apparently part of a larger crowd.

The photo is in colour but faded and slightly yellowed with age. In the centre is a man in his early fifties who Viv instantly recognizes as their former neighbour. He is a slim man who obviously kept himself in shape, his shirt showing arms taut with muscles. He has salt-and-pepper hair and a haughty expression as he stares almost angrily at the camera. She's about to click back to Carl's message when she notices something else about the picture. There, standing slightly apart from Declan is her sister, staring away from the camera, to someone or something out of shot. It's not as though she's standing *with* him, but she's definitely part of the same crowd of people. What is most arresting is the misery in her eyes. Viv gazes more closely at her sister's face. She looks slightly younger than the age she was when she died. Maybe only fourteen. But why does she look so desperately sad?

The message Carl has sent with the picture goes on,

I asked the Cockles but they had no forwarding address for him. I'm seeing my auntie later so will let you know if she's got any info. Cxx

Her mobile rings, the word 'Mum' flashing on the screen, and she's about to pick up when there's a loud knock on her door.

Cleo sits motionless, her eyes fixed on the caravan's door. She's breathing through her mouth to avoid the stench of stale cigarette smoke and petrol and the scratchy orange fabric of her seat is damp and cold. The only light comes from a small and dusty anglepoise lamp and her shadow is thrown huge against the wall. From somewhere outside she hears a radio's steady burble of pop songs and beyond that the low, distant noise of traffic.

Hunger gnaws at her and she eyes the greasy paper bag he left behind but though her mouth waters at the thought of food she will not eat it. What if he tried to drug her again? She wants her mum so badly that she can hardly breathe. She has to get out of here, away from him; she has to warn her mother about this man. And it is this thought, of the danger that Viv is in, that propels Cleo to her feet.

She looks around her. There's a small kitchen area with a sink, a stove and a cupboard with drawers. On the other side of the room is the seating area with a bolted-down table. Orange-and-brown stripy curtains hang at the windows and she goes to the largest window first, pressing against the Perspex, looking for any sign of weakness, but finds none. She tries the second, then the third, but they won't budge. She is completely trapped.

She creeps quietly to the toilet cubicle next. It's tiny with a shower above the toilet and a drain in the floor. Here, too, like everywhere else in the caravan, the Perspex window is boarded up on the outside. But this time, when she pushes at one corner, she feels it give a little; even better, the hardboard on the other side moves a fraction too, to reveal a sliver of light. Standing back from the window she considers its size. Small, but she thinks she might be able to squeeze through. Above the sink a mirror is screwed to the wall and for the first time she notices that it has a crack of about two inches in the bottom left-hand corner. She inspects it closely and works out that if she were to crack it more, there's a chance that she could slide a shard of it out.

And just as the spark of an idea ignites inside her, she hears the sound of the padlock rattling on the other side of the locked door, and she freezes in fear.

Marshall and Spilleti sit at Vivienne's kitchen table gazing at her, perplexed. 'Can I ask you where you were today?' Marshall says. Viv considers lying but, realizing it's pointless, says, 'I went to the village where I used to live. Where my sister was murdered.'

'I see. And why was that?'

She hesitates, thinking how to answer, but knowing

she can't tell him the real reason, she shrugs. 'Because I wanted to visit her grave. I wanted to feel close to her.'

He holds her gaze. 'You said when I phoned that you were looking for answers. Can you tell me what you meant by that?'

'I meant that I wanted to talk to my sister – it's something I do when I want help with something. I believe she's up there, listening.'

He stares at her for a beat or two, saying nothing, and she gets the impression he sees through her lies. 'It goes without saying of course,' he says, 'that if you hear from anyone claiming to have any information about Cleo's whereabouts you should tell us immediately. Any contact – phone call, text, letter – from her abductor, it's important that you let us know and that you never engage with him yourself.'

'Of course,' she says, holding his gaze. 'Have you managed to find anything out about Jack Delaney?' she asks.

It's DC Spilleti who replies. 'We have no reason to think that Jack Delaney has anything to do with your daughter's disappearance. As far as we're aware, he is still abroad as there's no record of him re-entering the country. His surviving family – two brothers – have had no contact with him since he left.'

'But they would say that, wouldn't they? And if he's in Canada, he would be there illegally. He can't stay there indefinitely, can he?' she says.

Spilleti nods. 'He didn't apply for a work visa, he went there as a tourist and then disappeared.'

'So how would he have afforded to live there?' Viv asks.

The detective constable shrugs. 'Casual, cash-in-hand labouring work is easy enough to get there, same as it is here,' she says. 'The point is, he could be anywhere.'

'Exactly. He could have come back on a fake passport.'

'Possibly.'

Vivienne sighs with frustration. 'And what about Aleksander Petri?'

Marshall and Spilleti glance at each other, and something in the atmosphere between them changes. Viv's heart leaps. 'What?' she says. 'What's happened?'

'Vivienne,' Marshall says, 'Aleksander Petri died in Kosovo in 1998. Whoever the man purporting to be him for the past eighteen years is, it's not Petri. He must have used Petri's papers when he came here seeking asylum.'

She stares at him. 'But . . . I don't understand . . . who is he then? Who is the person I've been . . . ?'

'As of yet, we don't know,' Marshall replies. 'Whoever he is, he was granted refugee status and eventually allowed to register as a practitioner here in Britain under Petri's name via the British Medical Association's Refugee Doctor Initiative. He has been working here ever since. We have circulated his photograph and have officers nationwide looking for him.'

She shakes her head, trying to take it in. 'But . . . Who was the real Aleksander Petri? Do you know?'

'He was a junior doctor at a hospital in Pristina. He died when he was twenty-eight.'

'How?'

'His family say he was murdered in 1998.'

'*Murdered*? By who?'

'According to them, by the Albanian mafia. The case remains open. The war was coming to an end, it was a time of great unrest . . . We may never know what happened to the real Aleksander.'

She shakes her head, trying to take it in. 'So who is the person I knew? And what does this have to do with Cleo?'

'That's what we're trying to find out,' Marshall says.

17

When Marshall and Spilleti leave, Viv continues to sit in her kitchen thinking about the man who'd come to her café week after week. She recalls how he'd said, 'War changes you, it makes you do things you'd never thought you were capable of.' What had that meant? Had *he* killed the real Aleksander? Was murder what he'd been referring to? But he'd also said his daughter believed something about him that wasn't true . . . she shakes her head in frustration; it's impossible to know what he'd meant.

Listlessly she picks up her phone and clicks on the texts she and Alek had exchanged over the past weeks, searching for clues. They make for meagre pickings: only ten messages in all, mainly brief and to the point arrangements to meet up. He had not once expressed his feelings for her in words, either spoken or written. Instead she had conjured evidence of how he felt about her by the way he touched and looked at her, the chemistry that seemed to her to crackle between them. She had imagined it all, of course, inventing affection that had never existed. She has, in fact, no tangible evidence of him feeling anything for her whatsoever. She had been entirely duped.

Suddenly her fingers halt and she stares down at one particular message. It simply says, 'Miranda Auerbach', followed by a phone number. It is, she recalls, the psycho-therapist Alek had recommended when she'd told him of her nightmares about Ruby. He had described Miranda as an ex-colleague – more than that, he'd said she was a friend. If that were true, might she know who he is, and where he is now? Hurriedly she googles 'Miranda Auerbach, therapist' and is directed to a website for a private practice in Kensal Rise, North London. She looks closely at the accompanying picture of a dark-haired woman in her mid-forties, then checks the time. She has mere hours left to save Cleo and absolutely nothing to lose. She clicks on the number and presses Call.

The phone rings once, twice, three times, and then a pleasantly professional voice answers. 'Miranda Auerbach speaking.'

Viv's own voice seems to leap from her throat, unnaturally high and loud. 'Hello, I . . . was given your number by a . . . friend . . .' she falters. 'I wondered if I could come and see you. It's rather urgent.' She clutches the handset tightly.

'Of course, let me look at my diary. One moment, please.'

'I really need to see you today,' Viv says quickly.

She can hear the desperation in her own voice and there's a brief surprised pause, before Miranda replies: 'I'm sorry, but I'm afraid that won't be possible. I could fit you in tomorrow for an initial assessment. I've just had a cancellation. Let me tell you a bit about . . .'

'No, that's too late.' Viv's voice breaks and she wrestles to get it under control. 'I need help today.'

'I'm very sorry, but I have other patients scheduled for the rest of the day, I couldn't cancel them at such short notice . . .' There's a note of concern in her tone now. 'I can hear that you're upset. Perhaps I could give you some other numbers to try . . . there's also the Samaritans. If you are worried that you might harm yourself, I would strongly encourage you to seek help from your emergency—'

'No,' Vivienne cuts in, 'I don't need any of those things! What I need is to see you today. Please.' Viv wonders whether to mention Alek, to say that he recommended her – perhaps that might convince her. But his name has been in the news regarding Cleo over the past two days and it might put Miranda off, make her even less inclined to get involved. She's still trying to decide when Miranda speaks.

'I'm sorry,' she repeats, 'but it would be impossible without letting one of my present patients down and I'm sure you can appreciate . . .'

Viv hears the sound of a doorbell ringing somewhere in the background.

'I must go,' Miranda continues. 'A patient has just arrived. But why don't you give me your contact details so I can call you back?'

Vivienne closes her eyes in despair, and without answering, hangs up the phone. She puts her head in her hands. She's running out of time and she has absolutely no idea what to do. When the phone rings and she sees her mother's name flash across the screen, her voice is barely audible when she picks it up and says, 'Hello, Mum.'

'Oh, thank heavens. Where on earth have you been, Vivienne? I've been going out of my mind.'

'Mum. Oh Mum . . .' the words emerge as a half-wail.

'What's happened? Is there news? Tell me!'

'The police were here. They haven't found her, or Jack, but they have found something out about Alek.'

'*Alek?*'

Quickly she tells her mother what Marshall had told her. 'I don't know who he is,' Viv says, her voice rising in distress. 'He might be a criminal, a murderer even, and I let him into my home. I introduced him to Cleo.'

'Oh Vivienne.'

And in those two words Viv hears the weight of reproach and despair she has levelled at herself ever since Marshall told her, and she closes her eyes in shame.

'What are the police going to do?' Stella asks.

Viv hesitates. She wants to admit everything – about the texts from Jack, his threats and demands, the terrifying photo he'd sent – but what if Stella insists on going to the police? What if she does that and Jack kills Cleo anyway? After all, they hadn't found him so far. Playing by his rules might be the only way of getting her daughter back alive. So instead she says, 'I don't know. They said they'd call me if there was any news.' She pauses. 'Mum, I need to ask you something. What do you remember about Declan Fairbanks, our old neighbour in Essex?'

'What? God, I don't know, barely anything. What on earth are you asking me about him for?'

'I just . . . something made me think of him, that's all. What was he like? Do you remember?'

'No. No, I don't, darling. I don't remember anything about him at all. Goodness me, don't we have enough to worry about without dredging stuff up about old acquaintances?'

When Viv finally puts the phone down she paces her kitchen restlessly, trying to decide her next move. Her exhaustion is laced with adrenaline that makes her feel sick and unsteady on her feet. Her thoughts return to Miranda and she comes to a halt. If there was even the smallest chance that this woman might know Alek's whereabouts, then she needs to talk to her. She could be her only hope.

She gathers up her coat and bag, intending to drive over there, but as she's heading to the door she catches sight of herself in the hall mirror. She's still wearing the clothes she had on on the night of the dinner party, with the addition of a hoodie and some trainers she'd flung on a while ago. Gingerly she smells herself and grimaces. Her hair is greasy, her face blotchy with grime and old make-up. She can't turn up to Miranda's looking like this, not if she's going to convince her to help. Quickly she runs upstairs and into the shower then throws on some clean jeans and a jumper, stopping for a few minutes to put on some make-up. Finally, snatching up her coat and bag, she runs from the house.

She barely notices her surroundings as she drives across the city. Peckham, Walworth and Bermondsey flash past her window before she crosses the Thames into central London. As she drives she thinks about Miranda, about whether she might know where Alek has run to, and puts her foot on the accelerator. Gradually, as she nears Kensal Rise, something else begins to occur to her. Could Miranda help her remember what happened the day Ruby died? Might she, if she underwent this EDMR therapy or whatever it was called, unearth something – some small detail – that could shine a light on it all? She thinks about the article she'd read about patients recovering long-buried memories from their past. Could that work for her? She'd resisted therapy all her life, but if there was even the slightest chance it could help her remember, shouldn't she give it a try?

Viv pulls up outside a large Edwardian house on a long leafy road in Kensal Rise. As she stares up at the front door with its row of doorbells, a twenty-something woman emerges from the basement steps before disappearing off, head down, along the street. A neighbour, Viv wonders, or one of Miranda's patients? Sure enough, when she descends the steps herself she finds a smartly painted door with a brass plaque bearing the words, 'Dr Miranda Auerbach' followed by an impressive collection of initials.

Steeling herself, she presses the buzzer and waits. The woman who answers the door is a few years older than she'd looked in her photograph, short but attractive with closely cropped greying hair. Her make-up-free face glows with good health and she has intelligent, inquisitive hazel eyes with which she is regarding Viv. 'Hello, can I help you?'

'Hi, yes . . . I phoned earlier. It's very important that I talk to you.'

The woman's look of confusion passes swiftly to one of realization then alarm. 'As I told you on the phone,' she begins, 'it isn't possible for me to . . .' Suddenly she looks past Viv, a flicker of relief on her face, and Viv turns to see a bearded man in his thirties coming down the stairs behind her. 'Hi, Rob, please, go on in, I'll be with you in a minute.' Miranda stands aside to let him through then turns back to Vivienne. Her voice firmer now, she goes on, 'As you can see, I'm rather busy. If you leave me your details, I'll be in touch directly to arrange a proper appointment.'

But Viv doesn't move. 'Five minutes,' she begs, then

in desperation blurts, 'It's regarding Aleksander Petri. I believe you know him.'

Miranda's expression alters. 'Alek? Do you know where he is?' After a moment's hesitation she stands aside. 'You'd better come in.'

Viv is led through to a small waiting area where the bearded guy is sitting reading a book. The room is cosy with brightly coloured throws and cushions on the sofa, the walls covered in abstract art prints. She can smell the scent of fresh coffee, feel the warmth pumping from the radiator. 'Rob,' Miranda says to him, 'I'm so sorry, but would you mind very much waiting for ten minutes?'

'Sure.' He shrugs, eyeing Viv with curiosity as Miranda leads her through another door.

In contrast to the room they've just left, Miranda's practice room is sparsely furnished with two low comfortable armchairs, a desk and office chair. Next to one of the armchairs is a small table with a box of tissues and a pot plant on it. The walls are painted a pale soothing green and hung with unobtrusive paintings of coastal scenes. A pretty yellow lamp throws out a soft golden glow.

'Now, what is all this about?' Miranda asks, indicating for Viv to take a seat and sitting down herself.

Viv talks quickly. 'My name is Vivienne Swift, and my daughter Cleo is missing. Alek was—'

Miranda's eyes widen. 'Yes, my goodness, you're . . . ? I've been reading about it. The *Guardian* mentioned Alek was wanted in connection with her disappearance . . .'

Her brow furrows in concern. 'I know Alek, it seems absolutely extraordinary to me that he could be connected to—'

Vivienne nods impatiently. 'Look, Miranda, Alek mentioned you to me. He said that you were friends. I wanted to ask if you have any idea where he might be. If you can think of anywhere he might have gone to hide.'

'No . . . I'm afraid I don't. I haven't seen Alek for quite some time.' She pauses then and adds with certainty, 'But I do know that he would never harm a child.'

'Then why has he disappeared? He was there the night she went missing, and he hasn't been seen since.'

'I have no idea,' Miranda says. 'I'm sorry Vivienne, I truly am. And I'm very sorry for what you're going through, it must be terribly distressing, but I don't think I can help you.'

Vivienne sees that she's telling the truth and the small spark of hope she'd been holding on to – that Miranda might lead her to Alek, who in turn might lead her to Jack – sputters out. She sinks back into the chair, burying her face in her hands.

'Are you all right?' Miranda asks gently. 'Can I get you anything? A glass of water?'

Viv looks back at Miranda's frank, patient gaze and shakes her head, overcome by hopelessness. It's only when Miranda passes her the box of tissues that she realizes she's crying.

Once she's composed herself, she says, 'Listen, the reason Alek gave me your name was because he thought you might be able to help me. I desperately need to remember something.'

'Go on.'

'A long time ago when I was a child, my older sister was murdered, I was in the house at the time . . .'

'Oh,' Miranda says, clearly taken aback. 'I see . . .'

'I gave evidence against her boyfriend, evidence which put him in prison. But all I can remember is what I told the police. I can recall the words I said to describe what happened, but I can't conjure any images to back them up. I was there that day, in the house at the time she was murdered, but whenever I try to recall what actually happened I have a full-blown panic attack and draw a blank. It's sheer terror, which is why I've spent the last thirty-two years trying very hard *not* to think about it.'

She takes a breath then continues: 'But the thing is, I think I was wrong back then. I think the wrong man went to prison for Ruby's murder, and now I need to find out who really killed her.'

Miranda pauses to take this in, and then she says, 'I'm so sorry for what you went through. It's not unheard of for a young child who's experienced trauma to bury the memory as a form of self-preservation. But I don't understand what this has to do with me?'

Viv sits forward and says, 'Alek told me you practise EMDR?'

She nods slowly. 'Yes, I do. Eye Movement Desensitizing and Reprocessing. It works by—'

Viv interrupts. 'I read that it can help people remember things they've previously buried.'

Miranda shakes her head. 'No, that's not what it's for at all. The therapy works by helping the patient cope with existing, distressing memories of a traumatic event, it's not about recalling events they've forgotten, you're talking about two very different things.'

'But it *can* happen, can't it?' Viv persists. 'I've read that it can.'

Miranda sighs. 'Look, it's true that it happens, I have colleagues whose patients have recalled details they've previously blocked out, but—'

'Miranda, please help me. I'm desperate. I have to remember what happened that day.'

'I'm afraid it's not as straightforward as that.' She looks at Viv with fresh sympathy. 'You are clearly going through an extremely difficult time with your daughter's disappearance, I wouldn't want to introduce this sort of therapy into the midst of such stress.'

'But you're the only hope I have.'

'I'm sorry, but it's too risky. I would be happy to help you in the future though. And I very much hope that you find your daughter soon . . .'

Viv looks at her, and she understands that, no matter what she says, however long she stays and tries to persuade her, Miranda isn't going to budge, that she's just wasting her time. She gets to her feet, grief and despair crashing over her, and without saying anything else turns and leaves.

It's freezing in the caravan. Cleo heard the van drive off at least an hour ago, and she has no idea when he might return. She needs to get out, she needs to escape and go home to her mum, but instead she's sitting here crying. 'Baby,' she mutters furiously to herself, scrubbing at her eyes and remembering how her father had told her that she needs to grow up. 'Stop being such a big baby.' But though she speaks in a stern brave voice she has to hug herself tightly, her arms around herself as though if she were to let go of her own shaking body it might fall to pieces.

She gets to her feet and goes to the kitchen area where every surface including the sink is covered in a thick layer of grime. There are two drawers which she opens only to find that they're both empty. Next she tries the door of the cupboard beneath the sink. It, too, is empty, but she notices how the door wobbles as she moves it, and on closer inspection sees that one of the hinges is half hanging off. It takes only a gentle tug for the two tiny and rusty screws to come loose, and then the thin metal hinge falls into her hand.

She stares down at it for a second or two before running to the bathroom. There she slides the corner of it carefully into the groove of one of the screws holding the Perspex window in place and finds, with a surge of exhilaration, that it fits. With all her strength she tries to turn it, but the screw won't budge. 'Oh God, please,' she says desperately, 'please turn!' She makes another attempt, gripping it so hard that it cuts painfully into her thumb. Still nothing. She tries again and again and again until at last it shifts. 'Yes!' Hope and relief explode inside her.

When she's home once more, Vivienne sits in the quiet gloom of her living room thinking about Miranda. On impulse she fetches her laptop, opens it and googles EMDR:

Eye Movement Desensitization and Reprocessing is widely used to help patients suffering from depression and anxiety caused by past trauma. Its high success rate means that it's fully supported by both NICE and WHO as a means of combatting the symptoms of PTSD. During therapy, the patient is directed to recall the traumatic event while following the left to right movement of a stimulus, for example, a flashing light. This movement replicates the REM period of sleep and by stimulating both hemispheres of the brain the left hemisphere is able to self-soothe the right. By bypassing the part of the brain that has become blocked due to the trauma, new neurological pathways are formed that allow the patient to reprocess the memory in a more healthy way. Gradually the recollection of the event loses its power to distress.

Viv closes the laptop, feeling none the wiser. She has no idea if such a thing would work on her, but an instinct had told her she could trust Miranda, she'd sensed a sympathy there. And then the realization hits her: the type of therapy is immaterial; the memory of what happened that day is in her mind somewhere, hiding in her subconscious, of that she's certain, she just has to make the decision to find it. For thirty-two years she has actively avoided thinking about the day Ruby died, an avoidance born purely out of self-preservation. But now she has someone far more important than herself to protect. There could be nothing worse than losing Cleo. And if she's going to fight through her panic to see what's on the other side, she wants Miranda there to help her.

She thinks about Alek. How desperate for money must he have been to do what he did? She remembers how he had talked about his own daughter – had his sadness for her been a fabrication too? Yet he had seemed so sincere when he talked about her. Something about his involvement in Cleo's disappearance doesn't add up. Suddenly, and with a jolt of adrenaline, she remembers he had once given her his email address and she flicks through her messages until she finds it. If his phone is turned off to avoid detection by the police, her calls and messages won't get to him. An email, however, might, assuming he's anywhere near a computer.

Quickly she begins to type. I cannot get Cleo back until I remember what happened to my sister. You have to help me, Alek. You have to make Miranda Auerbach help me. I'm not interested in you, or what you've done or where you are, but you need to convince Miranda to see me. Otherwise Jack won't get what he wants, and I will never get Cleo back. Please, Alek, please help me.

She doesn't know if she's appealing to him as a father, as someone who might have cared for her once, or as someone who might not get paid until Jack gets what he wants. All she knows is that she's desperate enough to try anything, even if it means grovelling to the man who's helped destroy her life.

She has no hope of meeting Jack's deadline now. All she can do is try to reason with him. She picks up her phone and types out her text: I need more time. Please, give me a little longer. I will find out who killed my sister, I promise. I just need one more day.

His reply comes almost instantly. I warned you.

Frantically she hits the reply button. I will find out. I will, I promise. Give me a few more hours. Please.

His next text arrives immediately. Too late, it says.

There, alone in her kitchen, she shakes her head in disbelief. 'No,' she says, 'No!'

If you hurt her I'll tell the police, she types desperately. They'll find you. They'll trace your phone. Please don't hurt her.

They won't find me, they'll never find me. But if you do tell them, I'll kill her. Your choice.

'Oh God,' she whispers as the sheer horror of his words sink in. 'Oh please God, no.'

Cleo doesn't notice the small black holdall in his hand at first. He doesn't look at her as he stands at the table and unzips it. It's only when he meets her gaze that something in his expression makes her look down and see what he's doing, what he's pulling from the bag. And she understands then, and her terror is so absolute that she is beyond shouting out, beyond screaming or crying or begging for mercy.

Instead she squirms away from him, pressing herself into the back of the bench. The low wail escaping from her mouth is unintelligible. She can't take her eyes off the meat cleaver in his hand.

'Keep still and this will be over with quickly,' he tells her. 'The more you struggle, the longer it's going to take. If I have to, I will knock you out.' Without warning, he lunges at her and grabs her chin, holding it tightly, his fingers digging painfully into her flesh. 'Is that what you want?'

She shakes her head.

Satisfied, he pulls a piece of rag from his holdall and ties it tightly around her mouth.

'Put your hand into a fist,' he says. She stares at him in uncomprehending panic. 'Do it!' he shouts.

Whimpering with fear, she does as she's told. He takes her fist and lies it on the table, pulling out her index finger so it alone points out. Then, pinioning her hand to the table with his own, he raises the cleaver. Instinctively she tries to pull away, but his grip is too strong and the blade falls in one quick movement.

For three seconds she feels nothing, only stares dumbly at the blood that spurts from the wound where he's cut it just below the top joint. And then the pain and horror arrive all at once and she is screaming against her gag.

Without releasing her hand, he puts the cleaver down and picks up a bottle of dark liquid, takes the cap off with his teeth, then pours it over the wound. It fizzes and burns and the pain is excruciating, but the bleeding stops at once. Spots of light flicker at the periphery of her vision, nausea rises in her throat and blank with shock she can only stare dumbly as he gets his phone and takes a photograph of what he's done: the mutilated finger, its severed tip beside it, the pool of blood. When he's finished, he takes out a roll of bandage and sets about dressing the wound with the sureness and dexterity of a doctor. 'Perhaps your mother will do as she's told now,' he says.

18

Vivienne has not moved since receiving Jack's last text, staring without blinking at his words, '*I warned you.*' It is only the thought of his further promise, that he would kill Cleo if she doesn't do what he wants, that jerks her into action and she picks up her phone and searches for the number of the Bird's Nest pub.

There's a low burble of voices and music when the phone is picked up. 'Bird's Nest?' a woman's voice says distractedly.

'I need to speak to Carl,' Viv says.

'Yeah, hold on.'

The phone clatters on the other end and there's an agonizing wait until she hears Carl's cheerful boom. 'Hello?'

'Carl,' she says, 'it's Vivienne Swift.'

There's a brief, stunned pause. 'Oh, hey, I was about to—'

'Listen to me. Did you find out where Declan Fairbanks lives?'

'Are you OK, Viv? I've seen the news about your daughter. Couldn't believe it. I had no idea when you came to see me, I only just put two and two together when I read your name. I'm so sorry—'

'Carl,' through gritted teeth she tries to keep her voice level as she cuts him off, 'I need to speak to Declan Fairbanks. Did you find him?'

'Oh, sorry . . . yeah, well kind of. My aunt seems to think they moved to Southend. She and his wife Linda exchanged Christmas cards for a bit. Apparently, she divorced Declan shortly after they left here.'

'Does your aunt have a phone number for him?' she asks.

'Yeah. Only she can't remember where it is. She's eighty-two, love her, and a bit forgetful, but she never chucks anything away, so she'll have it stashed somewhere, don't you worry . . .'

Viv's heart sinks. *Shit*. 'Southend,' she prompts. 'Is that all you know?' Something occurs to her. 'Do you know what he did for work?'

'Yeah, Auntie Sue said he was a surveyor, but of course he'd be long retired. Listen, Viv, does Declan have something to do with your daughter going missing? I don't understand . . .'

'I can't explain. But I have to track him down and I

244

need your help. Please, please can you try to find him for me, Carl? It's extremely important.'

'Of course I will. I'll do my best anyway.'

'Thank you . . . And, Carl? It's very urgent.'

'Yes, right, understood. I'll get on it straight away. But I don't understand what—'

'Please, as soon as you find out anything, call me back.'

No sooner has she put the phone down than it bleeps and she picks it up, her heart shooting to her mouth when she sees that it's another message from Jack. He has sent her a photograph and when her eyes make sense of the horrifying image she gives one low guttural wail of dismay and disbelief before flinging the phone away from her and running to the kitchen where she's violently sick into the sink. She stands there, gasping in panicked disbelief and when she hears the phone bleep from the other room she runs to it, snatching it up to read the new message:

You have until this time tomorrow before she dies.

She must call the police, she should call them this minute . . . but she doesn't move. '*If you tell the police I'll kill her anyway,*' he'd said. '*They won't find me. They'll never find me.*' She feels instinctively that he's right. After all, they hadn't so far. Her one hope is to find Ruby's real killer, otherwise her daughter will die. She's standing there, frozen in miserable indecision, when

245

her phone begins to ring. Her first thought is that it's
Carl calling her back, but the number flashing on her
screen is a London one she doesn't recognize. 'Yes?' she
says when she picks it up.

'This is Miranda Auerbach.'

Vivienne grips the phone more tightly. 'Yes?'

'I will help you.'

'Oh thank God, thank you,' she begins to sob.

There's a pause, and then, 'Alek emailed me.'

'Where is he?'

'He wouldn't say.'

'But . . . does he—'

'He has nothing to do with your daughter's disappearance. I believe him. He asked me to help you, and I will.'

'Thank you,' Vivienne cries. 'Thank you so much. I'll
be with you as soon as I can. I'm leaving now.'

'All right. I'll be waiting.'

When Vivienne knocks on her door, Miranda opens it
immediately, ushering her through to the same practice
room as before. 'Thank you so much for seeing me,'
Vivienne says when she's seated in one of the armchairs,
Miranda at her desk. It's dark outside and rain begins
to beat against the window. The lamp gives off its soft
golden glow.

Miranda regards Viv frankly. 'This is obviously a very
unusual situation,' she begins.

Viv nods. 'What did Alek say?'

'Not much. I don't know where he is, or what his . . .

246

situation is. I only know that he is concerned about you and insistent that I help you.'

Vivienne wonders bitterly if Alek's 'concern' is down to him not being paid until Jack gets what he wants, but keeps it to herself. Instead, she says simply, 'I think he helped the man who has my daughter. If you know where he is, you have to tell me – or at least tell the police. My daughter's life could depend on it.'

Miranda shakes her head. 'Vivienne, I have no idea where Alek is, but I'm as certain as I can be that he had no involvement with your daughter's disappearance. I know Alek well, he's a deeply troubled man, but he would never hurt a child. Never.'

She wonders if Miranda is aware of his false identity, whether she might even know what happened to the real Aleksander Petri, but the thought has no sooner entered her head before she dismisses it: it doesn't matter; she has no time for any of that. Her only concern is Cleo.

As if reading her thoughts, Miranda puts her hands together, leans forward and says, 'I said I'd help you. How do you think I might do that?'

Vivienne is glad of her no-nonsense tone, and, echoing it, says, 'As I told you earlier, when I was eight years old, my sister Ruby was murdered. I was in the house at the time. I believe the evidence I gave back then put the wrong man in prison. I've blanked out most of what happened that day. I need to remember as much as possible, even the smallest detail that might help me to find out who really killed her.'

'I see.' She regards Vivienne. 'And what exactly *do* you remember?'

'That I was watching TV in the living room when there was a knock on the door. Ruby went to answer it thinking it was Jack, her boyfriend, but it was someone called Morris from the local butcher's, dropping off something for our mum. Not long after he left, there was another knock on the door and this time it was Jack. Then they went upstairs and they started arguing. I heard Ruby scream, then silence, and Jack ran down the stairs and out of the house. I went up to see if my sister was all right, and . . . when I found her in her bedroom she was dead.'

Miranda is silent for a while, then she asks, 'And what makes you think that those memories are wrong? That someone else might have killed her?'

'Because I've never been sure that it's the truth. I know it's the story I told the police at the time, but I've always had a sense that there was something more, something I've forgotten.'

'And what happens when you try to remember?'

'I can only get to a certain point before I start to panic. It's like a huge weight pressing down on my chest. I can't breathe, it's terrifying. It's impossible to go any further. As a result I've spent my entire life avoiding thinking of it.'

Miranda nods. 'You were very young, at the time,' she says. 'It's understandable that you buried certain details of the trauma as a coping mechanism.' She pauses, then says, 'May I ask, what has your life been like in the intervening years? Do you drink or take drugs, for example, engage in any risky, sexual behaviour . . . ?'

Vivienne looks back at her impatiently. 'Sorry, is this necessary? I don't mean to be rude, but I don't have time to go through the ins and outs of my life. I only need to remember that day.'

If Miranda is offended, she doesn't show it. 'I understand, but it's important that I get a sense of you, of how you've coped with the weight of Ruby's death in the years since it happened, and how you typically deal with stress.'

Viv folds her arms and sighs. 'I drink too much, always have. I used to be very promiscuous, and had a period when I took far too many recreational drugs. I had a nervous breakdown in my twenties. I still have frequent nightmares, in which I open the door to my sister's room to see her murderer standing over her body, though I never see who that person is.' She looks at Miranda. 'When I wake I have the sense that the nightmare is what really happened, that I really did see Ruby's killer that day, and that the story I told the police is not completely accurate.'

'But why would you have lied?'

'I don't know! I was barely eight . . . I just don't remember . . .'

Miranda takes a notepad from her desk and writes something down, then says, 'Often patients who are dealing with buried trauma and the resulting psychological pain – whether manifested in upsetting flashbacks or night-mares or panic attacks – self-medicate with the use of alcohol, or drugs, or sex. It's all armour against having to deal with the upsetting event itself.'

Viv thinks about this in silence. 'I had a flashback recently,' she says. 'It was one I'd never had before, about our old neighbour, Declan. I thought of him and immediately this horrible, sick feeling of disgust and shame came over me . . . but when I tried to remember more it was as though my brain had shut down, and I couldn't go any further.' She looks at Miranda. 'But I think that he's a part of it all, that he's got something to do with Ruby's death.'

Miranda listens without comment, then asks, 'What's your relationship with your family like? Your mother and your daughter?'

She swallows the lump that forms in her throat at the thought of Cleo and says, 'I think I'm a good mother. Cleo and I are very close . . . or at least I thought we were . . .' She remembers the shock of finding out about 'Daniel' and a familiar self-reproach spills through her. 'To be honest, I only feel completely safe when I'm with my own mother. She looks after me, always has. Sometimes I think I'm far too dependent on her,' she adds.

'That's understandable. She was your one constant in a time of great turmoil.'

Vivienne leans forward. 'So, can you help me?'

Miranda regards her frankly. 'Well, as I've already told you, I'm not happy about introducing this therapy when your current situation is so stressful, but I told Alek that I would help, so I will.'

'And do you think I'll remember what happened that day?'

Miranda puts down her notepad. 'EMDR is about working through current memories, it's not about un-earthing lost ones, but it's true that some patients are able to remember more details of a traumatic event as the therapy progresses.'

Vivienne nods. 'OK, that's good enough for me. I just want to try.'

Though Cleo's finger throbs with pain, the bandage, so expertly administered, remains a pristine white; whatever it was that he poured on the wound, it certainly stemmed the blood. Still numb with shock, she remembers how carelessly he'd gathered up the scraps of rubbish when he'd finished, sweeping the bloodstained cloth, the cleaver, the half-full bottle of ointment into a dirty plastic carrier bag. The top of her finger, puckered, bluish-white and bloody, had been included in that discarded debris, and the thought of that makes sickness lurch up inside her.

Presumably he is outside somewhere; she hasn't heard the van drive off in the hour or so since he left her. *Perhaps your mother will do as she's told now.* What had that meant? Instantly her heart pounds harder at the thought of Vivienne in danger, and it is this that makes her rise unsteadily to her feet. The movement brings on a dizzy spell, nausea slipping and sliding in her belly, but it's nothing compared to the fresh spasm of pain that shoots from her finger to her elbow. It is all-consuming, stopping her in her tracks, and she clenches her jaw hard and makes herself wait it out, holding on to the table with her good hand, willing it to pass.

She hesitates at the toilet door. Does she dare turn on the light? Her fingers graze the switch, then on impulse she presses it. If he sees the faint flickering glow from outside it hardly matters at this point; he will not know what she's planning. She pulls the hinge from her pocket and puts it to the first screw holding the Perspex in place, crying out in relief when she sees that it fits. As she starts to apply pressure she hears a sound from outside and freezes in panic, but it's only the wind blowing so hard that it's lifting the board on the other side of the Perspex. The sight fills her with renewed hope: it must be looser than she thought.

At first she makes poor progress, the hinge slipping and sliding uselessly, but she keeps trying until at last the screw turns. Tears of relief spring to her eyes and she renews her efforts. Within twenty minutes she has managed to loosen all four screws. She gives the Perspex sheet an experimental tug, slipping her hand beneath it when it gives way to press against the hardwood that blocks the cavity. To begin with it holds fast, but summoning up her last ounce of strength she leans against it and shoves, and is rewarded by a mighty *crack* as the hardboard gives way.

The noise seems so loud that she jumps back in panic,

her heart pounding as she listens for a reaction from outside. Quickly she turns the light off and returns to the bench where she sits down to wait, her eyes wide with fear. But a minute passes, and then another, and still there is no sound of activity outside. If she can push the hardboard away completely, the hole should be big enough for her to fit through. Hope begins to rise inside her. All she has to do now is wait for him to drive away.

Miranda gets up and draws the curtains against the torrential rain and wind that's now battering against the window panes. In contrast, her practice room, with its plush cream carpets, pale green walls and subtle low lighting is still and quiet. Viv sits back in her chair, waiting apprehensively to begin.

'Have you read much about EMDR?' Miranda asks her when she's seated.

'A bit.'

'Well then, you'll know it's a therapy commonly used to help those suffering from post-traumatic stress disorder, or indeed anyone whose past experiences are affecting their mental health in the present. It allows the patient to revisit the traumatic experience, whatever it might be – a car accident, childhood abuse, or whatever – in a safe place and with the use of something called bilateral stimulation that neutralizes the feelings of panic as the patient remembers the traumatic event.'

'But how can you make revisiting the memory easier to cope with? How am I going to be able to go back to that day without it bringing on a panic attack?' Viv asks.

'We'll begin by exploring what happened immediately before you started to feel afraid, and continue from there. It's important to remember that *you* are in charge here. You can stop the process at any time you need to. You will not be forced to revisit anything that you don't want to. Most importantly, you will be aware that you are no longer the child you once were, that you are here, now, in the present, completely safe.'

Viv watches as Miranda gets up and fetches a black case from beneath her desk and returns to her seat. Opening it she sets up a tripod and attaches it to a slim, horizontal LED panel.

'OK,' Miranda says, 'as I explained, the lights will stimulate your brain in a way that replicates the rapid eye movement of the deepest phase of sleep.'

Viv eyes the LED panel doubtfully. 'And how exactly will that help me?'

'During this phase your brain achieves the deepest state of rest and self-healing. The stimulation of the left and right hemispheres promotes the brain's natural self-soothing mechanism. By replicating that state while you recall the traumatic event, the memory is reprocessed. This will enable you to gradually become desensitized to it, so that eventually you will be able to revisit that same memory without it triggering the anxious or panicked response it once did.'

Viv digests this in silence. 'And I might remember details I'd forgotten?'

'It's possible. As we gradually neutralize your panicked response, you might be able to move on from the memory and recall details that had previously been too traumatic to face.'

Vivienne looks at the clock. 'How long does it take, on average?'

'For some it can work very quickly, for others it could take a few sessions. But it's not something we can rush.'

Viv nods, her mouth bone-dry. 'OK,' she says nervously. 'Can we get on with it?'

At last, an hour after she'd pushed the hardboard from the window and felt it give way, Cleo hears the sound she's been waiting for: the slam of the van's door, followed by the growl of its engine fading gradually into the distance. Immediately she gets up and runs to the bathroom where she turns on the dim light. Then she sets about turning the already loosened screws, a task made more difficult by the trembling in her fingers, but at last she is able to pull the Perspex away. Next she presses hard against the chipboard, which again falls forward with a satisfying crack. It remains attached to the caravan, however, and though she pushes with all her might with her non-injured hand, she can't dislodge it. She will need to use both hands and all her strength if she's going to move it clear away.

She pauses to brace herself before stepping up onto the toilet, placing both hands on the hardboard and pushing as hard as she can. The pain is so excruciating it makes her cry out, but she persists until the board gives enough to reveal a glimpse of the dark and rainy world outside, and a gust of cold air stings her cheek. Panting with effort, she hauls herself up and propels herself forward. Her hand throbs as she knocks it, but she barely cares as she slides through the narrow gap, the ragged edge of hardboard tearing at her jumper and her skin until she lands on the wet and muddy ground outside in a heap.

She looks around her. It's pitch-dark and the rain is falling hard, her hair whipping around her face in the wind. The builder's yard is fenced in with a combination of high wooden boarding, wire fencing and slats of corrugated iron and she scans them rapidly, squinting in the darkness, to see if there are any gaps that she might climb through. And then she spots something that makes her heart leap. There, in the not too far off distance, are the lit-up towers of Canary Wharf. She's in London. Not only that, she's on the south side of the river. She had been so frightened that she might discover herself to be somewhere far from home, but she's here, in South London, and relief surges through her.

Her joy is short-lived. Before she can make good her escape, she hears the familiar sound of the van's engine, sees the sweep of headlights, and her heart drops.

*   *   *

The rain continues to pound on Miranda's window; they can hear the wind howling, pummelling the trees in her garden. 'I want you to try to clear your mind of the difficulties you are facing,' she tells Vivienne. 'Instead, I'd like you to think of a time and place where you felt happy – your home, or a favourite holiday, for example. Anywhere you like, as long as it's somewhere that you felt completely safe. Think of that place for me and try to relax.'

Vivienne nods, breathing slowly and deeply as Miranda has told her to. Searching her brain for a happy memory is harder than she would have thought. Her own home just makes her think of Cleo. Holidays, likewise: she can only picture ones she and Cleo went on together. She thinks of Stella's kitchen, but even that makes her feel panicky and anxious. And then she thinks of Unity House, of being around ten years old and sitting in the garden with Margo, picking beans from the vines. She feels a flicker of surprise, even shame, that this is what has occurred to her, considering what happened later, but nevertheless it is a moment in time when she remembers feeling truly relaxed and content, and she allows herself to savour it for a while, feeling again the warm sun on her arms, the comforting nearness of Margo.

'How anxious do you feel right now, on a scale of one to ten?' Miranda asks her.

'Um, not very, I guess. Three, maybe?' Nervously Viv clears her throat.

'Good. I want you to remember that you can return to this happy memory whenever you want. You are in charge here, Vivienne. You are completely safe.' Miranda leans over and switches on the LED box and a small green light moves from left to right, slowly and repetitively. 'Can you see the light?' she asks.

When Viv nods, Miranda continues, 'I want you to relax and watch the light and think back to the day when your sister died. Let's start by recalling the period immediately before anything upsetting happened, before you sensed any danger, OK? What were you doing, can you remember?'

'I was in the living room,' Viv answers tentatively. As her eyes focus on the moving light, she pictures the small, white-walled, low-ceilinged room and shivers; it was always cool in there, no matter what the time of year. Faded red velvet curtains hang at the windows, and the carpet is brown and worn. She smells the cottage's long-forgotten scent – a mixture of mothballs, dust and something else that's sweet and unidentifiable, but then it dawns on her that she smells the same thing in Stella's house in Peckham. It must come from Stella herself.

'OK,' Miranda says. 'Tell me what you're doing.'

'I'm watching TV,' Viv replies. 'I'm alone. Ruby's upstairs.'

'And what happens next?'

Viv tenses, her hands balling into fists as the first tendrils of fear grip her. Miranda leans over and turns off the lights. 'OK, Vivienne, that's brilliant, you're doing really well. Can you tell me how you're feeling at this minute?'

'Frightened, anxious,' She coughs nervously. 'On a scale of one to ten? About a seven . . .'

'OK. I want you to breathe deeply and think of your happy memory, can you do that for me?'

Viv nods, but says nothing. Miranda waits until her breathing returns to normal and then says, 'You are safe here, Vivienne, completely safe. What you were remembering happened a long time ago. I'm going to turn the light panel back on, and I want you to watch it as before, casting your mind back to the point you just remembered.'

This time, when Viv pictures herself in the room, she's surprised to find that the panic has faded a little. Encouraged, she allows the memory to unwind a little further. 'There's a knock on the door,' she tells Miranda. 'Ruby comes down from her bedroom to open it, because she thinks it's Jack. She says to me, "Don't tell Mum, OK, Vivi? Don't tell Mum that Jack was here." But when she opens the door it's not Jack, it's Morris.'

'Are you sure? How do you know, do you see him?'

'No, but I can hear them talking. And then he goes away.'

Miranda, who has been watching her closely, turns off the light panel and again asks Vivienne how anxious she's feeling.

'About an eight, it went down for a while, but it's gone up again,' Viv tells her. 'My chest feels tight . . . I'm frightened of what's going to happen next.'

'OK,' Miranda says calmly. 'But look, you're here, with me, and you're a grown-up. Whatever happened that day can't hurt you any more. It's all over. Here, today, you are a strong, adult woman, there is no danger here, you are completely safe.'

When Viv nods, Miranda says, 'OK, I want you to think of your safe place again, and I want you to breathe deeply. Can you do that for me?'

After a few minutes, Miranda turns the light panel back on and directs Viv to think of the same memory she'd just relived of Ruby running down the stairs, the sound of Morris's voice when she answered the door.

'How are you feeling?' she asks, as Viv retraces her steps along the memory.

'Better,' Viv says, relieved. 'About a six.'

Miranda nods and smiles. 'Well done, do you see what happened there? Before, when you were recalling this part of the memory, you rated it as an eight in terms of stress. But the next time you recalled the same memory your stress level went down to a six.'

Miranda looks pleased with her so Vivienne gives her a cautious smile. 'You're right,' she says. 'That's amazing.'

'It's because your brain is creating new pathways through which to recall the memory while being conscious that you're now in a place of safety, many years after the event.' She gives Miranda a reassuring smile. 'So, are you ready to go on?'

For the next hour they continue in this vein, edging along the memory inch by inch, Miranda turning off the light at each new remembered detail to bring Vivienne back to the present, ask her how she's feeling, direct her to her happy memory before returning to the day of Ruby's murder. Each time she does so, Vivienne finds that the level of fear has reduced, enabling her to edge forward to the point where previously her panic had prevented her from venturing.

But when they reach the moment where Ruby goes back upstairs, Viv feels the icy dread begin to soar, an inexorable rise of panic. Her breath gets shorter until she's almost panting.

'What's happening?' Miranda asks.

'Ruby's gone upstairs to wait for Jack. And then . . . and then . . .'

'You're OK,' Miranda says soothingly. 'You're absolutely fine. Let's stop for a break.'

But this time when the light panel has been turned off, the panic doesn't subside. Viv sinks her head in her hands. 'I can't do this,' she whispers, 'I'm too frightened.'

'Tell me what you're feeling.'

'Terror,' Viv whispers. 'I feel terrified.' She searches for the words to explain the sense of dizzying, vertiginous fear that has filled her, as though she's clinging to a cliff edge by her fingernails, her heart racing faster and faster. 'I'm terrified because I know Jack is going to come and knock on the door and he's going to go upstairs and . . .' She looks at Miranda, her face stricken.

'OK,' Miranda says reasonably. 'But the fear you're feeling isn't rational, is it?'

261

'Why not?'

'Because Jack isn't here, now, is he? Nobody is in danger in your current situation. What you're talking about happened a long time ago, when you were a child. You're no longer a child. You're an adult, sitting in a room in London with me. Nobody can hurt you. You are completely safe, aren't you?'

Mutely, Viv nods.

'OK,' Miranda says, offering a reassuring smile. 'You've done brilliantly. I think that's enough for today—'

'No!' Viv says. 'Absolutely not. That's not an option. I need to do this. I need to remember.' She lets out a deep breath. 'Could I . . . would it be all right for me to have a few minutes on my own? Would that be OK?'

'Of course. I'll go and make some tea. Take your time.'

When Miranda leaves the room, Viv gets up and stands at the window looking out at the rainy garden beyond her own hollow-eyed reflection. She thinks of the photograph she has of herself and Ruby, taken shortly before her murder. In the picture she is leaning in close against her sister's bump and they are smiling at the camera. The memory is so vivid, she can feel Ruby's warmth along her left side as she leaned into her. Every time she looks at that picture, she feels the loss of Ruby as the physical absence of that warmth, the left side of her perpetually cold, abandoned. Now, though, without Cleo, that coldness has spread to every corner of her, an icy expanse that she will feel every second until she sees her child again, that she won't be able to bear it if she doesn't – it is as simple as that, she will not be able to bear it.

She goes to the door. 'Miranda,' she calls. 'I want to go on.'

They are seated in the armchairs, the lights dimmed once more, the LED bar flashing its rhythmic pattern left to right, left to right. Vivienne has walked through the memory until the point where Ruby has returned upstairs after Morris left. She concentrates, casting her mind back until she is alone in the living room once more. Almost immediately the slow build of dread begins.

'Nothing can hurt you, Vivienne,' Miranda reminds her. 'Ruby's death was a long time ago. You are an adult now, and you are completely safe; what you are remembering is all in the past.'

Viv nods and she clings on to the feeling of being in Miranda's basement, her calm voice reassuring her, keeping her tethered to the safety of the present.

'OK, are you ready to go on? Can you recall what happened next?'

Her mouth dries, her heart pounds hard against her ribs. She makes herself take another step. 'There's someone else at the door,' she says. She is only dimly conscious of the tears streaming down her face.

'You mean you hear another knock?'

'No. Oh! They . . . they're pushing it open. Ruby must have left it on the latch – and whoever it is, is standing in the hall.' She has not remembered this before and she feels panic swirling inside her. 'I don't . . . I can't . . .'

'Who is it, Vivienne? Who's standing in the hall?'

'I don't know! I don't know! I can't see him and he doesn't speak!'

'OK,' Miranda says. 'OK, let's take a break here.'

But Vivienne pays no attention. She is standing on the precipice. She thinks of Cleo and something shifts inside her – something stronger than the self-preservation that has been keeping her memories locked deeply inside of her. She steps closer to the edge. And then she's there, in freefall, remembering.

'He's going upstairs . . .' she whispers. 'He's going up to Ruby's bedroom!'

'OK, you're OK,' Miranda says. 'Take a moment to breathe.'

But Vivienne barely hears her. 'I can hear Ruby shouting. She's crying and shouting and then . . . and then she screams . . . there's a loud thud, the whole house shakes . . .' Vivienne's breath is coming in rapid gasps. 'It's all gone quiet and I know something bad has happened. The other person, they're still up there.' Her voice rises in distress.

'Take your time, Vivienne, you're doing so well.'

'I get up and go to the foot of the stairs. I want to make sure that Ruby's all right, but I'm frightened. I'm so frightened . . .'

She doesn't notice Miranda leaning forward and

taking her hands in her own. 'Vivienne, you are OK, you are safe.'

'The other person is still up there with her. He's still up there in Ruby's room. I'm going upstairs,' Viv continues. 'It's quiet now. I'm going upstairs and I push open Ruby's bedroom door, and . . .' But the black weight is pushing down on her chest with such intensity that she can hardly breathe. 'No,' she cries. 'I can't. I don't want to!'

'Vivienne, we need to stop.'

'No,' she whispers, the world seeming to telescope away from her as she permits herself to see, finally, who's standing in the room with Ruby's body. 'No . . .'

'What is it, Vivienne, what's happened? What have you remembered?'

But instead of replying, Viv gets to her feet. She stares down at Miranda in dazed horror. 'I have to go. I have to go now,' she says.

Miranda gets up too. 'Please sit down, Vivienne. We need to talk about this. It's important that we—'

But as though she hasn't heard her, Viv rushes from the room.

Miranda follows after her. 'Vivienne,' she says, 'you can't go, not like this. You're in no state to drive home. Do you have someone you can call, who could come and collect you? Or I could drive you myself.'

Still dazed, Viv glances back at her. 'No, no. I'll be OK.' She reaches for the door handle and walks out into the street.

'Listen to me, Vivienne . . .'

She doesn't wait to hear the rest. And when she's sitting behind the wheel of her car once more the full force of what she's relived hits her anew. She fumbles in her bag for her phone and calls her mother. When Stella answers on the second ring, Viv manages only to cry, 'Mum, oh Mum . . .'

'What is it?' Stella says, her own voice rising in fear. 'Vivienne, what's happened? Is it Cleo?'

'I'm on my way home,' Viv says at last. 'Please, meet me there. I'll be forty minutes. Just come, Mum. Please come.' She hangs up and though she's shaking violently, she begins the drive home.

19

Cleo hears the van come to a stop by the gates. The doors open, and then there's the sound of his footsteps as he approaches the caravan. She has a split second to decide. When she hears the rattle of the padlock, she runs to the far end of the yard and hides behind a stack of bricks. She can hear nothing but her heart beating, the blood rushing in her ears, her panting breath, knowing that it's a matter of seconds before he looks inside and discovers that she's gone.

Even from fifty metres away, his roar of confusion and rage can be heard above the pounding of the rain on metal and concrete. He clatters down the steps of the caravan and runs to his van. She peeks around the stack of bricks and spies him opening the passenger side door and reaching in. He emerges holding a flashlight. His entire being radiates violence and she is more afraid of him than ever. He makes a circuit of the yard, darting around its edges, shining the light into every hiding place. He wants to kill her, of that she is in no doubt. He wants to kill her, and if he catches her, he will.

She is shaking so much that she's afraid she might upset the stack of bricks she's hiding behind. A few metres away, she's identified a gap between the wire fencing and adjoining panel of corrugated iron, but it's barely a foot wide. She's not sure she can make it through before he catches her. He draws ever nearer, swinging his flashlight, and she has to clamp her hands over her mouth to prevent her terror from escaping into the rainy darkness. She is going to be found and when she is her punishment will be far worse than a severed finger.

He's a metre away now, and still closing in. She could reach out and touch his shoe if she wanted. She feels her smallness, her powerlessness, and in that instant her fear is so great that she almost allows it to claim her. Though she knows what will happen if she does, she's ready to give up and scream for her mother, because she is only a child and she is no match for him and never was. But she shuts her eyes and wills herself to hold on, to be brave, a big girl; to keep still and quiet for a bit longer.

Above the drumming of the rain she hears a sound from beyond the gates that makes her open her eyes: a far-away siren. Already the sound is receding into the distance, but it's triggered a response. He swings around in its direction, then in one quick movement he turns off his flashlight and darts across to the caravan so that he is hidden from sight. She seizes her chance and runs as fast as she can towards the gap in the fence. It's too narrow to fit through, but she can see footholds above her that will allow her to scale the fence once he's out of the way. In the meantime she can only hope he will give up and leave soon.

Instead, he waits a few minutes then resumes his search. If he swings his flashlight in her direction she will be seen. She stands there, fists clenched, eyes tightly shut, praying. At last he gives a shout of frustration and heads back to his van. She stays still, the torrential rain soaking her to the skin, not daring to hope. And then she hears the slam of the door, the growl of the engine, followed by the sudden bright glare of headlights as he drives away. She closes her eyes in thanks, but her relief evaporates as it hits her with horrifying certainty that his next destination will be her home. He will go to her mother, who will have no hope of defending herself against him. She has to get there first. She has to get to her mother before he does. Quickly she scales the fence and hauls herself over to the street on the other side.

When Vivienne draws up outside number 22 Albert Road she sees Stella waiting for her on the doorstep, and she sits with the engine running, staring at the wet, bedraggled figure sheltering beneath her porch. She has no recollection of the streets she must have driven through to arrive here: everything is blank.

Stella's hair is plastered against her face and Viv is struck by how old she looks. When did this happen, the mother who had always been so strong turning into such a frail thing, her vitality ebbing away without Viv even noticing. An icy coldness spreads from her scalp down to her toes, her teeth beginning to chatter as it hits her anew that in a matter of minutes she will have to tell her mum what she knows, and in doing so change their lives forever.

'Vivienne,' Stella says, shivering in the cold as she gets out of her car and approaches her. 'What on earth has happened? What is all this about?'

But Viv doesn't reply. She passes her mother without a word, unlocks her front door and goes through to the kitchen. Stella joins her and the two women stand contemplating each other in silence.

It's Stella who speaks first. 'Vivienne, you're scaring me. What's going on? Please tell me.'

'I know who it was, Mum,' Vivienne replies. 'I know who killed Ruby.'

Stella stiffens. 'Well . . . it was Jack, Vivienne, like you always said it was. Jack killed Ruby.' She walks towards Viv and puts a hand on each of her shoulders, gazing at her with concern. 'Darling, what's happened? Are you OK? Do the police have any news?' When Viv continues to stare at her without speaking, Stella frowns. 'Vivienne, what's all this about?'

But although Viv opens her mouth, the words remain stuck in her throat.

'Talk to me!' Stella pleads. 'Have you heard something . . . about Jack? Please tell me what's going on.' She tries to lead Vivienne to a chair, but Viv doesn't move.

'It wasn't Jack,' she says at last. 'Jack didn't kill Ruby.'

Stella drops her hands in exasperation. 'For God's sake, Vivienne, why are you doing this? Don't you know how painful it is for me to hear you say such things?' She sits down at the table. 'My God, it's bad enough that Cleo's missing, I can't cope with this as well, I really can't.' She turns to her daughter and looks at her pleadingly. 'Come and sit down, darling, and let's talk sensibly.'

But Viv doesn't move. 'It wasn't Jack,' she repeats.

'Oh Vivienne, of course it was.' Stella sighs and speaks slowly and reasonably, as though to a wilful child. 'Jack went to prison. You told the police that he was there when Ruby died, that Ruby opened the door to him, that you heard them arguing, that you heard him kill her, then saw him run from the house. Remember?'

And Viv looks into the violet-blue eyes that are almost identical to her own and says, 'No. That's just it. That might be what I told the police, but it isn't what happened. I know the truth now. I've remembered. It wasn't Jack who killed Ruby, Mum. It was you.'

Vivienne watches almost dispassionately as the colour drains from Stella's face. She remembers how, in the care home that morning, Valerie Dryden had said to her, 'I'm so sorry we didn't help you back then, love. We wanted to. I wish we had.' At the time she'd supposed Valerie

271

was referring to the aftermath of Ruby's death, those cold dark days of bewildering shock and grief, but she understands now that she had been talking about Stella, about the person she really was.

'What are you talking about?' Stella says, managing to speak at last.

Vivienne learned to tell the warning signs young. The silent, brooding nights of drinking, the particular look in Stella's eyes that would alert you to the gathering storm. It became necessary to be ever ready for these signs, to become expert at appeasement, at invisibility, at contriteness. Just as important was the need to conceal what went on in their little white cottage. Vivienne had understood, almost before she could talk, that what mattered most to her mother was the admiration of others – that to cause the smallest fracture in her sense of self would spell disaster for them all.

But occasionally, just occasionally, the truth, like noxious smoke, would leak from beneath the cottage's doors or through half-closed windows, drifting beneath the noses of the villagers, only for them to turn away, pretend they could not smell it, choosing not to interfere.

When she was very young, Viv would play out with the other kids on the village green, always last to leave, putting off the moment she must return home for as long as possible. Valerie Dryden had found her lingering there once, long after everyone else had gone, and said, 'It's too late to be out, Vivienne lovey. You must go on home. Your mother will be worried.'

And something, she does not know what, had made Vivienne dare to take hold of her skirt and say, 'I don't want to. I am too frightened.' It was the first time she had asked for help and it would also be the last. Because Valerie had looked at her, so pityingly, but without surprise, before turning briskly away and saying, 'I'm sure it'll be OK, off you go.' Not wanting to get involved, to confront Stella Swift with her posh voice, her good looks, her intelligence, the quiet threat that lay beneath the surface of those beautiful eyes.

In the years after Ruby died, Vivienne had constructed a new set of truths to replace the reality of her childhood. The nights of drinking, for example. She'd taught herself to remember that this was something that came about in the aftermath of her sister's death, a natural response to the tragedy, lasting a few weeks, and not the constant feature of her childhood it had in fact been.

She, both smaller than her sister and more biddable by nature, had been her mother's favourite. It had been Ruby, so bold and defiant, who'd borne the brunt of Stella's rages. But Viv's own privileged position had been as precarious as it was hard won. Constant vigilance was required to ensure she did nothing to incite her mother's displeasure.

Her only refuge was her sister. Ruby, who would never fail to step in, to defend and protect her; Ruby, who had nothing to lose and who, the older she got, became ever more intent on breaking free. And then Jack had come along. The fact her sister had a boyfriend,

273

was growing up, the sudden shift in power adding to the pressure building between Ruby and her mother in ways eight-year-old Vivienne couldn't understand. She could only feel the air grow ever more fraught with danger – the tension tightening and tightening every time Ruby openly kissed Jack in front of Stella, or drove off in his car, a cigarette in her hand, a smirk on her face their mother was meant to see. Horrible and aggressive and awful as he was, Jack Delaney had nevertheless spelled escape and freedom, and both Ruby and her mother had known it. By the time Ruby's pregnancy began to show, life in the cottage had become intolerable.

Now, standing in her kitchen in Peckham, Vivienne says quietly, 'Jack wasn't there at all that day, was he, Mum? Only Morris knocked on the door, and then after that, you came home from work and you went upstairs to Ruby's room.' She swallows, remembering the argument that had exploded between them, the way it so often did in those final weeks. 'I heard you shouting, then a scream, then the sound of Ruby falling and then nothing. I went upstairs and there you were.'

The rain outside has turned to sleet that thuds against the window panes, and still Stella hasn't spoken.

When she saw her sister's body, Viv became hysterical. 'Mum, what have you done?' she cried. 'What have you done?' She ran to Ruby, kneeling down and shaking her. 'Wake up! Oh please, please, wake up!' She tried to lift her sister's head and her hand had been wet with blood where Ruby's skull had hit the windowsill.

And she remembers how quietly, how calmly, her mother had said, 'She's dead, Vivienne. Your sister's dead. It was an accident. It's not my fault she fell and hurt herself.'

She hadn't wanted to believe it. Pain and grief and fear had overwhelmed her as she cried, 'No, no, Ruby, no!'

And then Stella had come and kneeled down next to her, gripping her by the shoulders and looking into her eyes. 'Jack did this,' she said.

She'd stared back at her mother uncomprehendingly, then shaken her head. 'No! It was you. You hurt her. You killed her.'

But her mother had her so well trained. It only took a look, a certain tone of voice, to bring Vivienne into line. 'Listen carefully,' she said, each word precisely spoken. 'Jack did this.' And when Viv continued to shake her head, Stella had said very softly, 'Vivienne, are you disobeying me?'

She had frozen. 'I . . . no . . .'

'Jack Delaney killed your sister. You have to say it was him or I will go to prison, and it will all be your fault. That would be a wicked, *wicked* thing to do.'

And she relied so much on Stella's approval, had spent her short life ensuring that she always did as she was told, that she never disobeyed or displeased her, that almost without knowing it she had nodded. And with that nod she'd experienced a sort of disconnect, as if the world had divided in two, a rift in the universe where on one side lay her truth, and on the other, Stella's. And if she was to survive, if she wasn't to lose everything she knew, then Stella's truth had to become hers, too. She had no one else, no one at all now that she didn't have Ruby.

'You will tell the police that Jack did this. Won't you, Vivienne?' her mother said, her grip on her shoulders intensifying until Viv nodded.

'Jack did it. Jack killed her,' she whispered.

'Good. Good girl.'

And somehow, in the time it had taken for her to run to the wardrobe, to hide, it had become fact: Jack did it. It had to be Jack. It was his name she repeated over and over when the police found her, because the alternative, the truth, was too horrible to bear.

Vivienne stands in her kitchen, considering her mother in silence. Her brightly coloured dress is drenched, her hennaed hair falling in soggy rats' tails to her shoulders, her face haggard under the kitchen light. Where once she had been so impressive – someone to be admired, worshipped, feared – Viv is struck by how diminished she looks. She remembers how Stella had reinvented herself when they moved to the commune, how it was there that she'd begun to surround herself with the weak and the needy, people who would fawn over her, rely on her, feed the furnace of her ever-burning ego, bolster her image as brave survivor, a shining beacon to the poor battered women she 'helped'.

When the woman from the courts had been sent to listen to Viv's evidence, Stella had sat beside her, squeezing her hand tighter and tighter if she ever stumbled over her version of events. Later, when well-meaning professionals suggested therapy to help her recover from her ordeal, Stella had been firm: only she could help her daughter through her trauma, they were so close, after all, so tightly bound by their loss. Her message was clear: Vivienne should never talk about her problems with strangers, to do so would be a betrayal.

And Stella's insistence that only she could help mend her surviving daughter had been vindicated when Vivienne's first attempt at adult independence in her twenties had gone so disastrously wrong. Just one year away from Stella's guidance, and she'd suffered a complete mental breakdown. Boyfriends, too, were swiftly discouraged and disliked – especially if they showed the potential to undermine her control.

But now Vivienne looks at her mother, her hair wet, the hour late, something cornered in her expression, and she sees that Stella knows it's over. The spell has been broken.

The silence stretches, the rain pounds and finally Stella speaks. 'It was her own fault. The little slut deserved it.'

Cleo stands beneath the yellow beam of a street lamp, oblivious to the rain. The road is empty of cars and a high brick wall runs the length of it, the builder's yard on her right. She starts to run blindly in the direction she is facing. One road turns into another and then another, each one as unfamiliar as the last. She appears to be in the middle of some kind of industrial estate, amidst miles of empty lots or warehouses. On she runs with increasing panic until she comes to a road sign: Whitehaven Road, SE18. She's in south-east London! The relief and hope that this discovery brings gives her a new burst of energy.

She looks around, desperate for signs of human life but there are no bus stops, no shops, no houses; no one to help her. Then, just as she's about to start running again, she hears the sound of an engine. For one horrifying instant she thinks it's him, prowling the streets in search of her, and she waits, her heart in her mouth, knowing that she has no hope of outrunning him, that she has nowhere to hide.

But from around the corner comes a small red car. Without thinking, she runs into the road, frantically waving her arms, and it comes to an abrupt stop in front of her, windscreen wipers battling against the rain. The driver leans over and winds the window down. It's a woman of around her grandmother's age, staring back at her in alarm.

'You have to help me,' Cleo shouts through the noise of the rain.

'What are you doing here by yourself?' the woman asks. 'It's very late. Are you all right?'

'Please. Please help me,' Cleo pants. 'I need to get

home. I need to go to Albert Road in Peckham Rye. Will you drive me there?'

When she begins to cry, something changes in the woman's expression and she nods. 'Yes, yes . . . OK. Get in.'

Once in the passenger seat, Cleo feels the woman's startled gaze on her and quickly she stuffs her bandaged hand into her pocket. Oh God, why are they just sitting here? 'I'm in a hurry, I need to get home. Please . . . I'm sorry, but please start driving.'

The woman does as she asks, though maddeningly slowly. As they inch along, Cleo takes in the stranger's tortoise-shell glasses and woollen navy scarf, her dangly earrings in the shape of cats, trying to focus on the comforting ordinariness of these details.

'How old are you?' the woman asks. 'Are you . . . have you been hurt? Do you need to see a doctor? The police?'

'No. No. Please, I just want to get home to my mum. Please.'

'Yes, I'd rather like a word with your mother myself,' she mutters, putting her foot to the pedal at last. 'Peckham's not too far from here, though you'll have to direct me from the Rye.' She looks across at her, shaking her head. 'I do think I should take you to the police. If someone has hurt you, then they need to be—'

'Please,' Cleo says desperately, 'I just need to see my mum.' Something occurs to her and she asks eagerly, 'Do you have a phone I can use?'

The stranger shakes her head. 'I have one, but it's out of power I'm afraid.'

Cleo nods. 'Please,' she whispers. 'Please take me home.'

Viv sinks on to a chair. 'How did you make Morris lie for you?' she asks.

When her mother doesn't reply she looks up to see Stella gazing out at the dark and rainy garden. 'Well it wasn't difficult, darling,' she says. 'Let's face it, he wasn't exactly Brain of Britain material.'

Viv shakes her head in disgust. 'What did you do?'

'I told him that everyone would think he'd killed Ruby because he was there that day. Silly fool had only called round to catch a glimpse of your sister. His dad hadn't sent him there at all, he knew nothing about the chops. I told Morris his lie would mean he'd be blamed for the murder if he didn't do exactly as I said and say he'd passed Jack in the lane that day.'

'My God,' Vivienne shouted. 'He committed suicide with the guilt of it. He was a good person and you ruined his life.'

When her mother makes no reply, she asks, 'And what about Declan Fairbanks? What did he have to do with it? How did you make him lie too?'

Stella turns to look at her then. 'Oh, him . . . it was all his fault to begin with. We women are all victims really, aren't we, darling? It's always a man who drives us to our absolute limit, let's face it.' She sniffs. 'You should be proud of me for what I've had to overcome in my life. No, it would never have happened without him.'

And suddenly Vivienne understands. 'You and he were . . .' A memory returns to her, of getting up in the middle of the night to go to the bathroom, shrinking back into the darkness of her room when she saw Declan slipping from her mother's bedroom, shoes in hand. Was that what she'd half remembered the other day?

'Well, yes, darling,' Stella says. 'For nearly a year, in fact. He told me he was going to leave his dreadful little wife for me, the lying shit. In fact—'

But she is unable to continue, because right at that moment, a few feet from where they're sitting, a figure looms behind the frosted glass of the garden door. 'Jesus!' Vivienne shouts, jumping to her feet. Something hard hits the glass and when it shatters Stella screams and Vivienne cries, 'Mum, mind out!' But then, with a loud bang and a crack of splintered wood, the door flies open, missing Stella by millimetres.

And it makes no sense, it makes no sense at all for this man, whom she thought she knew, who had seemed so harmless and ordinary, to be breaking into her house and looking at her with such violent loathing. '*Ted?*' she says. 'What are—' but then she sees it. He's about five stone heavier, is almost entirely bald, his eyes are brown rather than the cold blue she remembers, but . . . 'Jack,' she whispers. 'You're Jack.' Thoughts race through her brain. Ted kidnapped Cleo? She confusedly

281

thinks back to the dinner party. How had he managed to drug her? And then a sudden image comes to her of Ted pouring drinks for everyone when he first arrived.

'Where is she?' he asks. 'Where's your cunt of a daughter?' He takes a step towards her. The soft Welsh accent is pure Essex now.

'What do you mean?' she asks, and her heart lifts with sudden hope. Had Cleo got away from him? Is she safe?

In one quick movement Jack crosses the room and grabs hold of her, manoeuvring her so he has her by the throat, a knife pulled from his pocket. She feels the blade against her skin and whimpers in terror.

'Who killed Ruby?' he says. 'I want you to fucking say it.'

Viv's eyes lock on to Stella's. Almost imperceptibly, Stella shakes her head. The familiar feeling of compliance comes over Vivienne, the compulsion to do as she's told, to please her mother no matter what. Her mouth dries. 'I . . .'

Jack tightens his grip. 'Tell me. You were there that day. You know what happened, so fucking tell me. And don't give me any bullshit about Morris. That retard didn't have the nous or the balls to hurt a fly. And if it was him, my brothers would have gotten it out of him. So who was it?'

She looks at her mother, her panicked thoughts racing. If she tells Jack the truth, he will kill Stella, of that she's certain.

'All them years I spent in prison,' he says, his mouth

so close that his voice rasps in her ear, 'fucking wasted because of you. My family gave up on me, you know that?'

Viv shakes her head, but the movement causes the pressure on her windpipe to intensify and she feels a burning pain.

'A lot happens in thirty years. People change their minds. My brothers went straight, didn't they? Pillars of the fucking community. Started filling our mum's head with all kinds of shit. Said that as I done my cellmate, I must be guilty of Ruby too. In the end, she believed them. Didn't want no more to do with me. Stopped writing, stopped visiting.'

Vivienne tries to speak, feels the words die in her throat.

'Couldn't even go to her funeral, you know that?' Jack goes on. 'Told I weren't welcome. My mum died this year thinking I killed my own kid! She died thinking that of me, hating me, and it's all your fucking fault!'

Viv tries again to form words. 'Jack,' she manages, 'Jack, listen to me . . .'

'Shut the fuck up!' he roars. 'It's time you listened to me.' She can feel the damp heat of his body next to hers, smell the sweat rising from him, the stale odour of his breath. 'My whole life, ruined. No family, nothing. All I could think about after my mum died was that she went believing your lies about me. It was because of you that I never got to say goodbye to her. That's when I started having a look at what you've been up to, how your life's been going since mine went down the shitter. Turns out it's been going pretty fucking nicely, hasn't it?'

His grip on her has started to slide, his hands sweaty on her neck, but he presses the knife closer. Viv feels the tip of the blade pierce her skin, feels blood begin to trickle down her neck. She looks at her mother, but Stella meets her gaze and says nothing.

'So who was it? You tell me. I know you know, because for you to make up that shit about me you must have had a pretty good fucking reason. You knew I wasn't there that day. You were protecting someone. Who was it?'

Viv's heart pounds. If she doesn't give Jack an answer, he will kill her, she's certain of it. She can feel his manic energy, sense his desperation. There's no way out of this situation for him and he has nothing to lose by killing her. And if he does, her daughter will be alone. Worse than that: Cleo will only have Stella to turn to. That thought, of Cleo in the world without her protection, jolts her into a decision. 'OK,' she says, her voice a squeak, 'OK.'

Jack loosens his grip a fraction and Viv raises her arm and points at her mother. 'It was her,' she says. '*She* killed Ruby. She killed her daughter and then she made me lie for her.'

For the first time in her life she sees real fear in her mother's eyes. 'No!' Stella says, backing away. 'She's lying.'

But Jack's staring at her, something altering in his eyes. '*You* did it? You killed her?' He lets go of Vivienne and moves towards Stella. 'You let me spend thirty years inside when it was you all along?'

'It wasn't my fault,' Stella cries. 'Ruby drove me to it! You don't understand! She—'

But in one sudden movement Jack slams her roughly against the wall. 'She was pregnant with my kid, you evil fucking bitch. You killed my son!'

'For God's sake, that baby wasn't yours!' Stella shouts.

The world stops. And then Jack, in a voice so quiet it's barely audible says, 'What the fuck are you on about?'

Stella's eyes are bright with excitement, her skin flushed a deep red. 'You stupid, stupid man,' she says. 'Of course it wasn't yours.'

And it's then that the last pieces fall into place for Viv. 'The baby was Declan's, wasn't it?' she says. 'Ruby was pregnant with Declan's child.' The revulsion and confusion that had plagued her hadn't been about Declan's affair with Stella. It all comes back to her in a rush of images. A summer's afternoon, walking home from school with a friend's mother. Ruby, fourteen at the time, was supposed to be there when she got in, but it was only when the front door had closed behind her that she'd noticed the cottage's unusual stillness. 'Ruby?' she'd called. 'I'm home. Where are you?' When there'd been no response she'd climbed the stairs and pushed open her sister's bedroom door. That's when she'd seen them together, in Ruby's single bed.

'Oh God,' she says. 'Oh God.'

But Stella's talking quickly, her voice shrill and pleading. 'Declan and I were happy. He was going to leave his wife for me. Then he started pulling away, losing interest, and I found out why. Ruby stole him from me, she took the only happiness I had!'

'She was a child!' Vivienne shouts at her. 'Fourteen! You should have been protecting her.' She puts a hand to her mouth, fresh grief coursing through her. 'My God, he was in his fifties. Oh, Ruby. She would have done anything to escape you, even if it meant getting involved with him!'

Jack, his face blank with shock, looks from one woman to the other. 'That old cunt who testified against me? It was his kid all along and you still framed me?'

'Oh please,' Stella cuts in. 'Don't come the innocent with me! You hit her plenty of times, the whole village knew it. And what about that man you nearly killed in prison? You're hardly blameless.' She turns to Viv, her tone plaintive now. 'Besides, I had to stay out of prison to look after you, Vivienne, darling. What would have become of you without me? I've sacrificed everything for you.'

And Viv sees that she truly believes it. Sees the martyrdom, the narcissism in her eyes, how the years of casting herself in the role of saint and survivor have allowed her to convince herself so completely of her innocence that it had been easy to fool everyone else. Vivienne is about to reply when Jack grabs Stella and shoves her against the wall so hard that her head hits it with a loud thud.

'You lying bitch!' he shouts. 'Thirty years. Thirty fucking years I was in for. My mum died believing I killed my own kid!'

'Jack, please,' Vivienne says, taking a step towards him. 'Please don't do this. We'll put it right. We'll tell the police you didn't do it, we'll . . .' But she's silenced by the look he shoots her.

'Fuck that. It's too late. She's dead. My mum's dead, everyone I cared about turned their back on me.' He looks at Stella, 'And it's all your fault.' Vivienne watches in silent horror as he raises the knife high. But it's not her scream that stops Jack's hand as it begins its plunge towards Stella's chest. It's the appearance of Cleo in the doorway, soaking wet, her left hand bound in bandages, an expression of horrified disbelief on her face as she takes in the scene before her.

'Gran!' she shouts. She runs at Jack. 'No! You leave her alone! You let her go!'

Viv is paralysed for an instant, relief and love coursing through her. And when Jack turns to her daughter with a cry of rage, the knife in his fist still held aloft, she acts instinctively, her mind blank of all thought. Opening a drawer, she grabs the largest knife she sees and runs at him. 'Stay away from my daughter!' she shouts. 'You stay away from her!' and she plunges the blade into his back.

He staggers forward, Cleo moving swiftly out of his

way, and then, like a tree, he falls. The three of them stare down at him, the smell of blood dank and metallic in their nostrils, the red pool creeping across the floor. Silence fills the room.

'Is he dead?' Stella whispers at last.

'I don't know.' Vivienne staggers in a daze to the worktop where her phone lies. 'Ambulance,' she says. 'And police.' When she's finished the call, she holds out her arms for her daughter and Cleo runs to them.

They wait for the sound of sirens. 'What will we do?' Vivienne asks, her teeth chattering with shock. 'What will we tell them?'

And when Stella speaks she looks her daughter calmly in the eyes. 'We will tell them that this is the man who murdered Ruby,' she says.

EIGHT MONTHS LATER

20

Vivienne eases her car into the flow of traffic and flicks the radio on, smiling over at Cleo as music fills the air. 'You OK, love?' she asks.

Her daughter rolls her eyes. 'You've got to stop asking me that all the time.' And then she smiles. 'I'm fine, Mum, honestly.'

'I know, I know. Sorry. It's just . . . well, it's a big day today, isn't it?' Viv turns back to the road ahead, marvelling once again at the recovery Cleo has made over the past eight months. Still, though, she can't help but glance down at her daughter's left hand, feeling the customary lurch of dismay that she knows won't ever leave her.

The specialist had told them that, thanks to its severed nerves, Cleo's hand would never regain full dexterity, but this news had been met with admirable equanimity by

Cleo. An excellent psychotherapist has been helping her to recover from the mental impact of her ordeal, and the strength and resilience Cleo has shown makes Viv glow with pride. But it is, of course, the revelations about Stella that have been hardest for them both to overcome.

For many weeks after her escape from Jack, Cleo would slip into Viv's bed at night, and the two of them would lie together in the darkness, talking, Viv stroking her daughter's hair, trying to answer her questions, while still reeling from shock herself.

It was on one such night that Cleo had told her about the letters she'd found in Stella's room.

'They were from her mum and dad,' Cleo said. 'My great grandparents, I guess.'

'What did they say?' Viv asked, confused. So far as she was aware, they'd cut Stella off decades before.

'They were really sad. The earliest ones were from nineteen sixty something and were begging her – Gran, I mean – to let them see Ruby. And there were others after you were born, pleading with her to let them see you too.'

Viv sat up in astonishment. 'But Mum always said they never wanted to meet either of us.'

Cleo had nodded unhappily. 'They said that Gran had to stop demanding money from them, that they wouldn't be blackmailed into paying to see their own grandchildren.'

'Jesus,' Viv had been aghast, and then she said, 'I wonder what caused the rift in the first place?

'I don't know. The early letters mentioned how she'd lied and stolen from them in the past, but it sounded as if they were willing to give her another chance for Ruby's sake. I think Gran was only seventeen when Aunt Ruby was born, wasn't she?'

'That's right.'

'One letter described how they'd travelled down to Essex to try and persuade her to let them see Ruby, but there'd been a big scene and Ruby had been so upset that they'd decided to stay away for her sake.'

Cleo had fallen silent, resting her head on her mother's shoulder, before continuing: 'One of the last letters was so sad, pleading to be allowed to go to Ruby's funeral.' She'd looked at her mother. 'They weren't there, were they?' she asked.

'No,' Viv said quietly. 'I guess Stella forbade it.'

'There's worse though, Mum,' Cleo went on. 'Gran took you to see them once, after Ruby died. She wanted money, in exchange for . . .'

She'd trailed off and Viv had looked at her questioningly. 'In exchange for what?'

'For you,' Cleo said. 'Apparently Gran had planned to leave you with them, on condition they gave her enough money to start her life again somewhere else.'

Shock and hurt had blossomed in Viv's chest. She remembered the day they'd gone to Shropshire, how she'd waited patiently at the gate with no idea of what Stella had been intending. Since learning the truth, she's found herself mourning the grandparents she'd never known, the reason for their absence so different from the story Stella had spun over the years. She will never know what went on between the three of them, what Stella had done to cause the rift, but she takes comfort in the fact they'd chosen to leave their money to her in the end, that they'd always wished her well.

'Do you think your gran knew you'd seen the letters?' she asks Cleo.

Her daughter shrugs. 'No, but I think she knew something was up. Once I'd read them, I found it hard to be normal with her. I guess I was treating her differently, being a bit off with her, and . . .'

'And your Gran couldn't cope with that,' Viv finishes for her, remembering the way Stella had become so icy towards Cleo. Stella never could tolerate anything less than absolute admiration and devotion.

They drive on in silence for a while and Stella thinks about the last time she'd seen her mother. She had deliberated long and hard about whether to tell the police the truth about Ruby's murder, but in the end it was a phone call from Carl that had made up her mind. He'd rung after seeing the news of Cleo's return, to tell her that he'd succeeded in tracking down Declan Fairbanks' last known address only to find out he'd died the year before. Morris of course was also long gone, and without those two key witnesses any case against her mother would inevitably fall apart. Stella was bound to deny it all, and Jack had already been found guilty of the crime decades before. Eventually, Viv had realized that the only way she could begin to get over what she'd learned was to remove Stella from her life completely.

The last thing she'd said to her mother was, 'Stay away from us. I never want to hear from you again. If you try to make contact, I'll go to the police. I'll tell them what you did, and I will do everything I can to make sure you go to prison.' And with those words, the love she'd felt for her mother, her fear of her, the control she'd had over her, shrank to nothing.

For her part, Stella had raised no objection. She'd closed the refuge down, sold the house and moved away, and Vivienne didn't know or care where to.

The inquest into Jack's death had been traumatic, but thankfully brief. The jury agreed that Viv had acted in self-defence to protect her family from the man who'd killed her sister and kidnapped her daughter. After all, he'd had a knife in his hand when he'd died, and Cleo's finger was proof of how dangerous he was. Jack's two brothers, now in their late fifties, had attended court to hear the verdict, and she had felt their eyes on her throughout. To her shame, she'd not been able to meet their gaze, knowing that their anger at Jack's conviction thirty years before had been justified.

Afterwards, the press attention had been so fierce that for a while Viv and Cleo rented a house some distance from their own – though ironically the same newspapers that had accused her of drunken neglect when Cleo first disappeared now hailed her as a hero.

She will never truly untangle the myriad complexities

of Stella, will never know how or why she became the person that she did. With the help of her own therapist she's come to understand that Stella was most likely suffering from a personality disorder, one defined by a sense of grandiosity, extreme narcissism and a pathological lack of empathy for others. It had allowed her, through sheer force of personality, charisma and cleverness, to convince everyone she met that she was nothing short of the perfect mother. Or, that is, nearly everyone.

Margo, of course, had seen through Stella from the start. And as she drives, Viv recalls that chance encounter with her in a supermarket a decade ago, how confused she'd been when, instead of the shame and guilt she'd expected to see in the older woman's eyes, it had been profound pity she'd seen there instead. Stella, jealous, threatened by their closeness, had expertly engineered Margo's expulsion from the commune – and Viv, to her eternal shame, had let her.

As Viv and Cleo draw up outside a familiar terraced house, Viv swallows her regret and sounds the horn, both of them smiling when Samar appears at the door, carrying a large rucksack.

'Everything OK?' Viv asks, when he gets in.

'Yep! I've dropped the keys off with the estate agent and the removal van has just left.' He shrugs. 'Guess this is it.'

The three of them gaze up at Samar's top-floor flat, his home for the last fifteen years. Like Viv's house on

Albert Road, it had become too full of memories for him to remain there.

'You ready?' Viv asks him gently.

He turns to her and nods. 'Absofuckinglutely.'

The three of them are silent as they make their way to East Dulwich, each of them lost in their own thoughts. Viv and Samar had had the idea of moving in together a few months after she and Cleo had moved back to their house in Peckham. They'd been in Viv's living room, talking over a bottle of wine. 'I can hardly bear to be in the kitchen any more,' she'd confessed. 'I keep seeing him lying there . . .'

'I know how you feel,' Samar had admitted. 'I hate being in my place, surrounded by memories of him. In fact, I'm thinking of selling up, making a fresh start somewhere new.'

That's when they'd had the idea of renting a house together for a year or so, in a new area, not too far from the café or from Cleo's school, but far enough away from their old lives to not be reminded constantly of Stella and Jack.

'Whatever will Neil do without us?' Viv remarked drily as they celebrated their plan. Amusing as it had been to observe him tying himself in knots to avoid her since she and Cleo had returned to Albert Road, it would be good not to have to risk seeing his weaselly face every time she stepped outside her door. She doubted she would ever forgive him for the things he'd said about her in the press.

She glances at Samar in the rear-view mirror and smiles. He's looking better these days; there's a lightness about him that she hasn't seen for a long time. For months he'd avoided talking about Jack. Whenever Viv had steered the conversation in that direction, he'd deftly batted it away. 'Don't worry about me, it's nothing compared to what you and Cleo have been through. I'm more concerned with how you are. Honestly, I'm fine.'

And he'd been such a huge source of support and comfort to the two of them that Viv hadn't pushed him. Besides, she'd been too preoccupied with the fallout of Stella's betrayal and Jack's violent revenge.

Then, a couple of months ago, as they were eating dinner together one night, Samar had finally opened up.

'How could I not see it?' he'd said. 'How could I have not known?'

'Sweetheart, you can't blame yourself,' Viv had told him. 'Nobody would have suspected!'

'Looking back, there were so many signs that he was lying to me. He was never much into the physical side of things, but I'd put that down to the fact he'd said he'd only recently come out and was trying to adjust. We'd always meet at my place, but I never challenged him or asked about his background. I was just so grateful to have someone who seemed to like me. I'm so bloody pathetic!'

Viv had gone to him and put her arms around him. 'Oh Sammy,' she'd said. 'You're not. Of course you're not.'

But he wouldn't be comforted. 'It's all my fault,' he'd

said. 'All of it. If I hadn't been so desperate for a boyfriend, he'd never have had such easy access to Cleo. I was the one who let him into your lives.'

'Sammy, he would have found another way,' Viv told him. 'Sooner or later he would have got to us. Cleo and I certainly don't blame you, so you mustn't either.'

Eventually Samar had dried his tears and said, 'I'm giving Tinder a wide fucking berth from now on, that's for sure.'

'Jesus,' Viv shook her head. 'We really do have the absolute worst taste in men, don't we?' and they'd caught each other's eye and laughed, slightly hysterically, for a very long time.

But despite her love life being the least of her concerns, Viv still thought of Alek occasionally. Even though she knew he'd had nothing to do with her daughter's abduction, the hurt she felt about his disappearance and deception still cut deeply. Then, one night, she had been about to close her café when Alek had walked through the door. She'd been entirely speechless when she looked up to find him standing there.

'Vivienne . . .' he said. 'Please—'

But Viv had cut him off. 'What the hell are you doing here?'

'Can I talk to you? Please, give me a chance to explain?'

She'd been on the verge of saying no, but instead she'd nodded curtly and indicated that he should take the seat across from her.

'I know you must be very angry with me,' he began.

'Where were you? Where have you been?'

'Vivienne—'

'You knew that Cleo was missing. You knew how desperate I was to get hold of you, but you disappeared into thin air—' She broke off, swiping away the angry tears that had sprung to her eyes.

'Vivienne, I am so sorry. When you rang that night to tell me Cleo had disappeared, that the police were on their way over, I knew that they would be knocking on my door within hours – naturally they would want to interview me. If they had investigated me, they would—'

'Realize your name isn't Alek and you're living here illegally?' she'd finished for him.

He nodded. 'I couldn't take that risk. I knew if I was deported, I could end up being killed.'

'*Killed*?' Viv shook her head impatiently. 'You said you wanted to explain, so go ahead. Why did you lie about who you are?'

'My name is Edon Bequi,' he told her. 'Aleksander Petri was my good friend. We were at medical school together in Pristina.' He paused, searching her face before he continued. 'Kosovo, by the end of the war, was a dangerous, lawless place. The Albanian mafia was very powerful, Pristina had become the drug and people-trafficking centre of Europe. My wife and I were young, we were newly married, and we wanted to get out, to move to Greece where we had friends and could start

300

a new life. But to do that, we needed money. Alek and I began stealing drugs from the hospital we worked at to sell to petty criminals, and it was OK at first. But it turned out they were mafia, and their bosses wanted more from us. First they wanted surgical equipment, then they wanted us to work for them in a medical capacity. At first we didn't know why . . .'

As he trails off, Vivienne pales, remembering reading about the Albanian mafia, about an organ-harvesting racket that had operated out of Kosovo towards the end of the war. Surely he couldn't mean that? 'Oh Jesus . . .' she murmurs.

'I wanted to get out, but my friend Alek didn't. He became too involved, though I'll never know how far he got into it. I could tell that whatever he was doing for them he had got in way over his head. One night he asked me to meet him, he told me that he'd stolen a load of money from one of the gangsters and he was planning on leaving Kosovo with it. I told him he was mad, that it was too dangerous and he needed to give it back, but he wouldn't listen. The next night he was shot. And then I made the worst decision of my life. I realized they would be after me next, so I went to his flat and I took the money and his passport and documents. Aleksander and I looked very alike, I hoped that I could pass as him. After that, my wife and I came here, to England.

'Things were OK for a while. I was granted refugee status and allowed to continue working here in London. Then Elira was born. At first we were happy. But after a while my wife missed her family and friends, she missed Kosovo and wanted to go back. I told her, even after ten years, it was too risky for me to return. I would be killed – the gangsters would have worked out I took their money. Gradually we became estranged, we were both lonely, angry . . .' he looks away, ' . . . and then I had an affair with a colleague.'

'Oh, Alek.'

'My wife found out and was furious. She took our daughter back to Kosovo and said that if I followed them she would tell the gang leaders where I was, and she'd tell the British authorities that I was here illegally. So I had to stay. I've sent every penny I've earned to Kosovo to pay for my daughter. Elira believes that I deserted her to stay here with a woman, that I don't love her, so every week I write to her to tell her how much I do.'

Viv stared at him, trying to process what he'd told her. 'What are you going to do now?' she said at last. 'Are the police still searching for you? You'll be deported, won't you?'

He nodded. 'I have decided to return to Kosovo. I want to see Elira, even if it is just once, and then I will leave. I have some friends in Greece, so perhaps I will go there for a while, at least until Elira turns eighteen and is old enough for me to explain things to her properly.'

Vivienne got up and began putting chairs on tables, too agitated to sit and look at him. 'I really thought you had something to do with Cleo's disappearance,' she said. 'You were acting so strangely that night.'

'That evening, before I came to you, I tried again to reason with my wife, to persuade her to tell our daughter the truth, to let me talk to her. But she wouldn't even consider it. Even though I send her all my wages every month for Elira, she will not forgive me for what I did. That night I was feeling very sad about my daughter and the sight of Cleo was too much. I'm so sorry for my behaviour, for complicating what was already so unbearable for you.'

The two of them considered each other in silence. As she gazed at him, Viv felt the stirrings of an old familiar longing, but determinedly she'd pushed them away. 'I'm grateful that you persuaded Miranda to see me,' she said at last. 'But I don't think I'll ever forgive you for complicating the police search, for disappearing when you knew I was so desperate. I do hope things work out between you and your daughter, though, I really do.'

'I am so sorry, Vivienne. I was very lucky to know you, and I hope that you will be happy.' He raised his hand as though to touch her face and Vivienne hadn't known whether she'd wanted him to or not, the same lonely part of her instinctively reaching for that same lonely part in him. But instead he got up from the table and left, the door scarcely making a sound as it closed shut behind him. She knew that she would never see him again.

* * *

The Saturday morning traffic creeps along beneath the cloudless August sky as the inhabitants of south-east London head out to enjoy the last days of summer. At last Viv turns the car into a pleasant tree-lined street on the edge of East Dulwich, draws up behind two idling removal vans and, switching off the engine, turns to smile at the others. 'Well,' she says, 'here we are!'

The three of them pause to look out at their new home and after a few seconds they see a woman with cherry-red hair come into view, followed by a removal man carrying a large box.

'Hayley!' Vivienne calls to her as they get out.

Hayley looks up and waves, and as they approach they hear her directing two other men where to take a sofa they're carrying between them.

When Viv reaches her she hugs her warmly. 'Thank you so much for your help. You've been bloody amazing.'

Hayley grins and turns to Samar and Cleo. 'Exciting, isn't it? The start of your new life?'

At this Samar smiles grimly. 'Christ, I bloody hope so.'

For the next few hours the four of them work hard, unpacking boxes, directing the removal men and slowly getting the house in order. They're taking a break in the kitchen when there's a knock at the door. Viv looks at Samar in surprise. 'Are you expecting someone?' she asks.

'Don't worry, I'll get it!' Hayley hurries from the room. When she returns she has three other people in tow.

Vivienne's jaw drops. 'Oh my God,' she whispers. 'I don't believe it!'

Standing in front of her are Jo, Christine and Sandra. 'Hayley said there might be a celebration in order!' Jo says, holding up two bottles of champagne and grinning broadly.

Vivienne falls on her unexpected visitors in delight. 'It's so lovely of you to come,' she says as she hugs them all warmly. 'I don't know what to say! I can't believe you're here!'

After she's introduced the women to Cleo and they have all been reunited with Samar, the seven of them sit at the kitchen table, smiling at each other over their glasses of champagne. Jo, in her late fifties now, is rosy-faced and comfortably plump, her olive skin shining with health. 'Hayley told us that you were in touch,' she says to Viv. 'We couldn't wait to see you again.' She hesitates then adds, 'We were so sorry to hear about what you've been through – and about your mother.'

The other women nod. 'We couldn't believe it,' Sandra says, glancing at Christine. 'I don't think we'll ever forgive ourselves for not realizing what Stella was really like. She had us completely fooled.'

'We only wish we'd helped you back then,' Christine adds quietly.

Viv smiles at them gratefully. Only Samar and Cleo know the whole truth about Stella – Viv will never tell another soul about how Ruby really died. But she had told Hayley enough about her and Ruby's childhood to ensure that, when it came to Stella, the scales had well and truly fallen from her eyes.

After Viv has assured them that their apologies are not needed, Jo pours them some more champagne and as if by mutual agreement, that's the last they talk of Stella, each of them keen to keep the day as one of celebration and reunion. Instead, Christine and Sandra tell Cleo what the commune had been like, Jo and Hayley joining in with anecdotes and stories that Viv has long forgotten. For a time those days of camaraderie and awakening come flooding back. Viv listens with delight, affirmation that not all of her past had been something to regret, that there were people who loved her, times of real happiness too.

Later, after Samar has gone out for more wine and Viv is ordering pizza for everyone, there's another ring on the doorbell and when Jo goes to answer it she returns a few minutes later with a new visitor in tow. When Viv hangs up the phone and looks around, her heart shoots to her mouth at the sight of the elderly woman who enters the room with a walking stick. 'Margo,' she whispers.

When Margo reaches her she takes both of Vivienne's hands in hers. 'Hayley invited me, I hope you don't mind . . . ?'

Mutely Viv shakes her head and Margo stands back, drinking her in. 'Well, look at you,' she says. 'What a beautiful woman you've become. Just as I always knew you would.'

'I can't believe you're here,' Viv says, 'I've thought of you so often lately . . . I guess you heard about everything.'

Margo nods. 'Yes, I did, and I'm so sorry.'

'This is my daughter,' Vivienne tells her, as Cleo comes forward and shyly says hello.

The other women come to Margo, then, embracing her, everyone talking at once as they sit down at the table. When the pizza arrives and the wine is opened and conversation fills the air, the women reminisce with such fondness and laughter it is as though Nunhead and Unity House was only yesterday, and still Viv can't take her eyes off Margo.

Eventually, when Cleo offers to show the others around the new house, the two of them are left alone together.

'Come and sit by me,' Margo says.

When Vivienne goes to her she blurts, 'I'm so sorry that I didn't believe you back then, Margo. I know that Stella planted those things in your room. She was jealous, I think. She never could stand me being close to anyone but her. But I'm so sorry that you had to leave, that she treated you like that.' She blinks away tears. 'I'm so sorry about all of it.'

Margo puts a hand on her arm. 'It's I who should be sorry, I've felt terrible for all these years that I left you to that woman.'

'Did you know all along about her?' Viv asks.

Margo sighs. 'I've never disliked anyone on sight the

way I did Stella. There was something I sensed about her from the start – the way she was with you disturbed me, and I wanted more than anything to try to show you that there was more to life – more to *you* – than her control.' She smiles sadly. 'But my influence could only go so far: she was as wary of me as I was of her. I think she knew that I saw through her.' She pauses. 'I don't blame you for what happened, I never have. Just like I never blamed any of the other women for being taken in by her. Your mother was a master manipulator, but I trusted that one day you would see the truth and I was right.'

'But why didn't you deny it, when it happened?' Viv asks, her eyes searching the other woman's face. 'Why did you leave the way you did when it wasn't you who'd stolen those things? Why didn't you tell me then that it was Stella who'd put them there?'

Margo shrugs. 'Sometimes you have to wait until a person's ready to hear the truth. When we were all standing there in my room that day, when your mother pulled those things from my drawer, I had a decision to make. I could take the blame myself or tear your whole world apart and force you to see what Stella was like. Hayley has told me a little of the childhood you endured, and if I'd known the full extent of your mother's abuse I would have done everything I could to get you away from her, but I had no idea – and you were so young, so vulnerable . . . I could see you needed to trust in your mother's goodness, and I didn't think you would

308

have believed me.' She sighs. 'Besides, I was ready to go, I'd been thinking of moving on for a while, it seemed the right thing to do at the time.'

There is the sound of footsteps on the stairs, Cleo calling, 'Come and see the garden, it's massive,' and Vivienne and Margo smile as the others troop out after her.

A silence falls between them and Viv wants to tell Margo that a small terrified part of her had always known the truth about Ruby's death, had spent her life refusing to let herself believe it. Miranda's therapy had worked so easily because it was only when Cleo's life was in danger that she allowed herself to face it. But as she meets Margo's gaze she understands that, though Margo doesn't know the full, horrifying extent of her mother's wickedness, she has guessed that there's far more to her and Stella's estrangement than the explanation Viv had given Hayley. Vivienne puts her head in her hands and begins to cry, then, and Margo draws her close and puts her arms around her. She smells in the folds of her clothes and in the scent of her skin that recognizable Margo smell she'd known so many years ago.

After a while, when Vivienne has dried her tears she says, 'I still have days when I think I will never ever get over what happened, that I can't forgive myself for not saving my sister. I sometimes think that it will never let me go, that I'm not strong enough to bear it.' She glances up at Margo. 'And Cleo is doing so well, but for months

309

it didn't look like she would ever recover from what that bastard did to her. I was terrified she'd be destroyed by it, and it killed me to watch her suffer. She's so much better now but sometimes I'm frightened that neither of us will ever truly move on from it all.'

Margo is silent for a while as she strokes Vivienne's hair, and then she says, 'When I met you at Unity House I saw a little girl who had been through such unimaginable trauma, who had lost everything she knew and loved, yet had emerged with the courage and strength to be one of the sweetest, most curious, most loving children I'd ever met. You are still that person, Vivienne. And you have brought up a daughter to be a strong, incredibly brave young woman too. Nothing can take that from you. You will survive this. You might not think so yet, but you will, both of you.'

After a while the two women rise together and, going to the window, look out at Cleo, Samar and the others chatting on the lawn. Quietly, Viv asks Margo, 'That charm, from your bracelet. The one you left in your room for me to find. What did the symbol engraved upon it mean?'

Margo smiles. 'Freedom. It means freedom. I knew you'd find it sooner or later.'

They go outside to join Cleo, Samar and the four women who have arrived out of Viv's childhood to be made miraculously real; flesh and blood and kindness and quiet strength solid against the hazy summer evening sky. Cleo looks up from laughing at something Jo has said and, seeing her mother standing there with her hand outstretched, crosses the lawn towards her and takes it in her own.

Acknowledgements

My thanks to Julia Wisdom, Kathryn Cheshire, Anne O'Brien and the rest of the fantastic team at HarperCollins UK. Huge thanks also to my agent Hellie Ogden at Janklow & Nesbit UK. Thank you to Dr Laura Haigh, Professor Jamie Hacker Hughes and Marcus Jones for their invaluable advice, and to Alex Cree for reading and critiquing along the way. Finally, big love and thanks as ever to David Holloway.